GIRL W

THE
GIRL WHO PAINTED

For those who have lived through the whirlwind of love

"Boy, if ever thou dost love,
In the sweet pangs of it
Remember me."

Count Orsino
TWELFTH NIGHT

Russell Bower

FORGOTTEN TIMES PUBLISHING

Works by Russell Bower include:

FICTION	*PLAYS*	*BIOGRAPHICAL*
The Girl Who Painted	Mr Kett	A Childhood of the Mind
Moonbow*		A Thousand Thirsts
I'm Thinking of Arabella*		Please, Sir!
Who Steals a Goose*		
Five Faces of Love		

* *These novels comprise the triptych Scenes of England*

Published by Forgotten Times Publishing

A CIP catalogue record for this book is available from the British Library.

ISBN 978-1-9996803-2-2

Book layout and cover design by Clare Brayshaw
Cover image © Jiri Vaclavet ? Dreamstime.com

The Girl Who Painted is entirely a work of fiction.

The excerpt from the lyric of the song *Let's Play at Make-Believe* by Willam Oppenheimer 11 is from the musical SHOWBOAT. Permission from Imagem Ltd. to quote part of it has been applied for. To date, March 2018, no reply has been received.

Prepared and printed by:

York Publishing Services Ltd
64 Hallfield Road
Layerthorpe
York YO31 7ZQ

Tel: 01904 431213

Website: www.yps-publishing.co.uk

CHAPTER 1

She got there before dawn, parked the car, set up her gear on the cliff.

Along the sweep of Eastborough Bay lay what was left of night, the shore an arc of darkness, sea in shadow, sky scarcely touched with pallor. She didn't want tints of sunrise. She wanted to capture the almost-darkness, the mystery of a sea beyond the curve of the living world on which life passed from life to death, from death to life again.

She worked quickly, the darkness thinning even as she unscrewed the caps from the tubes. She identified on a piece of paper the tones of a sea between knowing and unknowing, felt enough had been captured.

The man who was watching her from a clump of horse angelica began masturbating. Idly. Openly.

She brush-sketched a bush, the rigid hawthorn intertwining with the female spread of the bramble. Noted the flowers, the pale centres – how curious to see Alphonse at choir practice yesterday. Had almost forgotten him. Used to get on well together, she and Alphonse – he'd never got in touch. Ages since the Fenleys moved away, never so much as a card! Now here he was back in Kirkhaven – *Emilia Brainbox!* Rotten sod! Calling her that old junior school name.

The smile froze. Saw the man, what he was doing.

Wasn't a big man. Flaunting himself, maintaining his erection with his left hand, inviting her to watch him.

She couldn't speak.

Wanted to run away.

Couldn't run away. Wanted to scream, shout out.

She refused to shout, couldn't bear even a sound to link her to him.

Idled with himself, watched her, dared her to stop him. He left his spy-place, went a step or two closer, awkward, tracksuit pulled down.

Emilia grabbed a brush, held the point towards him, warned him.

Made her feel less vulnerable. She was angry, her opportunity for painting being lost, the man imposing himself on her.

He was intent on himself, worked up. She sketched him in her mind, small man, hair parted on the right, the tracksuit a pinky-purple. Saw the angle of the head, a droop of the legs, surprisingly low part of the abdomen the penis was attached to. Kind of revenge, noting him, painting him in her mind.

She pretended to be looking along the cliffs, watched him with the side of her eye. Wanted him to concentrate on himself, get it over with and go away, so she forced herself to look at him, eye to eye, saw him for what he was, a failure, gratifying himself by proxy.

His moan like that of a disappointed child. Arm hardly moved. Stared down at his penis, the knob the colour of plum. He groaned again. She gripped the brush. Her legs wouldn't move, wouldn't take her nearer.

He shook himself, pulled his tracksuit up, gave her a look as though she should have done better. Then slouched off, grass tangling his feet.

She wanted to pack up, go home, wanted to hide somewhere warm and secure. She looked around at the easel, the paint, the paraphernalia of picture making, wished it would gather itself up and put itself in the car. Then remembered she'd still got to fulfil that birthday card contract. Material was here at hand, ready to be made use of.

She sat down, forced herself to concentrate.

She sketched the centre of a blackberry flower, its bouquet of stamens, sketched two or three blackberries against matt green leaves.

She hadn't been physically hurt. But he'd intruded into her privacy, into the images she was trying to shape on the sheet in front of her. It had been a kind of rape. When she got home she'd sharpen the brush handles.

Looked at her watch. It was time she went. She didn't want her mother to have breakfast alone.

She cleaned her brushes, closed the palette.

Had the feeling someone was behind her.

Her insides tightened. Her hands lost their strength. Could hardly grip the brush to defend herself.

She wheeled round.

Her eye took in images of blue-green shadow, stalks of flower of grass, spiky, straw-coloured. Nothing else.

She waited a moment, panting in spite of herself. She strode across to the bush and looked behind it.

No-one. No trace of him.

Listened for a sound of movement. Almost wanted to hear him, wanted to stab him and get her revenge. Wanted someone to take her part, do it for her.

She went back to the easel, sketched what she remembered of him. A graphic enough representation. Honest, him standing there rubbing himself, eyeing her.

Honest as the blackberry bush flaunting its flowers for pollination.

She put her gear into the rucksack, folded the easel and made her way to the car. She moved about as usual, aware of the dawn-coloured green of the grass, the flush on the leaves of the bushes, tried to paint out, paint out, paint out that other image.

She put her seat belt on, took in the view around her. Dog roses bloomed, may hung on the hawthorn, petals of cream-washed paper. Insects swirled, settled, swirled again.

One day she'd get even with him. One day she'd make him pay.

CHAPTER 2

He twisted over in bed, glad the furniture was visible, the darkness beginning to lift. Knew he wouldn't get back to sleep.

He'd got to apply for his own job! To think that others – colleagues less experienced – could even be considered!

Not that there was much to worry about. Weren't going to get a better manager than him. Track record unblemished – profits never been better at the company – knew Small Boats Assurance from the bottom up – like he knew the boats on the rivers, the broads, estuaries.

He went over the tedious tale again in his mind, the decision to put him in charge of the Audley House branch at Kirkhaven so the firm could expand into insurance for sea-going craft. He'd been the best in the field and had got the job, his future assured.

Wasn't his fault one or two idiot directors of Small Boats Assurance had persuaded the board to diversify. Wasn't his fault a shark in the form of Leisure Nation, seeing S.B.A was now a competitor, had opened its jaws and swallowed the firm up. And what the new firm had also done was to note that Alphonse's base, a pleasant Georgian dwelling known as Audley House, was a desirable location. Too desirable to be left in the hands of a chap who insured small boats.

The first news he'd had his job was in jeopardy was when his post was advertised and a job description issued. In due course, along with other candidates, Mr Alphonse Fenley had been invited for interview.

Today was the day.

Outside Head Office a statue of the founder stared down. Alphonse stared back, wasn't sure to be glad or sorry his career wasn't in the hands of such as him; but at least the old sod looked as if he knew his business, which was unlikely to be the case with the present mob.

He went inside.

A girl whose name disc called her Rita told him to wait. She would let him know when Mr Presdel was ready.

Alphonse glared, swore at her mentally. Was used to managing things, not being told to wait by regimented little bodies with regimented little minds the likes of Rita.

Big Dick Dickson flicked up in his mind. Swore at his face too. Dickson! Jesus!

Used to work in a junior capacity – very bloody junior – in another branch. Somehow had got the ear of the directors – somehow gone on courses. Then disappeared. Then got short-listed for this job. As regards ability Dickson didn't pose much of a threat, pushy little bastard. His forte was knowing which bandwaggon to climb on – - –

Over at reception the girls were quietly at work. Computer tapped quietly, an aquarium bubbled quietly – every bloody thing quietly, regularly, according to plan. Ovary-land, land of the bland, land of the usual. God help anyone who showed initiative.

There's this row of hooks, he was telling his friends, *men have to hang their bollocks on when they come in of a morning. When they leave at night they collect them along with their coat and umbrella.*

He glanced about him to see the best place for the hooks. Or there could be an ornamental piece of iron-work, a bollock-stand with various pegs. User-friendly Rita would be in charge. If you couldn't produce your docket you didn't get your bollocks back. Her flat little voice, *Have your docket ready if you want your bollocks back. Hurry up please, I've got my typing to do.*

There'd be pairs that hadn't been collected for years. Belonged to blokes who didn't seem to miss them, accountants, clerky types. Sometimes the office had to have a bollock sale to make a clearance. Sent the proceeds to Help the Aged.

He imagined telling Emilia. Pictured her face when he told her. Remarkable face actually, green eyes, black hair, almost a Red Indian profile. There'd be little reaction. Her hand would remain steady. That was the word for Emilia. Steady. Not quite the I-paint-with-my-prick attitude of a Renoir. He imagined the stereotyped scenes she'd paint – local churches, market town scenes, children on the beach. Nicely done – bought by middle-aged couples to hang in the hall to impress visitors.

Knew he was being unfair. But had she been fair to him last night? *What about sex?* she'd asked when they'd had a chat after choir. *Have you had intercourse yet?*

Caught him by surprise, girl he hadn't seen since they were kids, suddenly demanding, "Have you had intercourse yet?"

As if she had every right to know.

"Haven't seen anyone I've liked enough to do it with," he'd said.

At which she'd smiled – as if she'd got one over on him.

What about you? he'd asked. Instead of answering she'd got talking about this exhibition of hers – coming up in a couple of weeks.

Be make or break, she said. If the pictures didn't sell she'd have to find another job. But as her mum had got cancer it was good not to have to work set hours.

Was sorry to hear about her mum being ill. Had always liked Mrs Connaby. But she'd brought it up as an evasion. As regards sex Emilia was obviously a well-travelled young woman.

A girl came in carrying a box file. Blonde. Eighteen or nineteen. White blouse sleeves buttoned round shapely wrists, the curve of her tie hinted at her bosom. She didn't speak but her face greeted him. Then she'd gone.

His life had changed. He knew his life had changed.

He watched the door she had gone through. Willed it to open, willed her to come back. But she didn't come back.

He believed she'd worn a short black skirt. Could imagine it brushing against those young legs. Felt vaguely improper for thinking it.

Well-proportioned door she'd gone through, semi-circular arch above it, and fanlight. She'd be sitting at a desk. Other people in there, men who'd ogle her, go over and lean close, talk about work, but nosing her perfume, her skin, the smell of youth. And she, half aware, half innocent, only a junior, with that early-morning look about her as if she'd suddenly arrived on earth out of the mist.

He felt in a blaze. Loved it now, this ovary-land. Never mind Audley House, friendly and efficient though it was, this was where his heart was. She was here, other side of that door, maybe at a desktop, face softly reflected in the screen, neat knees together under her desk. As soon as he got the manager job he'd get her transferred away from the likes of Mr Presdel and his staff.

He'd never have believed he could feel so swept away. Wanted to touch the carpet where she'd walked, wanted to run his hands over the indentations her shoes had made.

He knelt down as if to re-tie his shoelace, let his fingers caress the fibres. Wanted it to be a spell, a primitive, to capture a soul by magic. Yet part of his mind was alert to being thought a fool, and when he looked round there was Rita – staring as if seeing a man doing up his shoe-laces was too much for her poor brain.

He ran his fingers across the carpet pile deliberately. Bent closer, studied the pattern.

"See this?"

"See what?"

He got to his feet.

"Doesn't matter."

"What is it?"

He shook his head.

"Don't usually spend my time – "

Bent down again, picked something small from the carpet. Held it up to the light, seemed to put it in his top pocket.

"What is it?"

"Amber."

"Amber?"

She seemed amused, more agreeable.

"You've been seeing that film."

He shrugged. "Please yourself."

Then added, "Grows in good quality carpets."

The phone went. She continued her assessment of him over the handset.

"Mr Presdel will see you now," she said, indicating a corridor. "I thought it came off the beach."

His retort died on his tongue.

In the aquarium luminous fish darted like bits of rainbow. A circular fish, mouth on one side, tail on the other, slowly rose, dignified, from behind plants bright and blue as plastic. In a shimmer of bubbles another creature – made entirely of orange. A comfortable threat-free world. He walked past, on his way to his future.

Paused at the door, checked his trouser fly, knocked.

CHAPTER 3

Some days Jean Connaby preferred to get dressed in the bathroom because the mirror was too misty for her to see herself in. Knowing she had cancer was bad enough; what it had done to her was something she tried not to look at.

She held a couple of silk scarves against her skin, chose the pale green one Emilia had bought her. She liked the healing possibility of greenness next to her throat, almost believed this last day or two that nature had started a little repair. She had looked worse, would probably do so again, but on good days there was hope.

She patted her remaining hair into shape, remembered she'd left a matching headscarf in Emilia's room, smiled to see it draped around a dark blue vase. The girl lived for her art. Jean imagined her draping and re-draping the scarf, shifting the vase to alter the effect of light and shadow. Her world must seem an endless possibility of things to capture in paint.

The phone stirred. She directed attention to her posture, allowed herself not to feel hurried. She guessed who it might be – and before lifting the handset attended to her poise, was sitting on her sitting bones, her throat at ease.

"Thought it might be you, Valerie."

She was about to have breakfast but if Valerie desperately wanted to come round –

"No, I don't insist you come round, Valerie, but if you say you want to talk about it – something I ought to know? Well, if you'd like to come round..."

Jean put the phone down. Another mole-hill, no doubt, in a long line of mole-hills. Made one wonder what was underneath, pushing them all up.

She went through to the kitchen, laid the breakfast table ready for when Emilia came in. She felt guilty, being the centre of her daughter's attention these last months. Emilia had enough to do without spending time on a sick mother – but nothing was too much trouble for Emilia. And this being as positive a thought as the world had to offer she lay down, let the settee bear her weight, her care...

The doorbell rang.

The fluted glass sliced a figure that was not Emilia's.

"My dear, you're wearing green!"

Jean directed attention to preventing her throat tightening with irritation at Valerie's battery of superstitions.

"I really don't think we should encourage bad luck, Jean. Wearing green indoors! Too much like nature!"

The word made Valerie shudder.

"Nature is best left outdoors – where it belongs."

Jean sighed. Valerie was always like this: narrow, inflictive.

When she came back with the tea she asked how Cecily and Robert had enjoyed their holiday in France.

Valerie's face sharpened. Same old story, she said.

"`Robert goes to bed to sleep, Mummy,'" she mimicked. "`And I'm still only a young woman!' I don't know who she takes after. Not me, I can tell you."

Valerie took a sip of tea, sat fiddling with the flap of her handbag. Jean would have liked to try to soothe the tension in the shoulders but knew Valerie would be wary of the touch of a woman with cancer.

"That's what I mean about nature, Jean. Cecily blames Robert's trouble – though I should call it a godsend – blames it on those chemicals he used to handle. Says they've changed his nature. The more that sort of nature is changed the better, I say!"

Jean watched her, puzzled at the energy output of the little figure. This wasn't the molehill her sister-in-law had come round to talk about. The business of her daughter Cecily's unsatisfactory marriage was old hat. "She's got those three children," Valerie was saying, "so he can't have neglected her every night, can he! Don't know who she takes after!"

Jean was lucky having a daughter like Emilia! Cecily's trouble had always been the hordes of boy-friends. Men were a mixed blessing, putting it charitably! Girl who kept clear of men was sure to do well.

"Emilia's been a brick."

"No young men in the offing, I suppose?"

Jean said she didn't enquire.

"I'll be told if there's anything worth telling."

Valerie disapproved. It was possible to be too laissez-faire! A parent-child relationship needed both parties to make it work.

Jean's attention wandered. She'd heard these views countless times, hadn't the strength to endure them.

She swivelled her chair round to face the sun. She closed her eyes, grateful for the blessing of the elements. The only voice she wanted to hear was Emilia's.

"You sure you're well?" Valerie demanded. "Emilia's going to have a late breakfast, isn't she?"

Jean didn't answer. She didn't blame her daughter for making the most of the morning.

"Or am I boring you as well as everyone else?"

Jean allowed her consciousness to return. Valerie hadn't unburdened herself. Deep down the mole was still working away.

"So how are Cecily and Robert?" she asked.

"If you mean the marriage, the same as ever. I told Cecily years ago: `*You tell Robert it's his*' I said. `*He's as good a catch as any.*' `*It could be his*', she said. `*Never mind could be*', I said. `*You tell him it is.*'"

Jean tried to sound interested. Was what Valerie always did, tell you she was desperate to get something off her chest, then have to be prompted to come out with it.

"I loathe the colour green and all that fertility," Valerie said. "Too much made of fertility altogether."

Jean followed the psychological signposting.

"So how's my brother-in-law, then?"

The body stiffened, the arms rigid as sticks.

"Kendal? What about Kendal?"

She crouched over the question like a cat, daring Jean to snatch it into the conversation.

"You must have wanted to talk about something when you rang," Jean pointed out.

"Kendal's well enough. Since you ask."

Jean rested her hands palm upwards in her lap. She didn't mind waiting.

"You want to try living with what I live with," Valerie said.

Her voice tightened.

"All these years I've kept it to myself! But not any more."

She hugged herself, rocked herself on the chair in anguish.

Jean offered no comfort. She'd seen how shallow anguish was with some people.

"You've been a good wife to Kendal," she murmured.

Like breath on a glowing stick.

"Day and night I have!" Valerie flared. "And little pleasure in it for me, I can tell you! And this is been my reward! Makes my blood boil!"

"Reward?"

"For protecting him. Being put in the position of protecting his good name – and mine, more's the pity! Connaby! How I loathe the name!"

"You've had a shock?"

Valerie's chest heaved. "That's one word for it. It's like you see in a film. And you wonder why the woman didn't put two and two together years ago – "

Suddenly, "What would you think if you'd found a schoolgirl's cardigan in your house?"

"Which is what you found?"

"In your own house. What would you have thought, Jean? You seem to have an opinion about most things."

"So what did Kendal say about it?"

"I just happened to be glancing through his briefcase while he was having his wash. And there it was. In a carrier bag. A young girl's cardigan. Dark blue. School uniform thing. Hidden away in his briefcase."

Her voice was confrontational, as if Jean was to blame.

"Did you mention it to Kendal?"

"Mention! I should think I did mention! `What do you call this?' I said. `Hidden away in your briefcase.' `Oh, that's Pauline's,' he said. I said, `I know it's Pauline's. I can read the label. More to the point,' I said, `what's it doing in your briefcase?' `Private matter,' he said. `She popped in to see me about something. Must have fallen off her bag when she put it down.' `Popped in!' I said. 'I know all about popped in where you're concerned!'"

Normally Jean would taken a patient's hand, let it lie in her own hand. But Valerie was beyond normal comforting.

"He said Pauline had got something on her mind and wanted advice. I said, 'Why didn't Pauline ask her parents for advice? She's only a schoolgirl.' He said, 'They're the very people she can't ask. And on no account must they know she's been to see me, either from you or anyone else.' And this is my own niece, Jean! My own sister's daughter! I said, 'I wasn't born yesterday. Going in to see a solicitor for advice she could ask of her parents!'"

Nevertheless, Jean reminded her, young persons were advised to seek help nowadays. And Kendal was her uncle, after all.

"Knowing that little madam," Valerie said, "I don't know what sort of advice she's looking for from a grown man. Or perhaps I do!"

Jean's small reserve of energy was almost gone. Knew she wouldn't be up to coping with her sister-in-law much longer.

"So what happened to the cardigan?"

"He took it. He didn't want that sort of evidence lying about. No flies on Kendal."

"So why," Jean asked,"should he bring the cardigan home in the first place. Especially if there'd been any hanky-panky. I mean, how old is Pauline?"

"Thirteen. And precocious with it."

A car pulled into the drive. A reflection of redness across the ceiling confirmed it was Emilia's.

Jean closed her eyes, thankful.

So what was Valerie going to do?

What could one do, Valerie asked. Ought to have taken the cardigan to the police, of course! Or gone to a solicitor. Trouble was, all these solicitors hung together. Probably tell Kendal everything she told them.

Jean noted the more open voice, the easier diction. A lie from start to finish. Kendal a child-molester! Quite impossible.

Still no movement from the car. She longed to hear the door slam, Emilia's footsteps up the drive.

She got to her feet, dizzy from weakness.

"Excuse me. Must see if Emilia's all right."

Noted that even in a situation like this Valerie didn't forget to wear her affronted look.

CHAPTER 4

She wanted him punished. wanted to pick him out at an identity parade, give evidence against him in court, see him sent down.

"Now you can do it all day long," she'd jeer.

Yet she hadn't been disgusted. It wasn't what the man had done, the simple biological act; it was that he had done it visibly. It was rape. Rape of the mind. She had wanted to paint, observe a scene. Instead she'd had her mind filled with what he wanted to do.

Bizarrely, she had the feeling her dad was alive again, that she could tell him. The rock of her life, her dad had been. Still was, at times.

She didn't disclose her sketch to the police. She gave a verbal description and an account of the incident; and felt depressed at the routineness of it all, the way they wanted to phrase it, as if normal language wouldn't do, as if her account was being stored for uses that weren't her concern. She wished she hadn't bothered.

"I've been telling your mother not to wear green," Valerie said. "No need to invite bad luck into the family. We've got enough of that already."

"What an old wives' tale, aunt! Green is a lovely colour."

"You'll find there's more in these old wives' tales than you think, one of these days," her aunt said. "Doesn't seem to have done your mother much good."

"So what about people who don't wear green?" Emilia asked. "They always have good luck, do they?"

She noted her aunt's outfit, her black and white check jacket, her red handbag, red shoes, red fingernails. And a tight black skirt a mile too short for those spindly little legs. Like an elderly woodpecker, pecking at everything in sight. Yet after the episode on the cliff even that sharp little voice was a comfort. At least nothing alarming could come from it. Valerie was unlikely to say anything she hadn't said countless times before.

"I've seen what bad luck can do to a family," Valerie persisted. "Most families don't need any more bad luck than they've got already."

Emilia pointed out that Valerie had got a lovely daughter and a lovely husband and didn't want for money.

"I wouldn't call that bad luck if it was me."

Inwardly she didn't want to quarrel. She wanted a family she could talk to, even hide in for a while. And here was this aggressive little woodpecker pecking away, her words flying off like splinters.

"Your mother can tell you what a lovely husband I've got!"

"You tell your own tales, Valerie," Jean said. "I'm not saying anything about Kendal."

She closed her eyes, glad of the sun on her eyelids.

"So I will, then," Valerie said. "Now you've got it out of me. It would be as well if Emilia knew how things stand."

"Knew what?"

"That your uncle brought a young girl's cardigan home. That's how lovely he is. In our own home!"

Emilia carried on with her cereal. She had had years of Valerie's innuendos.

"What do you mean, brought it home?"

"In his briefcase. He'd hidden it in his briefcase."

Emilia poured a coffee.

"So what colour was this cardigan?"

"Colour? Blue. You know what colour school cardigans are."

"And the buttons? What colour were the buttons?"

"I don't know. Blue, I expect. To match."

"Nothing green about it, then?"

A cheap point. But she would use anything to defend her uncle.

"No, it wasn't green," Valerie snapped. "And neither were the knickers I found in a drawer in our bedroom."

"Valerie – !"

Jean sat round at her, amazed at this new twist in the allegation.

"It's all right, mum."

"I'm glad you think it is all right, Emilia," Valerie said. "I came here this morning because there were things I thought you ought to know."

"Such as?"

"Such as that in our bedroom, in our own bedroom, I found a pair of girl's knickers, navy blue knickers, Emilia, and if you want to know what I did with them I hung them on the lampshade, the pink lampshade, beside your uncle's bed. That's what I found and that's what I did. And that's what I think you ought to know."

Emilia's head spun. But she knew if she got upset her aunt would take it as a victory. Her aunt always regarded other people's bad luck as a victory.

She asked if her aunt had still got the knickers.

Kendal had been too sharp for that, Valerie said. He wouldn't want that kind of evidence left about. If I'd thought about it I'd have hidden them up and gone to the police. But I hoped – "

Emilia resumed her breakfast.

"Hoped what?"

"I hoped I could save my marriage, Emilia."

Jean noted the quieter voice. Realised she'd begun to feel afraid of the woman.

"You know whose knickers they were, Emilia?" Valerie asked. "Pauline's. Your little cousin Pauline's. Rich, isn't it?"

"You think you can't save your marriage?"

"I thought it right to let you know. In case Kendal should need – somewhere."

It was as if someone unhinged was uttering words at random. Uncle Kendal was a solicitor, lived in a nice old house, was a rock in her life. Might *need* somewhere?

Yet the woman sounded reasonable.

"What about Cecily in all this?" Emilia asked. "Does she suspect what you seem to suspect?"

Valerie looked away.

"She's our daughter," she said quietly. "I couldn't tell the girl that."

Her eyes were moist. Emilia knew it was a ploy, wasn't going to be deceived by a few crocodile tears.

Valerie put a hanky to her cheek.

"You're all I've got. You and your mother. Except for my sister, and she doesn't count."

The painter in Emilia noted the quality of light in a moist eye, how it lay forward, diffused.

"Something that might interest you, Mum," she heard herself saying, "Alphonse told me last night he's never had sexual intercourse."

She turned to her aunt as though what she'd said was their usual sort of table-talk. Inwardly she was astonished. Her mouth had blurted it out – formed the thought and blurted it out!

"Don't you think that's an extraordinary admission for a young man to make, Aunt?"

Jean noted the excited voice. Emilia was usually so calm, the last person to be unsteady. Yet this morning there was this brittleness.

"I mean," Emilia was saying to her aunt, "suppose some young man had confessed to you when you were young that he'd never had sexual intercourse, wouldn't you have thought it rather unusual? "

Valerie stood up and brushed her skirt down with the back of her hand.

"If that's all you can say," she said quietly. "I didn't think when I came here, Jean –"

She drew her jacket to her, as if afraid the very furniture would contaminate it.

"I didn't think I should be made fun of."

All she had wanted was moral support, she said. She'd have thought she was entitled to that, but it seemed she was mistaken.

"Just one thing," Emilia persisted when she and her aunt were on the drive. "Are we to keep what you said about Uncle Kendal to ourselves or are you going to tell anyone else?"

Valerie drew herself back, looked her niece up and down.

"I'll decide that, thank you! Not you!"

People, she said, had better remember her husband was a lawyer. People who chose to make allegations of that sort had only themselves to blame for the consequences. She'd spoken in confidence and been insulted for her pains. She would keep her own counsel from now on.

"One thing I will say, young lady. If it was my mother who was ill like that, I don't think I'd go out and leave her on her own so much. But standards obviously vary."

"I wish I'd stabbed the little bitch."

"I wish you had, dear. If it would make you happy."

Emilia and her mother were washing up. They made it a jokey occasion, wanted to feel close to each other.

"It's like a cloud lifting, seeing the back of her."

Emilia's arms felt trembly. She wanted the comfort of being near her mother. There were hours of painting awaiting her, not least the work on the sketches she'd done on the cliff. If only her mother were well, she thought, if only she had a normal expectation of years and wasn't going to be snatched away so soon!

Outside the kitchen window the fruit trees were in leaf, the grass was sprinkled with daisies. They were images of hope, of ordinariness. Emilia tried to pull them into her mind to blot out what was going crazy elsewhere.

She put the breakfast things away; helped her mother through to the living-room.

"Why on earth Uncle Kendal married her!" she exclaimed. "They're as different as chalk and cheese."

"Perhaps you should ask him."

Jean took her daughter's hand, wondered at the tension in it. She knew what a drain she was on Emilia's resources. It was more than the girl could cope with, looking after a terminally ill mother as well as trying to get started in a career, as well as keeping the house going. As for the future, things would only get worse.

She moved her finger-tips over Emilia's hand, surprised that Valerie should have been able to upset the girl so.

"It's me," she thought. "And the longer I go on being ill, the more I'll drag her down."

"Funny thing to say," Emilia said. "Chalk and cheese."

"Like neither chick nor child," Jean said. "Neither hair nor hide."

"Cool as a cucumber..."

"Black and blue..."

They chatted on, glad to be shot of Valerie, glad of inconsequential things to occupy them.

"You're so kind to me, dear."

Jean's eyes closed. Emilia studied the brown patches under the eyes, the pale skin tight around the mouth. And found herself wanting to sketch the face as a memento. "Even on the day of her death you'll be wanting to use her," she accused herself.

Valerie's face came into her mind. Like that of a bird, ravenous, for ever pecking at the world, at her marriage, her husband. In search of what?

"Never had sexual intercourse!" Emilia mused. Hadn't realised the thought was in her head, let alone in her mouth..

She smiled at her mother's sleeping face, loved the comfort of leaning against her.

The ship of death. A line from somewhere – then the line, the feel of an antique ship, rising and falling, restless at being at anchor.

Something like terror shivered her. Aware of her mother's quiet breathing, she asked in her thoughts, "When that ship has sailed and I'm sitting on this settee alone, where will you be then, my dearest?"

CHAPTER 5

The young waiter in La Golondrina was eager to please, pencil and order sheet in hand, green apron freshly laundered.

She'd have a lemonade for now, she said. She was waiting for a friend.

It was a pleasant old building, with its dark timbers and polished floorboards. Not much trace of lavender and beeswax, she sniffed, more oregano and basil.

The waiter was soon back, wiped the base of the glass with a napkin before setting it down. Something observant about the boy; he seemed to see what he looked at.

"New here?" Emilia asked.

"Art college. Just done my first year."

He pulled a sketchbook out of his apron pocket.

"Enough subjects to sketch here," he said, indicating the groups of diners, "to last me years. Not that I get the time."

"If you get a moment – I'd love to have a glance. Being in that line myself."

"Sure," he said. He was called away, looked back at her. "Sure."

He seemed like an ally. She felt in need of allies.

Alphonse came in.

She was more pleased to see him than she'd expected.

"All very pleasant, Emilia," he said, smiling. "How did you know it was my birthday?"

He looked like the boy she used to know at school, even without the freckles. She quite liked it that his hair was starting to recede prematurely. Made him seem dependable.

"Engraved on my heart," she said.

He enjoyed the sarcasm. Easy to feel fond of Emilia for short periods.

What about doing the same thing next week, he asked. His treat.

Exactly what she didn't want, she said. This expectation people had! Why was everyone so habit-forming?

He wished he hadn't asked, wished she didn't look so attractive. So damned antagonistic. Had probably been on the pill so long she rattled.

He asked after her mother.

Had always liked her mum. Living opposite he used to call round, and Mrs Connaby took it as natural that the kids were fond of each other. He remembered her as someone he was completely at home with.

She insisted on living as normally as possible, Emilia said. And on Emilia doing the same. A neighbour came in Wednesdays so Emilia could go to choir.

The waiter took their order, seemed to enjoy writing on the order sheet. Almost seemed to say, "There!" when he'd finished.

"Youth!" Emilia laughed when he'd gone. "He's going to show me his etchings."

Alphonse looked around at the tables. The blonde wasn't at any of them. One or two girls reminded him of her, until he looked more closely and saw they were nothing like. But she might come in. Any moment she might come in.

"Ever thought of marriage?" he asked.

Emilia leaned back in her chair, seemed to weigh him up as a prospect.

"Would depend," she said.

"On?"

"Whether I needed anyone to pay the mortgage. That shock you?"

"Seems a shade mercenary."

"All marriages are mercenary."

Alphonse had in mind a girl whose face had greeted him, had scarcely been out of his mind ever since.

"Wouldn't love come into it?" he asked. "Whether you were in love?"

"Love!"

She made it sound like the ultimate waste of time. But something about her glowed, and he wished she would be one thing or the other so he could be definite about her.

The waiter brought the meal.

"Can I get you anything else?"

"I think we'd like some wine."

Alphonse was non-committal, didn't want to be obliged to her.

She ordered a carafe of red. When he brought it the waiter lit their candles, left her his sketchbook.

She raised her glass.

"So here's to Alphonse Fenley."

He watched her take a sip, didn't raise his glass. Knew she was being insincere.

"So here's to all young strugglers, then," she said.

She raised her glass in the direction of the waiter.

Alphonse wanted to say there was candlelight in the wine, that her black hair and green eyes were seductive, that there were strugglers young and old who had their expectations. But because she could make him look a fool in a moment he said nothing.

"I feel quite touched," she said, turning a page or two of the notebook. "Letting me see this."

She skimmed it through. It showed no great promise. The boy would be even more pushed than she to make a living from art.

"What's it like?" Alphose asked.

"Deserves a bit of help, maybe."

"Like the rest of us," he said.

She put her fork down.

"Funny thing you should say that, Alphonse," she said.

For some reason his heart sank.

"I've got something to tell you. It happened that morning I went painting."

He remembered talk of her wanting to paint a dawn scene.

"Get what you wanted?"

"Got something else as well."

Her voice rang like a challenge. He wished her manner was more confidential.

"This man – he came out from the bushes. You can guess what he was doing."

He nodded, hoped he had guessed wrong.

"You don't have to talk about it if it upsets you."

"I don't care about being upset," she declared. "I'm upset already. Or are you afraid it'll upset you?"

"You're all right physically?" he asked.

"No, I'm not all right. And shan't be till the little bugger is caught."

He hated her being so loud. As though she wanted the other diners to hear.

"So what did he do?" he asked quietly.

Immediately regretted it.

"Masturbated. Right in front of me."

She saw him wince. Was glad he was embarrassed. The more uncomfortable she could make him the better. She hadn't been spared and didn't see why anyone else should be.

"He took his time – I was helpless to do anything about it. That's what made it worse, feeling so bloody helpless."

Alphonse was aware of people at nearby tables, the waiter taking an order, Emilia making no attempt to be discreet.

"He came out from these bushes – holding himself. I mean you don't – there he was – absolutely masturbating in front of me. I didn't mind what he – I didn't mind that so much – it was being so helpless – him inflicting himself."

But people eating didn't want to hear about someone wanking, for God's sake. A voice in his mind asked, Why her? Why did he do it to her? Because he could see she was experienced? The fact was she'd played with fire and now she'd got burnt.

"Did he touch you?" he murmured. "Not rape, was it?"

"Not in that sense."

"Well, was it rape or not?"

"Not physical rape. More mental rape."

Rape! Everybody saw things they preferred not to see, he said. They didn't go round saying they'd been mentally raped.

"What I hate is the way it keeps coming back into my mind."

Things do float back into the mind, he said. Uncomfortable things do keep coming back. It's what minds are for.

And privately added, She's probably helped one or two to do it in any case.

"As if he's done it in front of you dozens of times?" he asked. "In imagination?"

"That's what makes it like rape – "

"Must be worn out, then."

It suddenly struck him as humorous, Emilia having some little jerk continually appearing in her mind, masturbating away.

"Can't you deliberately recall him?" he asked. "Recall him into your mind and make him do it – do it and do it till he's exhausted? Then order him, `Come on, another twenty times'? And watch him getting weaker and weaker. Till it drops off?"

He tried not to laugh, then couldn't help it and laughed aloud.

He could see she was riled, as if he'd betrayed her.

"Be able to recognize him, would you?" he asked.

The waiter had finished with the next table and turned to them.

"If I saw him again," she burst out, "I'd stick one of my paintbrushes right up his penis!"

Alphonse closed his eyes.

"Can I get you a sweet?" the waiter asked. "Or a coffee?"

Emilia said she'd love a knickerbocker glory. Alphonse felt it easier to say he'd like one too. The waiter took their plates.

"Have some more wine," she said when he had gone. "You look as guilty as hell."

Alphonse leaned across the table.

"Because you're being overheard!"

She leaned forward too, aggressive.

"Then they shouldn't bloody listen!"

"They can't bloody help it. Everybody in the restaurant can hear you."

"You don't have to identify with them. I just asked you to hear what happened."

She was a queen, a primitive chieftainess, not afraid to make a scene or be sullen. He admired her, hated her.

"Give us a kiss."

"Sod off! If men got this sexual harassment it'd be a different world."

Here it came! The feminist whinge.

"You aren't harassed either," he said. "Except this once on the cliff."

"I thought I could talk to you," she said. And heard her aunt in her voice.

The waiter brought two garish volcanos in tall glasses. He set Emilia's down with what seemed extra attentiveness, his glance brushing over her as he left.

They ate without talking, each in thought, both angry.

Alphonse scraped the fruit from the base of the ice-cream. He'd enjoyed the meal, he said, in spite of her being so argumentative.

"You'd be argumentative if you'd been through what I've been through."

"Been through!"

Everyone was mentally raped sooner or later, he said. Any brutal experience displaces innocence. Emotional violation is the price we pay for being alive. To be immune from the loss of innocence is like being perpetually unborn.

"Anyway," he said, "I still think it would help if you deliberately went over the incident in your mind. Over and over. Deliberately, rather than letting it take over your mind at random."

"Maybe I'll try it," she said.

Her voice was different, suddenly agreeable.

"Maybe I'll try fitting other faces to him when I do," she said.

He didn't care for the way she was looking at him.

"Not my face, thank you very much."

It was time to go to choir. She asked the waiter for the bill. Soon she was laughing away, chatting about the sketches. Not perturbed now, Alphonse noted. But a penis in orgasm would be of little consequence to a woman of her experience.

He felt bitter at his own inexperience. Had been too cautious about mixing himself with this and that girl, whereas people like Emilia took for granted what he'd been naive enough to believe were intimate and marvellous. But one day he'd meet the blonde, and be glad he'd waited for the marvellous things.

"Got many paintings for your exhibition?" he asked.

They were walking across the park on their way to choir.

She'd have to work day and night, she said, to get enough finished.

He asked if she only painted what she thought she could sell.

As a rule, she said. She painted to eat.

"Do you ever paint anything you wouldn't sell?"

She stopped still. Looked as if she'd been bowled out.

On the river of death a ship fought against a strengthening current.

"That interview of yours," she said. "How did it go?"

Fairly well, he said. But there was this chap Dickson. He told her how Dickson had originally worked in his office, how he had got in with the directors and been on courses, and then seemed to disappear, and how he was the one person he had felt uneasy about before the interview.

But in the event Dickson wasn't a candidate at all.

"When I went in, there he was. On the bloody panel!"

Horse chestnut trees that had bloomed week before stood in pools of petals. The blossoms that remained had less colour, as though they'd been switched off.

"There's a scene!"

She studied a tree, its mass of bloom fallen, the grass beneath like foam. She took out pad and pencil and did a sketch. It seemed she was recording the wrong bits, more like a negative, the shades and highlights peculiar, like looking at the tree through defective spectacles.

He asked if he could see more of her work.

"You can always come to the exhibition and buy something."

It was meant as a joke. But he was beginning to think it would have been better if she'd never recognised him that evening at choir.

"I wonder why he picked on you," he mused, wanting his own back. "That pervert."

She completed what she needed of the sketch, put her things away.

"Maybe he thought he could widen your life," he persisted. "Took you for a poor little virgin – "

"What do mean, took me for a virgin? I am a bloody virgin!"

His look of surprise annoyed her.

"Yes, Alphonse Fenley. Surprising as it may seem."

"But when I asked – and you didn't say anything – I thought silence gives consent."

"Not in my case it doesn't! And nobody'd better think it does!"

She kicked up splashes of creamy-brown blossoms.

"I just hope some bloke catches him at it some time and gives him hell. I've hardly painted anything since it happened."

"I wouldn't mind sorting him out."

She stopped, eyed him up and down.

"Seriously?"

Sounded almost appreciative.

"You'd have to mind you didn't kill the little sod. I wouldn't want you ending up inside so I'd have to visit you – at least, not till my exhibition's over."

They walked on, their feet occasionally in step, arms sometimes touching. He guessed she was too despondent to notice.

"Means a lot to you, this exhibition?"

"Make or break."

He let his arm pass round her, his hand lightly on her hip.

"Things that bad?"

It wasn't that she was expecting to be slung into the workhouse, she said. But if she couldn't keep herself and buy extras for her mother by her art work she'd have to find a proper job – with regular hours and away from home all day long.

"And with Mum as she is..."

It was why she liked early morning work, so she could be back by the time her mum needed her.

"Now with this little creep on the prowl – "

"We'll sort him out," Alphonse said. "You'll see."

They were almost at the end of the park.

"Must have been strange," he said, "biologically speaking. Seeing this bloke masturbate in front of you like that."

"I kept thinking it'd fall off."

It wasn't what he meant, couldn't be bothered to explain.

"What about you?" she asked. "Do you go quick?"

He might have known it with Emilia! Always back to the personal!

"What about you?" he asked, evasive. "Do you?"

"Hardly ever bother."

"Same here."

They were at the green gate that let on to the road. He felt he was the keeper of some gorgeous animal that didn't know if its claws were out or in.

"Maybe if you showed me," he joked, "I'd show you."

"If I ever got that far – !"

CHAPTER 6

Weeks passed.

He made it his practice to go home by way of Head Office, but by the time he was able to leave work the rush hour was over and it was never the blonde who came out of the revolving mahogany doors. Sometimes he found time to drive past in his lunch hour; and if of an evening he roved round the town he might see a girl who made the heart leap, but at a second look was always disappointed.

He came to believe she was a dream, an ideal in flesh and blood who had walked across an office floor and then ceased.

It didn't stop him looking for her. Her face, the way she walked, the just-so shape of her – hundreds of times such figments appeared, every time came disappointment. But the fire burned. Day and night her absence was with him. She had existed once, every morning he had hopes of what the day might bring.

The interview over, he settled back into work, and feeling he had a point to prove worked harder than ever. His office was efficient. Business increased, his department was the most profitable wing of the company. But whereas success had once been a joy it was now a battle, one he meant to win. He had a score to settle. Against whom he wasn't sure. Sometimes it was the interviewing panel, sometimes the parent company Leisure Nation; sometimes life itself. Life was a thug. Had little sympathy for the likes of him. Small wonder the world was bitter, the way it was treated.

He and Emilia were in Gerald Paine's house along with the rest of the choir waiting for the choir master. Normally a stickler for time, Gerald had failed to come through from the other part of the house. Had been rumours of rows between Gerald and Pamela for weeks. Those who'd got here early said they'd heard the mother and father of rows upstairs.

Would probably blow over, some said. Others weren't so sure. They knew Gerald. Once he got an idea into his head he kept it there; and inflicted it on others. Wasn't a popular man, even with the choir, brilliant though he was at getting them to sing. The choir had been born just after the war, but standards had been low. Gerald had transformed things. Had got rid of a boughful of sopranos, brought in real voices, insisted on everyone being able to sight read. That was his virtue. His weaknesses were equally public.

From upstairs came sounds of breaking crockery and raised voices.

"And that's the man whose hands we're in!"

Beryl and Albert, founder members of the choir, were long-time critics of Gerald Paine and all his works.

Never used to have this kind of behaviour with Dr MacDonald, Beryl remarked. As she remarked every week.

She checked her watch.

"And the choir supposed to be practising for the promenade concert!"

She looked around the room, reprimanded everything she looked at: ornamental swallows swooping down the chimney breast; turquoise dancer holding out the hem of a short pleated skirt; brass ploughman on the mantlepiece trudging behind a big brass plough drawn by a small brass horse; ashtrays, pottery boots, mugs from Gran Canaria, evidence of the kind of man the choirmaster was.

Emilia's cousin Cecily came in.

Alphonse recognised her at once, sensed the impact she made, the way the men stopped talking.

"No Gerald yet," they said.

Everyone knew she'd been quietly crazy about Gerald for years.

"Another row?"

"Probably blow over," they said, not wanting to worry her.

She made no secret of it, even to Gerald. Made her all the more popular, married woman with three children though she was. Gerald practically ignored her. He had eyes only for Pamela – or Doreen – whoever had smitten him lately. Even the women liked Cecily. She was always open about it, and no threat.

"Emilia!" she exclaimed, seeing them. "And boyfriend! Emilia, I'm so pleased for you!"

Then she placed him.

"Alphonse! After all these years!"

She held their hands, gazed from one to the other.

"She's waited for you, Alphonse. Ever since schooldays. And now you've come back to claim her!"

"So what was the holiday like, Cecily?" Emilia asked.

"There was this man there," Cecily said. "Known as the husband. Otherwise the children and I had a very nice time."

And Robert?

"Robert did the organising, Emilia. So Robert is very well."

Their bed never needed making, Cecily observed. Just a moment's smoothing as if it had never been slept in. Or as if it had only been slept in.

Gerald came in. He had been crying.

Tall, awkwardly put together, he was suddenly a presence waiting for them.

A presence for Cecily too. A dog seeing its owner after weeks away couldn't have had a more yearning look than hers seeing him.

But the choir for Gerald was an impersonal thing, an instrument in four sections needing constant tuning, a sound-maker that on occasion almost came up to expectation.

He was ready now, the music alive in him, every bar awake in his mind.

"Shall we start with *Fair Phyllis*? To lift our spirits."

Having perfect pitch he gave each section its note by humming it. He rarely accompanied with the piano. He preferred to rely on the choir's ability to sight read and his own vocal assistance.

He spread his hands.

Up and down...

He stopped them. He wanted a cleaner attack. And attention given to the p's and d's.

Up and down he wandered...

Not sharp enough. It was a matter of finish, he said. Finish was what counted. In this up and down job.

A smirk at the double entendre, then he was waiting, his hands gathering the choir, drawing the singing out of them, cleanly, exactly in key.

Fair Phyllis I saw sitting all alone,

Feeding her flock near to the mountain side...

In Emilia's imagination the man wouldn't finish. He idled with himself, came towards her, awkwardly because of his tracksuit pulled down...

The image arrived, developed and vanished, and all between the beginning and ending of a bar of music.

Up and down he wandered
Whilst she was missing.
When he found her,
Oh, then they fell a-kissing...

Gerald drew out the final chord, snapped it off clean.

At the moment of silence he relaxed, inclined his head, acknowledging them.

The choir buzzed, believing they'd never sung it so well.

"Now we'll have – "

Gerald fished about amongst a heap of scores.

"*To see, to hear, to touch*... Here we are – "

"Yes, Mr Paine," a voice said. "And here we are!"

Beryl's eyes were glassy behind her spectacles. She unrolled a sheet of paper at him.

"This is the programme we agreed a month ago. Which we've never yet managed to get through. It's *God's Cheerful Floweres* next, not another madrigal."

Gerald stared around at the walls, startled.

"I thought," he whispered, "I thought I heard the voice of the Philistine!"

"It's *God's Cheerful Floweres* next," Beryl insisted. "We've agreed a programme and we must stick to it. It's only a few weeks till the concert."

"It isn't the Philistine!" he breathed. "It's Beryl!"

"Not only Beryl," Albert said. "If we don't stick to the programme we won't know where we are – "

"Stick to a programme? You two stick to it. Then we'll know where you are!"

Gerald grinned as though it was witty. Emilia guessed he'd had a drop. And had forgotten what the programme was.

"We've already agreed what we're going to sing," Beryl said, "and the order we sing them. You're making the choir too airy-fairy. If you're not careful, it'll be too highbrow for anyone to come to."

Gerald stared, angled his head at her like a chicken.

"Then I'll announce that one of God's cheerful flowers will sing it as a solo."

"Albert and I started this choir," Beryl said, "to entertain the public. Not to go on the Third Programme."

Gerald shuffled the scores into a heap.

"I didn't volunteer to train this choir," he said quietly. "I was asked. I've got plenty to do without training a choir, much as I like doing it. If people don't want me to do it, either they can leave or I will."

He opened the door.

No-one moved.

"If Gerald doesn't take us," a voice said, "I shall resign."

It was Christine, a soprano who had joined since Gerald took over.

There were murmurs of agreement, remarks that the choir was better than it had ever been.

Albert got to his feet.

"Come on Beryl. Gerald."

He gestured them towards the piano.

"It's only one item. Nothing to break the choir up over. Let's see if we can't come to some agreement."

Beryl smoothed out her copy of the programme, and she and Albert went through the items that the three of them had already agreed should be included. Gerald ignored them, his face averted, chin raised.

Then he muttered something, glanced coldly down the list, and Albert and Beryl, suddenly victors, gathered up their scores, gave each other a how-near-to-the-madhouse-can-you-get look, and went back to their places.

They would include the extra madrigal Gerald wanted if there was time during the concert; and from now on Albert would keep an eye on the sequence of items.

"A short burst on it first, then," Gerald announced, "then we'll tiptoe through those delightful floweres to please Beryl."

He had the grace to smile as he said it.

He gave the note, spread his hands.

Come again...

As for coming again, he declared, half of them hadn't come the first time.

"Which doesn't satisfy anybody."

Emilia wished he'd shut up. But supposed it argued a kind of honesty in him.

Come again!
Sweet love doth now invite
Thy graces that refrain
To do thee due delight
To see, to hear, to touch, to kiss, to die,
With thee again,
In sweetest sympathy -

An outside door was flung open. A car started up, screeched out of the drive and roared away in the direction of Kirkhaven.

Gerald was running from the house after it, his long hair dishevelled.

"Pamela!"

Later, those who had the best view at the window said he stood at the gate like an old testament prophet, arms outstretched at the receding car.

"Pamela!"

If ever a man looked distraught, they said.

He sank to his knees, covered his face.

People left quietly. Even those who made a joke of it did so discreetly. It seemed only proper.

CHAPTER 7

He saw her back to her car. Waited for her to start up and drive off.

The engine lumped over a couple of times. Then failed.

She turned the key again. And again.

"Battery's dead." He lifted the bonnet. The terminals were green with corrosion. She had no idea how long she'd had the battery.

Too late to get a new battery tonight, he said. If he got it started with jump leads there was no telling when it would let her down. Or where.

He'd get a new battery for it in the morning and fit it tomorrow evening. He could give her a lift home if she liked.

On their way to his car she asked if he'd mind if they went round to Robert's first. She'd told Cecily she'd let Robert know she'd be a bit late.

Why wasn't Cecily going home like everyone else, he asked.

She wanted to see Gerald was all right, she said.

Couldn't she phone?

Then realised.

"Oh, what a tangled web we weave ,

When first we practise to deceive -"

Emilia coloured.

"Don't suppose she'll stay long," she said. "I expect she's sorry for him."

Daddy was at home, Alphonse thought, getting the children to bed, reading them a story in bed, perhaps. Whereas Mummy? Mummy was reading the choirmaster a story. In his bed.

"You're quiet," she said. "Don't you approve?"

He felt sorry for Robert, the two women against him. Yet he admired Cecily for going for what she wanted.

"I think life's a beginner."

He felt her stare.

"A sort of learner driver. Hasn't quite got the hang of it yet."

They were through the worst of the traffic, were in the suburbs the other side of town. The sky was a wall lit by an unseen fire. Street lamps were beginning to glow amongst the ornamental chestnuts either side of the road. Something of the late evening fire was on her face. He touched the back of his finger down her cheek.

She didn't move away, didn't respond.

"That's why there are these echoes in life," he said. "It sees something going on, and imitates it."

"What echoes?"

"Haven't you noticed? The way things come in twos?"

He could feel her attention. It was what he liked about her.

"You have this experience," he said. "Then life goes and copies it."

He turned off where she indicated, down a tarmacked lane, the high hedges meeting overhead.

"As if it's got nothing better to do."

He let the car glide, the headlights sliding over tree trunks and hedgerows and forming pools of shadow on the road ahead. It was nice having Emilia beside him, her face faintly lit by the glow from the dashboard.

"Easy to read things into a theory," she said.

"But you've got to try to account for things. Otherwise, what's the point of it all?"

They drove a while without speaking.

"I had something like that happen to me," she said. "Things happening twice, I mean."

The man on the cliff for one, she said.

"And the other?"

To do with someone else, she said. Supposedly inflicting himself on a young girl. "Except I don't believe a word of it."

He waited. But she wouldn't enlarge.

The headlights picked out the entrance, a solid-wood, stockbroker-belt gateway. Alphonse drew in, parked on an expanse of shingle.

The house stood amongst trees, as did stables, and a gentrified garage.

Emilia rang the bell.

"Calls it The Warren, for God's sake," Emilia said.

"What would you call it?"

He felt defensive of the man, Robert looking after his children while his wife played away.

"Pseud's Corner, I should think."

The door opened. A pink-faced man with thinning white hair was delighted to see her.

They couldn't stay a moment, Emilia said. They had just called to say Cecily might be a little late.

"She's re-living the holiday with some friends.She didn't want you to worry. I said I was sure you could cope."

"She might as well enjoy her youth," Robert smiled. "It's her birthday tomorrow."

He asked no questions. Alphonse noticed how innocent the eyes were in the man's young-old face.

"Can I offer you a drink?"

Emilia declined. Alphonse felt he ought to follow suit.

"So you're a chorister too," Robert said. "Cecily is always saying how friendly everyone is there. Even the choirmaster."

"She sings his praises?"

Robert laughed. Alphonse liked him. The man deserved better of his wife. Yet he could understand how driven Cecily must feel, how her thoughts would fly again and again to that one face.

He pulled into the slip road outside Emilia's home. Opposite was the house where he had lived as a child. It looked much as he remembered it, red-tiled, trellis by the white front door.

"Where little Alphonse Fenley used to live," Emilia said.

He knew she was trying to be agreeable. He didn't respond.

"Still got the sulks?" she asked. "Cecily's a big girl now."

"Just trying to work out who's the pseud. That's all."

She noticed he hadn't undone his seat belt.

"Like to come in and say hello to Mum?" she said. "Now you're here?"

Only a courtesy for bringing her home, she thought. Needn't think he was getting his feet under the table.

CHAPTER 8

"Still the same Alphonse!"

And she was the same Mrs Connaby. Thin, the flesh gone from her face, but still the woman who had always treated him as a friend rather than a child.

When he'd finished his training, he told her, he'd started at Small Boats Assurance, had recently been promoted and transferred to another branch, so now here he was back again in a rented flat in dear old Kirkhaven.

"And when I joined the choir the other week Emilia was there too. It was like old times."

"Except you didn't know me from Adam," Emilia said.

"Time fulfilling itself."

The conversation twisted and turned, the years since he had left were gone over, but under it the remark glinted. Typical of Mrs Connaby's way of thinking, as if time was as alive as we are. He wanted to ask her, wanted her to explain, but talk had turned to the time Dr Connaby had built a pond in the garden and Alphonse and a friend had stocked it with fish. He remembered the evening. The fish had queued up to hook themselves on the lines. He recalled thinking how pleased Emilia would be, how she would look at him when the rudd flicked their tails and swam out of the jar into the pond. Nowadays he disliked that side of himself, of always having a motive for what he did, whereas his friend had fished for the delight of it.

"We got them in the Spring Deek," he remembered.

"Deek?" Emilia mocked. "Do you mean dyke?"

"We always called it the Spring Deek."

"Could be Middle English," she said, "before ee turned to I."

She gave him a look, daring him to contradict.

"Now he'll call me Emilia Brainbox," she told her mum.

He liked the way she looked after her mother, her concern that the small table wasn't too far away or the chair too hard. He saw how pleased Mrs Connaby was with her daughter, wondered about the way he treated his own mother, whether her eyes lit up when she saw him. Was afraid he knew the answer.

The phone bleeped.

Jean picked it up.

"Love to see you," she said into it. "Be as soon as you can."

"Kendal," she explained. "Wonders if it's all right to drop in on his way home. He's in the car now."

They wouldn't hear of Alphonse leaving.

"He can come up and see my etchings while you old ones have your chin-wag," Emilia said.

Alphonse wished her eyes would dance at him the way they danced at her mum at the remark.

"Of course I remember Alphonse."

Kendal smiled at Emilia, linking them.

"Intelligent young lad."

"You could have the wrong Alphonse," Emilia murmured.

How at ease they all were, Alphonse thought, Kendal sure of their affection, Jean and Emilia so at home with him. A kindly, sturdily built, comfortably dressed man,

Kendal asked after this and that detail of their life as if their affairs were his business.

Alphonse envied him, the intimacy. He himself was always on the edge of things, outside the groups of people in his life. He didn't think it was lack of confidence – though if he could be sure he'd hang on to his job he might start to feel more in the centre of things.

"Alphonse is going to come up and see my etchings," Emilia told them. "I think?"

"Of course," he said.

He was seeing the heart of Emilia's world, he realised: her mother, her uncle, her paintings, her home. It was the girl herself who was such a flickering flame.

Jean and Kendal went over to the window. He stroked her hand, wondered if she hadn't lost a little more weight.

"I'm well enough," she said, understanding the interest in her knuckles. "I eat well, do my usual things. I'm no worse."

In the north-west the sky still had a touch of colour. Along the avenue lamps glowed under ornamental trees. In a few hours, Kendal mused, daylight would return, the sun would emerge from its shallow arc, birds would sing, the shadows would melt away. It was hard to accept that this metaphor of renewal wouldn't apply to Jean, that the slight figure reflected beside him in the window would never recover.

"Twelve years come September the Fenleys moved," she said.

He squeezed her thin shoulders.

"The year Johnson made the pond."

The year Johnson died, she could have added.

She drew the curtains. It seemed appropriate.

"Alphonse caught some fish for it. We were talking about it when you rang."

"So he would have known Johnson?"

"He used to call round for Emilia. Used to be sweethearts, I thought. Don't know if people have sweethearts any more? Seems to be partners now – or lovers."

They sat together on the settee, the mention of Johnson another bond between them.

"Alphonse seems a nice chap," Kendal said. "Single?"

Jean studied him.

"Didn't Valerie mention it? Apropos something I wouldn't otherwise mention?"

"Remind me."

"Emilia came out with the remark when she was here. She said, `Alphonse tells me he's never had sexual intercourse!' Just came out with it. Absolute show-stopper."

"What did Valerie say to that?"

"Cross. Hadn't come here to be laughed at, she said. She left soon after. So to answer your question, yes, I should think he is single."

Kendal's eyes softened. "I hope it goes well for them – if it goes at all, I mean. They seem to like each other?"

"So far as I can tell. Emilia's got a lot on her plate – what with me, and her exhibition. But I think she'll do well enough. Alphonse calls her Emilia Brainbox."

Kendal laughed with her.

"She doesn't take after me."

"Though you're the very one she does take after," she murmured. "As well you know."

They sat a while, unwilling to disturb a reverie of what life might have been like.

Jean moved to an upright chair, the back legs of which rested on blocks of wood. She sat lightly, her head poised on her spine, each foot flat on the floor.

"Relaxed and poised," Kendal said, quoting her. "You take this illness – very well."

"I don't know that I do," she said. "But there's no point in reverting to bad attitudes at a time when I need good ones more than ever."

She allowed her hands to rest palm upwards on her thighs. When she was easy she asked him. Would he like to hear what Valerie had told her about him?

"As opposed to anything she may have told you she told me."

"I think I can bear it."

It was more a case, Jean said, of whether she could bear to repeat it.

"It's awful to realise that so far as she's concerned you're a destroyed person. What sort of woman would want her mind full of destroyed people?"

"Full?"

"You. Me. Emilia. Even Cecily to some extent. We're all damaged goods in Valerie's book. I take it she never promised you a rose garden?"

"Didn't need promises – that time of life."

Jean watched him. Well as she knew him, her brother-in-law – more than a brother-in-law – there were times when it was difficult to distinguish the man from the lawyer.

"She said she found a cardigan, a schoolgirl's cardigan, in your briefcase. You can guess the implication she put on it."

"A blue cardigan," she added. "Hidden away in your briefcase."

"Hidden?"

"That was how she described it to us."

"Us? She told Emilia as well?"

"Emilia came in while she was here – I told you her outburst about Alphonse."

"How did Emilia take it?"

"She's got little time for Valerie, I'm afraid."

"And you?"

Jean didn't respond. She put it down to habit, this trick of firing questions when he was under pressure.

"As to the fact of there being a cardigan I was open minded," she said. "What we didn't believe was that there would be anything wrong in it being there."

She surveyed him dispassionately.

"Was there a cardigan?"

It was his training, she guessed, that made him pause before answering.

"Of course there was a cardigan."

He sat with his thoughts, his usually mobile mouth compressed.

"It's all private, Jean. She knows damned well it is. My niece Pauline, Freda's daughter – she called in at the office – asked if it was possible to see me. I didn't have a client just then so of course I listened to what she had to say."

For a moment his eyes held her.

"I don't know if you know the family? At any rate, when Pauline had gone I found the cardigan on the floor, so I took it with me. She very much didn't want her parents to know she'd been to see me. Unsurprisingly."

"I'm not sure how long they're not going to know, Kendal. Valerie was obsessed with it when she was here. She's sure to tell Freda. She's her own sister, after all."

Kendal took it calmly as he took everything calmly. But under that well-set head, she wondered, under the greying hair, how calm would he be when she told him the other thing?

"She says she also found a pair of Pauline's knickers."

His face barely altered.

"A pair of Pauline's knickers. In a drawer in your bedroom."

He didn't wear the incredulous, indignant look she might have expected; more one of anxiety.

"Which she said she hung on the pink lampshade."

"That I brought in?"

There was no point trying to comfort him. His thoughts had found themselves in a strange place. It was beyond her power to help them get their bearings.

"You don't think," he asked, "she's going mad?"

It was answer enough. She couldn't have borne it if he was flawed. But she wanted him to be forewarned.

"She doesn't suspect about Emilia?" she asked.

"Not in the least."

There was no emphasis in his reply, merely certainty.

The occasional call of a bat came from the warmth outside. The curtains beside an opened window stirred and fell still.

"You will be careful, my dear?"

He put his arm round her. He'd take every care, he said. He'd sleep alone, he'd employ a professional food-taster and check the lavatory for explosive devices.

She held his hand. She didn't want to be alarmist. But if Valerie was malicious enough to confuse fact and fiction it was equally possible she could confuse right and wrong.

Except for the dusk that lingers after a summer sunset the studio was dark.

Emilia left it unlit.

"I feel I can undress my mind – in the twilight."

He felt she had put him on trust with the remark. Almost as if they were in church.

"That's when I can think better," she said. "When I feel I know who I am."

She leaned back against the edge of a table, apparently oblivious that they were a young man and young woman alone together. He knew anything other than friendship would appal her.

"You seem to get on well with Mum."

It was more than that. He and her mother were kindred spirits. But he couldn't tell her.

"So Kendal's your uncle?'

"Dad's brother. Pops in to see mum on the way home sometimes."

"Married?"

"To Aunt Valerie, unfortunately. Or extremely unfortunately."

It was a comfort to know Kendal had made a misjudgement. He liked the man the better for it.

She switched on some low-hanging lights.

Alphonse half expected to see a studio with pictures hung round the walls. And found himself in a workshop. Here was this glamorous girl in her short skirt and wool jacket – and all around, a muddle of hard work. A heap of sketches, a couple of half-finished paintings, picture frames of various sizes, easels, boards, rag, tubes of water-colour with dried squeezings of colour round the tops, pots sprouting brushes, plastic palettes with last times' mixings unwashed away, sketch pads, toilet rolls, packets of Arches paper wedged between the back leg of the table and the wall.

No shelf labelled inspiration – except for a few art books between a pair of bookends.

"They're made!" he remarked. "Hand made!"

Emilia was searching through a heap of unfinished sketches.

"God, you're observant, Alphonse."

"But they are," he insisted. "And made out of virtually nothing! And there was I thinking there was a tube of something labelled magic."

"Ah, well!"

As if it was what a wally like him would think.

Their eyes met briefly, amused.

He went over to the studio window. Close by was a disused builder's yard with saplings sprouting up amongst the dozen or so huts. Further off lay the main part of Kirkhaven. A myriad arcs and lines of streetlights threaded the blackness, the movement of traffic like pin pricks of light gave the impression of a vast urban swamp, brilliant, threatening. Beyond that, the sea, moving and rattling in darkness. Nothing of it defined Emilia.

She joined him at the window.

"I was trying to see what you look at every day," he said. "To see what makes you what you are."

"Sugar and spice."

He asked if she'd ever painted the view from her window.

"People like to buy what they recognise," she said. "A town at night looks like most towns at night."

"A girl's got to live," she explained. "Sugar and spice don't come cheap. I have to paint what'll sell. Till I meet a big fat sugar-daddy one fine day."

"Sugar daddy!"

She heard the disapproval.

"Getting prudish?"

"I think it's a wonderful idea."

He was annoyed with himself for being concerned. But he wouldn't want her to throw herself away.

"You asked me if I ever painted anything I wouldn't sell," she said.

She went over to the pile of incomplete paintings, found the one she was looking for. But he was irritated with her, didn't want any favours.

"Don't show me anything you don't want to."

She held it up for him to see.

"Don't know what you think – ?"

A painting of an antique vessel, a Roman slave ship, perhaps a Greek war galley. The colours recalled those in Egyptian tomb paintings. Instead of a sea the vessel floated on a silken scarf puckered underneath like ripples and arched over behind in a crimson wave.

He liked it. A curious, restless craft. Wouldn't mind going for a cruise on a ship like that, he said.

This ship didn't go on cruises, she said. Only a voyage.

"What voyage?"

It was the Ship of Death, she said.

He studied it again. The background was as yet only pencilled in. Maybe it was the way the ship seemed to want to move out of the picture – the impression of something insecure.

"Based on D H Lawrence's poem."

She handed him a poetry book open at *"The Ship of Death"*.

And launching there his little ship,
Wrapped in the dark red mantle of the body's memories,
The little slender soul sits swiftly down and takes the oars
And draws away, away, away towards the dark depths
Fathomless ahead, …

He imagined the vessel moving away, gliding into the shadows of an unknown shore.

What if it were himself, he wondered, and one of his loved ones about to go to such a place?

"I want it to have a cargo of thoughts."

Thoughts of what, he asked.

"I want to tell my mum things. So when she dies she'll know my thoughts, what I feel about everything. She'll take with her what we've shared – and I'll be here, remembering what we shared."

He was aware of the pale walls of the studio, the uncurtained blackness of the window, the paraphernalia of painty things – and Emilia, vulnerable, standing as she might have stood as a child, her fingers screwing and twisting the paper she had used as a bookmark for the Lawrence poem.

When her dad died, she said, it must have been like leaving a young stranger behind. They weren't distant, she and her dad, but she didn't know him.

"I mean, I even knew my teacher better than I knew my dad. I loved him like anything – but he didn't know what was going on in my head. I can't tell you how much I regret that – him going away for ever, like a stranger. But with my mum, I want to know her, I want her to know me – so she'll take part of me with her."

He suddenly felt closer to her. She seemed more real, more human. Yet he felt inadequate, unable to meet her at that level.

"Symbolically, you mean? Like the ship is symbolic?"

"She'll take our sum of thoughts with her."

"Is that what you believe, we're still mental entities after we're dead?"

"We can believe that," she said, "or that our minds dissolve like our bodies. If that's what you meant?"

He didn't answer, uneasy about such things.

So far as she understood it, she said, the universe was based on intelligence.

"I mean, it's taken the combined efforts of the greatest minds in history to find out the little we do know about it – which would hardly be the case if what they were trying to find out about was not based on intelligence."

And since the universe seemed made of mind as well as matter she didn't think it unreasonable to suppose that mind continued after death.

"I mean, matter can neither be created nor destroyed, so why shouldn't that apply to mind?"

"Even when the person is dead?"

"I'm not talking about brain function," she smiled.

"How full is this ship?" he asked.

"Oh, there's tons of space," she joked. "You could add your thoughts in if you like, not that they'd take up much room."

She was standing close, the other side of the painting. She had told him her tenderest thoughts. And he had intellectualised the conversation, been less than honest.

"Nice meeting your mum. And seeing the picture – "

Afterwards he thought he'd said it was great. Or impressive. He believed he'd used the word *upsetting*.

What he remembered most was that she contrived to be at the doorway first. And turned and faced him. It took a moment for her intention to register, the girl deliberately standing there, facing him, not letting him pass.

He leaned to kiss her.

It happened before he was aware, her turning away at the last moment so that he brushed her cheek instead.

"Alphonse!"

As if it had been his intention, as if he had done something brutish.

"You trying to set me up?"

He didn't wait for an answer. He pushed past and went

downstairs. But she came downstairs with him, and when he stopped at the living-room door, not sure whether to interrupt her mother and Kendal, she said they'd love to see him. As though the kiss incident hadn't happened.

"Alphonse is off to get some badly-needed beauty sleep," she told them. "I hope you two have been behaving yourselves."

"And you," her mother laughed.

"Oh, Alphonse does nothing but talk."

He was awaiting the result of an interview, she added.

"So wish him luck."

Mrs Connaby's hand was warm, friendly. He was amazed how herself she was, how caring. Didn't seem possible she'd got the skids of death under her.

Kendal wished him well, seemed to regard him as a son come home.

Emilia went to the car with him. He didn't speak, could hardly trust himself to. She was like one of those methane flames flickering on swamps and decayed vegetation, here, then here, then over there.

He wished her luck with her exhibition.

"Thank you for coming to see mum," she said. "I could tell she was pleased."

"See you," he said. But didn't look at her.

He started the car.

"I hope there's good news about the interview," she said. "And thanks for bringing me home."

He drove off. Didn't bother to wave.

CHAPTER 9

"Who're you looking at, pratface?"

Hadn't realised he'd been looking their way. Seven or eight of them, hard-faced, hard-eyed, chasing about, swearing and catcalling in the mouth of the arcade.

Alphonse walked on. He'd come to have a look at the Kirkhaven he used to know.

"You I mean! Pratface!"

He visualised seizing the ringleader by the T shirt and hoisting him over on to the concrete. It irritated him to have to walk away. He wished he'd kept physically fit, wished he could have smashed one or two of them in the guts.

The insults faded behind him. Little more than school kids, their strength was in the pack, physically heavy some of them, tattooed, their hair tied back. With so much scum on the streets one needed to get fit.

He decided he'd go for a swim. It was years since he'd swum in the sea. It was fine evening. He'd go there and then.

He walked on, hoping to find a shop that sold swimwear, found himself in a run-down area where shops sold second-hand furniture, second-hand clothes. The only place to get swimwear was back where the yobs were, a cheap-and-cheerful store where you could get kiss-me-quick hats, multi-coloured buckets and gob enhancing candy-floss.

He felt a tightening in his stomach. The yobs were there in force, shouting and swearing. He tried to walk like Gary Cooper in High Noon. It was easy for Gary Cooper. Death from a bullet was heroic when everyone was on your side. There was nothing heroic about enduring insults and God knows what from a bunch of yobs.

"You cunt, Sandra!"

"Fuck off yourself!"

They were milling about in the road, kicking a yellow ball across the pavement into the arcade. They had little concern for the passers-by trying to avoid them, nor for the child crying by a pillar box and pointing to the ball. If it came his way, Alphonse thought, he'd rescue it and give it back. It was like when he used to play football at school, the ball never went near him. But by the time he came out of the shop the child had his ball back and Sandra, her red and orange hair resembling the rays of the rising sun, was bending down talking to him.

Alphonse felt he ought to have got the ball for the kid. Next time, he promised, he would.

The draught of wind off the water tingled his skin like an adventure.

The sea was calm, darkened by a movement of air, otherwise smooth in brilliant blue fields from Kirkhaven harbour in the north to the Eastborough headland in the south.

Alphonse crossed the esplanade and sea-wall, went down to the beach. The smell of the sea brought back childhood days of learning to swim, the sea cold round your privates, the gasp as you kicked away and pulled on the water with your hands and squeezed it away with your legs and found yourself swimming on the back of the sea and heard it ringing in your ears; and realizing that under you were fathoms of water all the way down to the crabs in the darkness at the bottom; then turning over to float on your back, the sea comfortable under you, and the sky and sometimes a skylark miles above you; and then swimming back, finding it further away than you'd thought, your feet reaching down, feeling nothing but water, and swimming again, and still the suffocating yards of water between you and the beach – and at last your toe touching sand far below, the sea trying to drag you back at every step; and then you emerge, like coming home from battle, sea-drops on the body like medals.

He sat down on the shingle. The tiny waves sighed like quiet breathing, then dying back, almost to stillness.

People swam, paddled, played on the beach. Further out a group of people clambered about on a diving raft, diving off the edge or from a board a few feet up from the raft floor. Two or three young men were taking turns to practise their dives, swimming round back to the raft for another go. One of them poised himself on the board, arms forward, head up. He went up on tiptoe, gave a spring and curved down, his feet following his body in like a spear with hardly a splash.

"Nice one," a girl said.

A blonde said.

The little blonde from Head Office said.

She was with friends. She sat on the edge of the raft, her legs in the water, the sinking sun painting her gold.

He'd found her. Appropriate. This was where she came from, a diving raft on a calm sea in the setting sun. Life had opened its door.

Another girl went and sat beside her, their feet idly paddling the water.

The man hauled himself back up on to the raft.

"Pretty to watch, Richard," the blonde said.

He touched her hair with his fingers as he went past, waited his turn for another dive.

Like being at a play. The only part Alphonse wanted to watch was that played by a girl who sat swinging her legs in the sea, body gilded in the evening sun.

Richard stood on the board, backwards this time, concentrating on his balance, his arms angled, his heels over the end of the board. He was beautifully built. Alphonse wasn't envious. The chap had worked at his diving, had made the best of himself.

At the moment of the spring a wave came from nowhere, lifted the raft as he curled forward. His head cracked against the board. He slid into the sea.

A couple of the divers were in in a moment, looking for him under the surface. No sign of them. The wave, a foot or more high, rolled shorewards and broke, followed by three or four more.

A head appeared, then others. Richard was being brought ashore, unconscious.

Alphonse was on his feet, shouting, ran for the lifeguard whose binoculars were on boys on an inflatable raft out in the bay.

"Bring that!"

The lifeguard pointed to a rescue float, was already running down the beach, first-aid kit in one hand, blankets in the other. By the time Alphonse got there and pushed his way through Richard was in the recovery position. Bright red blood streamed from a gash in his forehead, rivered down the side of his face into the sand.

"Open that pad up."

Alphonse ripped the wrapping off a pad in the first-aid box and as soon as Richard resumed breathing the lifeguard pressed the pad on to the wound, tied the bandaging tightly round the head.

Someone knelt beside him, started wiping the blood and froth off the swimmer's face. The blonde, dabbing at Richard's face, dabbing the blood out of his eyes and nose. She was almost leaning on Alphonse, her bare arm brushing against his arm. He could smell her wet hair, her warm salt skin.

"Lift his head a bit," she said.

"Steady," the lifeguard warned.

"So I can get the towel under him."

Alphonse eased his head up a shade, she had the towel under, was smoothing it out.

"To keep the sand off," she said.

Her mouth was pretty, lips pleasantly full. Her hair more of a tawny colour now it was wet.

"Look at that!"

She was gazing at the pad, already growing crimson.

"Only blood," the lifeguard said.

"That's all right, then."

Her voice was pleasant, ready to make a laugh of things.

Richard had opened his eyes, was focusing on the faces ringed above him.

"Let's have that here."

The lifeguard indicated the rescue craft. Flat and light, its other purpose was to act as a stretcher in cases like this.

"I'm all right," Richard said. His face looked deadly.

"Get it close."

Alphonse had become the lifeguard's lieutenant. When he wanted Richard transferred to the stretcher and the blanket put over him it was Alphonse who took the other end of the stretcher to carry the casualty up to the lifeguard station where they wrapped a heat insulating blanket round him under a couple of ordinary blankets.

"They go cold in shock," the lifeguard said. Then he was on the radio for an ambulance, a minute later had his binoculars back on the boys on the inflatable raft.

One of the swimmers said he'd go in the ambulance with Richard; another said if they gave him a call when they left hospital he'd go and pick them up and run them home. Richard's bike was a different matter. Everyone else seemed to have come by car.

"Does he live in the town?"

They told him where.

Alphonse said he'd take it home for him. If he could have the key to the lock from his clothes.

"I'll tell his people he's O.K."

Her name rang in his brain. Even the wheel rim chafing on the back brake of the cycle he was wheeling had a stab at it: Amanda! Amanda! Amanda!

Amanda the Golden. On a raft. On a blue sea. In the evening.

A car hooted. A wine-coloured 2CV passed him. Amanda was waving to him out of the passenger window.

"Thanks," she called. "Thanks ever so much!"

The bright little car hooted again. An arm bare to a short blouse sleeve waved again.

It was a dream bursting. He'd woken up after being asleep all his life. Everything was bright and beautiful after all.

The air smelt clean and cold and seaweedy. Kirkhaven was alive, the streets, the shop fronts, everything quivered brand-new and wonderful.

"They'll just give him the once-over," he told Richard's parents. "He was more concerned about his bike than his head."

The news struck the woman in the chest, knocked the breath out of her. She was all questions, flustered out of her mind.

The wave, he said, came from nowhere. Pure chance. Richard wasn't in the water long, but they had to be on the safe side. He was in the best place for an hour or two.

She went back indoors. She had to get ready to go and see him.

"Could have been a big boat out there," Mr Wigby said. "Hell of a wake, these big boats. Seem to come from nowhere, waves."

He offered Alphonse a lift home.

He preferred to walk, he said. Time he started to get fit.

He walked.

There was a beach, and the water so calm the waves barely unfolded, rising a little and flattening as though asleep. There was a raft out to sea and people diving. Then there was Amanda, and Amanda pushing down beside him, hair wet, body warm, her arm against his arm as she wiped the blood away from Richard's eyes.

And a glance.

It was the start. He knew it was the start.

When he realised he was lost he didn't care.

He liked these back streets, these houses with doors that opened on to the pavement, their individual colours that took no account of what would "go" with the neighbouring house, street after street of identical houses – and all different; some rough cast, some bare brick, some stone clad, some painted red, some cream – houses lived in by people, he thought, not emanations from some clerk's drawing board.

He saw St Lawrence's church.

Had never been in it, but he liked the fact there was no churchyard to separate it from the public. Except for its railings it lay alongside the pavement like a row of terrace houses. He liked it for being what it wanted to be.

"I was built as the house of God," it proclaimed. "If you don't like it you can get stuffed!"

The sunset turned vivid; its light took the upper section of the tower, the black square-cut flints glowed like apricot.

"Try that, Emilia!" he thought. "Put that in a painting!"

But he felt generous to the girl. She couldn't help her nature, and was kindness itself to her mother. He hoped her exhibition here went well.

He leaned against the wrought iron gate to take in the change in his life. He'd seen his work of art. From the soles of her sandy feet to her tawny wet hair she was alive in his mind. There was no going back. Even if he never saw her again things wouldn't be the same. He was too stirred up, could never be what he was before.

A car hooted and drew up.

"You needn't queue up yet," Emilia called. "The exhibition doesn't open till Tuesday."

He was pleased to see her, accepted her offer of a lift to his flat.

"No trouble starting now," she said, meaning the car.

"That remark of your mother's," he said. "About time fulfilling itself. I hadn't thought of it like that."

"Like what?"

"That things come true – they work out right."

Her mum wouldn't be that simplistic, she said.

"Things obviously don't work out all right – as Mum knows better than most."

"I don't mean they work out happily. I mean they work out in more detail – more clarity."

He was back on the beach. Saw Amanda idly paddling her feet to and fro, the water swirling, trapping the little hairs against her legs.

"As if the picture gets clearer rather than fainter."

He sat forward, an idea suddenly alive in him.

"It's like a sketch. Something happens in your life. Maybe you don't understand it at the time, just get a few impressions. Then something like it happens again – and it's more complete. Like your sketch of that ship! It's not complete to start with – but later it's completed – fulfilled."

They're like little boys, she thought, seeing him twist on the seat, his eyes full of his idea. She envied men their uncomplicated outlook, their enthusiasms.

He turned towards her.

"Life is an artist!"

He was almost oblivious of her.

"It does a preliminary sketch – some event happens – then it develops it. That's why things seem to have an echo, seem to happen in twos. It's the fulfilment!"

He looked so pleased with the thought she didn't like to say it was bullshit.

"Life is an artist! Experimenting."

His eyes moved over her face, scarcely seeing her.

"We think events are all there is, that they are what they seem. But what if life itself is experimenting, trying something, then trying again? As if life itself is a living thing?"

She wanted to tell him he had confused the issue, that of course life couldn't exist without creatures to live it. It was like saying that dreams existed independent of the dreamer.

"You ought to come round and talk to Mum."

He felt confident with her again, able to wind her up. She sensed it and felt easy. Could be herself more with Alphonse than with anyone.

He pointed her across to a 1960's block of flats. She found a place to park and drew up.

They sat a while, neither wanting to seem dismissive.

"I've been wondering whether to tell you something," she said.

But when it came to articulating the tale her aunt had told them she hesitated. It was too bizarre.

"Well, don't relapse into Nordic gloom," he said. "Come in and have a coffee."

She undid her seat belt.

"Mustn't be long. Though it's a treat to be away from painting. I've been on them all day."

The flats were made of glass and thermoplastic tiles. Alphonse's was along a blue and white tiled corridor, one of fourteen blue and white tiled corridors. He unlocked door two hundred and forty-four, ushered her into a room with a white polystyrene ceiling, magnolia walls and a window at the end overlooking a supermarket. There were a couple of white radiators, white doors to the kitchen and bathroom, a bed along one wall.

"Like it?" he joked.

The kitchen was more agreeable, bright with orange and red pots and pans, and posters of healthy-to-eat vegetables.

He put the coffee on.

"You don't have to tell me – whatever it was," he said. "You won't forfeit your coffee."

"Something Aunt Valerie told us."

"I'm thinking of giving notice to quit," he said. He hadn't got a place in mind. He'd have a look round. But he was hanging on to see if he'd got that new job.

"I don't believe it in any case," she said. "What she said."

"Because you don't like her?"

"Because it's not true. I wouldn't believe it even if it was true."

"Yes you would," Alphonse said. "You might not like living with it, but you'd believe it if it was true."

"It's an allegation of child abuse."

She hadn't meant to say it quite so bluntly.

"And you're afraid it is true."

Her aunt had found a girl's cardigan in Kendal's briefcase. Kendal had said it belonged to a girl who had come into his office asking for help.

"His niece," she said. "On his wife's side."

She felt she had to tell all – about the blue cardigan, the buttons, the navy blue knickers, the pink lampshade, the bedroom drawer. And the impression she had had of her aunt's relentless sensibleness.

"And this is Cecily's mother talking about Cecily's father?"

"She doesn't want Cecily to know. Which is something in her favour, I suppose."

"Yet she made sure you knew. And your mum."

Alphonse let his attention drift over her. It was unfair the girl should be so surrounded with ill luck.

"What I'm afraid of is who she'll tell! She's quite implacable."

"Who can she tell?"

"People who matter. Who can damage my uncle. He being a solicitor."

"But what can she say? I found a girl's cardigan in my husband's case, and a pair of knickers in our bedroom. But I've no evidence because I foolishly let my husband take them away."

"They were blue knickers and she hung them on a pink lampshade."

"Ho, that makes all the difference, madam. They weren't just knickers, they had purple spots on. And you saw them `anging on a pink lampshade? Not everyone would `ave noticed that. Don't you worry, ma'am. `E don't stand a chance. We'll soon `ave `im behind bars, the swine.' Seems all of a piece. I tell you a lie to upset you for some reason. The evidence which I could have kept has vanished because I was silly. I've made you uneasy about someone you trust. And if you talk to anyone about it you're risking trouble."

He felt pleased, coming to a decision so quickly. Especially in a matter to do with Emilia B.

"But why would she want to make it up at all? And why all the detail about the knickers?"

Alphonse supposed that anyone who invented something liked to protect the invention. Even a lie.

She was relieved he was so positive. Not that she was convinced. Yet she knew the allegation was impossible.

"Where's your tea towel?" she said, indicating the sinkful of unwashed dishes. "I'll give you a hand for a couple of hours."

"You go and get your pictures finished," he said, not sorry to have her feel indebted. "I'm not going to waste my time with a pretty girl letting her do the washing up."

He put his hand on her waist to usher her out of the kitchen. When she didn't move he kissed her. She didn't resist, didn't kiss him back, merely stood still with her eyes open, allowing him.

"You'd better go," he said.

She stepped back into the living-room.

"Unless you'd like to come to bed."

She looked at the high ceiling, the bare walls, the grey curtaining over the window.

"Not in a room like this, thank you very much."

He saw her down to her car. She was parked outside the Turner House garages.

Suddenly she came up close. Staring at something behind him.

"That's him!"

A man stood near the garages, holding a bicycle.

"Your man on the cliff?"

"Is he looking this way?"

"Not specially."

But he had the impression they were being watched.

"Have a proper look. Is it?"

In spite of herself she shivered.

"That's him!"

"You get in and start up. Don't drive off. Shan't be a minute."

He said goodnight, waved absently, and wandered away. As if he had something on his mind.

As he got level with the man he suddenly snatched the bike away and threw it down.

"You watching me?"

"You?"

The man seemed amused.

Before he knew what he was doing Alphonse launched a punch, his fist travelling inches.

It was a childhood rage, out of nowhere.

"You heard!"

The man tried to hit back, got a harder thump. In the stomach.

"Wanker!"

The man turned towards Emilia's car, tried to grin. Alphonse pushed his head against the garage.

"C – rist!"

He was holding his ear, amazed at the attack.

"If I see you here again – or wanking on the cliffs – "

"I'll have the police on you – !"

Alphonse brought his head down into the man's face.

"If you're here when I come back – !" he said quietly.

He hurried away, got in the car.

Emilia drove off.

Alphonse got his breath back. Found he was shaking.

"Drive to your house," he said. "I'll walk back."

"Think you hurt him?"

"Christ knows."

He was amazed how angry he'd got. But felt revenged. They hardly spoke the rest of the way. It was a shared time, a bond that didn't need words.

Emilia pulled into her drive.

"Like to come in for a coffee?"

"If anything happens about this," he said, "say you'd lent the car to me. In case he made a note of your number."

"Stay if you like," she said.

The lights were out in the house. Her mum would have gone to bed. He knew she meant in another room.

He'd go and see where the bloke had got to, he said. If he was still there he'd thump him again.

CHAPTER 10

He heard the letter come despite the gusts of rain on the window.

A long white envelope on the doormat.

Surely not the police!

He recognised the firm's letterhead. Perhaps he hadn't got the job after all. Perhaps failure hadn't been as slim a chance as he'd thought. He'd face up to it though. It wouldn't be the end of the world if he didn't get it. Yesterday he had seen Amanda, had felt her bare arm brush his arm. Yesterday he had beaten the bloke up for Emilia, had kissed her and she hadn't demurred. And yesterday he had enjoyed his work at the Audley Road office as usual. Nothing disagreeable about a continuation of yesterdays.

He opened the letter. A glance was enough.

"The successful candidate was Mr Owen Evans...we should like to thank you...further posts will be..."

He felt numb. The interview had gone so well. There had been no trouble with the questions, he had demonstrated his skills, he was on top of his job and everybody knew it. Even Big Dick Dickson -

That smooth bastard!

"...the successful candidate was Mr Owen Evans..."

He washed and dressed in a daze. Read the letter again. It was unbelievable. But he did believe it. Wouldn't be such a thump in the guts if he didn't believe it.

Now it was a case of facing failure. Publicly. The news would race round the firm. Alphonse Fenley couldn't keep his own job.

He supposed he'd locked the door of the flat. Couldn't remember. Couldn't be bothered to go back and check.

When he got to work he'd say it was no more than he'd expected, seeing who was on the panel.

But mentally he had been preparing for the new job, had anticipated accepting their congratulations, determined not to bask, not to ease up. Now it would be a case of having to apply for something else. If anything else turned up.

"Alphonse! I can't believe it!"

Tina was kind. Tina was always kind.

"I don't know how you can be so laid back about it," Doreen said. "And to think he got it," jerking her head in the direction of a certain office.

"If they turned you down," Stuart said, "what chance have the rest of us got?"

The phone went.

Tina held her hand over the mouthpiece.

"It's Owen Evans. He wants you to spare him a few minutes. He's in the sub office."

Owen Evans had rearranged the furniture a little, chiefly by seating himself behind the desk.

He gestured Alphonse to a seat. Alphonse's congratulations made a pleasant noise, but Evans's ears were already tuned to higher things.

It appeared that the directives from Head Office were going to require a more statistical response from Audley Road than heretofore. He was sure Fenley could see his way clear? And the presentational side, by the way, was going to transfer to Head Office with immediate effect, a move long overdue in Mr Evans's humble opinion.

"Don't you think, Fenley?"

The unbearable thing was he was such a poor specimen! But what did that say about Alphonse Fenley?

"Between you and me," Mr Evans said confidentially, "when I get a toehold here I shall want – someone with ability? Know what I mean? If all goes well."

And made what was supposed to be a meaningful wink.

Alphonse tried not to appear sceptical. The last thing he was going to do was help Evans out.

When Fenley had gone Owen Evans relaxed. The first sweep of the broom had gone well. He would be able to push harder in future. Where Fenley went the others would follow.

Both men knew that Head Office would be the place where the action was. And that Fenley's role was going to be downgraded.

CHAPTER 11

Valerie was emptying the last of Kendal's clothes drawers when the phone buzzed.

It was Freda. Sounded desperate.

"I can't tell you over the phone."

Near to tears. Promising start.

"Lunch? Today?" Valerie eyed the piles of clothes about the floor. She wouldn't want Kendal to know she'd been searching.

"I've got all of hour's work here."

But her sister had got to talk to someone or she'd go mad.

"I can't go on like this – "

"Pauline all right?" Valerie asked.

Pauline was all right, Freda said, because Pauline was in France on a school visit. It was when Pauline was in England that was the trouble!

Valerie's heart leapt. Maybe it wouldn't take an hour, she said. She'd really fly.

She was there before her sister. Par for the course. Freda got other people worked up on her behalf, then couldn't be bothered to turn up on time.

The sisters seldom met. Had never got on together even as children. Now that Freda had come back to Kirkhaven after all those years in London Valerie felt no closer to her. The woman even sounded like a stranger with her London accent and that free and easy way of talking. But her troubles were a pleasure to look forward to.

The Twelve Apostles was an old-fashioned restaurant with solid dark furniture and clean white table cloths. Valerie asked for a table for two in the corner.

Freda emerged from the loo.

"I saw you come – in your new yellow car. But I just had to go. My insides are that churned up. I'm nearly out of my mind wondering what to do."

The waitress came for the orders, the order book pressed to her aproned young stomach as she wrote.

"And a pot of tea to be going on with," Valerie told her. Freda looked as if she needed a pick-me-up.

"And how's Paul?" she asked.

Useful speculation she thought. Freda had made an unfortunate marriage. Her husband, it turned out, had criminal connections, came from a gangland family. But they were likeable enough, the Smiths, and Freda had never assumed that the flow of ready cash came from anywhere but the stalls in the various street markets the family had an interest in – until brother-in-law Peter got done for GBH, and then other matters came up which Paul was involved in, and both brothers went down for eighteen months. Since then life for Freda had gone along smoothly, much as life on the side of a volcano goes along smoothly if one ignores what might be building up underneath.

"Nothing to do with Paul," Freda said. "I could have handled that. It's my daughter Pauline."

The name was music. As was the heavy way Freda had said "My daughter Pauline".

"Now look, my dear," she said gently. "I've got something I want to share with you. It's not very pleasant but I must tell somebody. There's no sense you and me bottling things up. So you tell me what's worrying you, then I'll tell you what I've got to put up with."

"I hardly know where to start," Freda sighed.

Pauline hadn't been her usual self for months, she said. At first Freda had put it down to her age. Had been the same herself. A shame what some girls had to put up with every month. Enough to pull a horse down, let alone a young girl. But when Freda suggested she go and see a doctor she wouldn't hear of it.

"`It's not that, I tell you!' Stamped her foot as if I'd said something dreadful."

The girl was so withdrawn. Like living with a corpse. No-one could get through to her. And tears! There'd be tears at the least thing.

"Doesn't feel as if I've got a young girl in the house. It's like I say – like living with a ghost."

"You don't think she's – - ? Do you?"

Valerie was cautious of floating the idea. But Freda had faced that possibility.

"At least I'd know where I was if she was pregnant," she said.

"So you've got no idea what the trouble is?"

"Ah, but I have," Freda said. "At least, I've got an idea where it is."

She'd taken the opportunity while the girl was in France of cleaning up Pauline's bedroom. And had found a little red notebook. Freda had thought she used it for school notes but when she happened to glance in it she found it was her diary.

"So you've had a chance to read it!" Valerie exclaimed. "Did you find anything out?"

"It's a diary, Valerie. A private diary!"

"It's no use you wearing that holier-than-thou look with me, Freda. If you can find out what's on the girl's mind it's your duty to read it. Your duty as a mother. You've got to read it."

"Would you have read Cecily's private diary?"

"I used to read everything of Cecily's. I encouraged her to write her secrets down, then I'd read them when she'd gone to bed."

"Even when she was Pauline's age?"

"You've got to monitor what's going on, Freda, otherwise how can you give them a sense of right and wrong? Unless, of course, you don't care how they end up."

"Of course I care. I can't sleep with the worry."

"Then you want to look in her diary and find out what the trouble is. Have you any suspicions?"

The tea arrived.

"I'm afraid I have, Valerie."

Her voice was near to breaking.

"And that's why you rang," Valerie said.

She poured the tea.

She didn't like to see her sister quite so drained – though it was a price she was prepared to pay.

"You don't have to beat about the bush with me, Freda. I might not be so shocked as you think. I might even be able to help."

"I think Pauline's being abused."

The cup seemed to jump in Valerie's fingers, spilling tea on the tablecloth.

"Oh, my goodness!"

She was trying to wipe it away when the waitress arrived with the meal. Not to worry, the girl said. She could soon change the cloth.

"What ever!" Valerie said when she'd gone. "Whatever gives you that idea, Freda?"

Freda knew it sounded preposterous. It was hard to believe one's own child would be abused. But it seemed abuse was commoner than one had thought.

"You mean sexual abuse?"

"I mean sexual abuse, Valerie."

Freda looked straight at her sister. She wasn't going to allow Valerie to take a high moral tone on the subject.

"I mean the sexual abuse of a young girl by someone she knows, Valerie!"

It was like sunrise! Valerie tried not to show it. But her suspicions had been vindicated. She had been vindicated!

"What gives you that idea?"

Freda drank her tea. Carefully replaced the cup in the saucer. The days of allowing herself to be bullied by her sister had long gone.

"Pauline gives me that idea, Valerie."

"I thought you said she was in France? And you didn't know what the trouble was?"

"Which is true. But as a matter of fact I did read Pauline's diary."

"You said you hadn't."

"I said no such thing. All I said was it was a private diary. And I asked you if you used to read Cecily's diary and you said you used to read her diaries and letters and everything."

Freda hadn't changed, Valerie thought. Still the hypocritical humbug she'd always been! If it hadn't been for that little matter between herself and Kendal she'd have walked out and left the woman to stew.

Freda took a red notebook out of her bag, put it beside her plate and started her meal.

"Aren't you going to tell me what it says?" Valerie asked.

"If you're sure you want to hear."

"Isn't that why you asked me here? So you could get things off your chest? Otherwise I've got better things to do, Freda."

Freda took her time, enjoying the spectacle of Valerie unable to take her eyes off the book and dying to know what it said.

She read slowly, knowing it would irritate.

Fourteenth June. That's this year. He's still abusing me, horrible person, in the family and everything. I don't know who I can tell, I wish I could tell someone but D would be so cross if he found out, someone would probably get killed and I'd get the blame for that too. Now ... says if I tell anyone he'll say I let him do what he wanted the first time. I always feel ill now. M keeps taking me to the doctor.

Seventeenth June. Now I've gone and forgotten my cardigan. I hope to God M and D don't find out it's missing, I wish I was dead. Perhaps I'll get an illness and die so I'm out of it. What does he want me for when he's got a wife?

Freda read ahead silently for a moment. Then slipped the book back in her bag.

"Nice business, isn't it?"

"As a matter of fact, Freda," Valerie said quietly, "it was rather what I expected."

"You expected Pauline to be abused?"

"That cardigan she said was missing," Valerie said. "I found it."

"You?"

It was unbearable. That Valerie of all people should have known about the cardigan!

"Found it! Where?"

"No need to sound quite so belligerent. I happened to be looking through someone's case a day or so ago – and I came across it. A navy blue cardigan. Had Pauline's name stitched in red on a name tag."

"Why on earth – ?"

"If you remember," Valerie said quietly, "I told you at the beginning I'd got something to tell you. So now I'm telling you."

"Why ever didn't you give it to me back?"

"Because it disappeared again."

It was in Kendal's case. Valerie just happened to be looking through it while he was upstairs, and lo and behold, there was a cardigan. In a paper bag.

"He obviously wasn't expecting it to be found."

The pleasure on Valerie's face was undisguised.

"I don't know whose side you're on," Freda said. "Pauline's being abused, and you sit there as if there's something wonderful about finding my daughter's cardigan in a briefcase. I want the man responsible for abusing her caught. And if it happens to be your husband, Valerie, I'm sorry but he'll have to be dealt with the same as anyone else."

Valerie didn't look unduly upset.

"I hope he is dealt with, Freda," she said calmly. "I hope he's severely dealt with. As much as you do. But he can't be dealt with until he's found guilty, and he can't be found guilty until there's proof."

Just like she was as a child, Freda thought. Good at arranging other people's affairs.

"That's why I was so pleased about the diary," Valerie said. "It's the first bit of evidence we've got."

"Evidence! I can't let the girl know I've been reading her diary!"

"You can't afford not to. The first thing you've got to do is have those passages photo-copied in case she takes it into her head to destroy it."

"The girl's nearly over the edge – "

"You can't take notice of a child, Freda. Just tell her she's got nothing to worry about. You and I can see that Kendal is brought to justice."

"If I tell her I've been reading her diary – "

"Tell her it fell out of her bag – open at the place. It's up to you what you tell her. The people we must tell are the police."

"But Kendal's your husband!"

"Ask yourself, Freda, do you want Pauline to live in misery? In some evil person's power, just because you're too squeamish to help? Do you call that being a mother? Just because you're afraid of upsetting her for five minutes?"

Freda's attention drifted away. Telling Valerie had been a mistake. There was no comfort in the woman.

Outside the leaves of the trees hung palm down in the rain. Like dripping hands.

"What was Kendal's explanation?" she asked suddenly. "You must have asked him about the cardigan."

"He said Pauline dropped in to see him. As if a girl of her age would "drop in" to see a solicitor! He's got some hold over her, Freda. That's why she was seeing him. Why else would he have had her cardigan in his briefcase?"

Freda shook her head, defeated.

"It isn't getting pregnant, so much. It's if she tries to get rid of it."

"Or tries to get rid of herself!"

Freda closed her eyes. "If she knew I'd told you – "

"No need for her to know anything," Valerie said. "I shan't tell her. Ask her if her trouble is anything to do with her uncle. It didn't mention uncle in the diary so you wouldn't be giving anything away. See how she reacts. If you think it sounds like Kendal, let me know. I'll get in touch with the police."

"Easy enough for you. It isn't your daughter."

"Easy?" Valerie flared. "Have you thought of my side of all this?"

Freda had very much been thinking about Valerie's side of it. Had noted her sister's Pompeii-red suit, expensive black silk scarf, the jewellery – had seen her arrive in her smart new yellow hatchback.

"You'd have an awful life," she conceded. "Kendal in prison, hardly any money, everyone pointing you out – maybe saying you drove him to it. Your life would be ruined."

"So you please yourself," Valerie said. "You'll either do what's right by Pauline, whatever she says in a burst of pique, or you won't do what's right by Pauline. You'll just let things go on as they are, getting worse and worse. But if it does turn out that Kendal is involved, I hope you'll let me know as soon as possible. My life is on the line as much as yours."

"Why don't you divorce him? You're prepared to put the police on him. Why don't you divorce him and have done with it?"

"Divorce? Oh, no, Freda. What Kendal needs is punishment. After that I might think about divorce."

CHAPTER 12

She put it down to the weather. Rain and strong winds since first thing. Half the morning gone, no-one even been in to look! No-one was going to get soaked struggling to get to a picture gallery.

It was a nice feeling, having the fruits of her labours around her in the church, all fifty-two of them, completed, framed, hung to the best effect. She was pleased with their range, from landscapes to children on the beach, industrial sites to rural pubs. But she knew that if by the end of the week she hadn't waved bye-bye to a good few of them her days as a professional painter would have to end. Children of her labours these paintings might be, created for sale they definitely were.

She moistened her brush, resumed work on a birthday card for Taurus, one of an astrological series she was under contract to complete by the end of July. A great black bull reared up in a meadow of buttercups, front feet pawing the air, its hooves yellow with crushed flowers. Emilia stroked her brush along the abdominal curve from hind leg to pizzle, then touched in the horns, the swing of the tail.

The vestibule door swung and closed. A man of about thirty shook the rain off his coat and umbrella. His suit, his white shirt and dark red tie, everything about him proclaimed Business Man. He said hello, looked around at the paintings. Went from one to the next, systematically, giving a few seconds to each, as if on the lookout for something with a suitable C.V.

"Which one's your favourite?"

Maybe the one of the ship being loaded with grain for the Scotch whisky distillers, she said.

Why was it her favourite?

"Because of the light on the water. The clouds kept coming and going – made it difficult to get."

And she liked the lines of the ship, especially as it settled under the weight of the cargo.

He had a closer look. Seemed to study the corners of the picture. He came away, then turned and looked again.

He'd have it, he said. It would do nicely.

She tried to look unsurprised.

If it was her favourite, he asked, why wasn't it the dearest?

Because it wouldn't be many people's choice, she said. She could charge more for what most people wanted.

"Even so, your prices aren't high."

He asked if he could pay by cheque. And could he collect the picture Sunday morning. Friday and Saturday were both out for him.

They exchanged cards. He was Terry Bracondale. The card heading was *La Golondrina.*

He gave her the cheque.

"I don't need this," she said, handing the cheque guarantee card back.

His reaction was sharp.

"You must."

"I can't be bothered to write the numbers down."

He frowned.

"Have you ever been let down?"

"Only once. By an accountant."

He gave his purchase another look.

"I see it's got a gas module in the background. Is it there to make a contrast – the new technology as opposed to the traditional?"

She remembered considering whether or not to include the huge silvery construction, had decided to do so because it would form an non-competitive mass away from the centre of interest.

More a matter of balance in the composition, she said.

He studied the painting again as if determined to understand what she meant.

He noticed the Taurus painting, went round the desk to have a better look. She mentioned her contract for an astrological series.

"Not that I believe in this astrology nonsense," she said.

"Don't you? What do you believe in?"

The question rather caught her out.

"Genes, I suppose," she said.

"You don't believe in anything beyond? Fate, God, Destiny?"

"I certainly don't believe life can be foretold. Do you?"

"Of course it can, statistically. It's the basis of the risk business, knowing probabilities."

She considered the implications of the claim. Then peeled the back off a red tab, stuck it in the corner of the picture. Trust a male to come out with such a tangential remark: life can be foretold – statistically!

"An interesting thought," she said, "an insurance company basing its premiums on people's star signs – Leos more likely to have a car crash than Virgoans, girls born in Aries more likely to be raped than girls born in Gemini. You'd end up with everyone wanting to be born in October."

He seemed to consider the remark. Then said "Hm!" as if there might be something in it.

Three or four holiday-makers drifted in out of the rain.

"What about you?" she asked. "You a horoscope addict?"

"I try not to be addicted to anything."

He checked the card she had given him.

"If it's not inconvenient," he said, "I'll call round for the painting Sunday morning. Not sure if that's a prediction or not."

He did his coat up before leaving, watching her, as if he couldn't quite slot her in to his scheme of statistics.

CHAPTER 13

The diving-raft crashed down the back of a wave, slid sideways up to the brow of the next, hung for a moment before crashing down again. A seagull landed on the handrail, perched precariously, head pulled down into its feathers. Then glided forward, poised against the wind.

To the south the blue Clean Beach flag rattled from the mast of the lifeguard station; to the north plastic covers shivered against a stack of roped-round deckchairs. Whichever way he looked the scene was disheartening. No divers. No glowing bodies. No Amanda.

Would have been easy to idealize her, invent some dreamy version of a goddess. But he didn't need to idealize her. She had wet goldy-tawny hair, there was sand on her skin, she smelt of sweat and salt. She had knelt on the sand pushing a tufted yellow towel under Richard's head, water dripping from her hair, tied-back hair with a blue ribbon, the water draining through little hairs in front of her ears, little gold hairs made visible by drying water -

An elderly woman was pushed along by the wind, green trousers and anorak tight against her at the back, ballooning out in front, her two alsatians half-heartedly chasing each other on the beach until one stopped suddenly, crouched, quivered, gave a couple of scratches when it had finished, and lolloped off to join its companion –

Amanda had held the ends of the towel tight, edging it under Richard's head, her back bare down to where the swimsuit came round from her hips, her backbone an indentation in an undulation of curves. She dabbed at Richard's face with a towel, roughly, like wiping a garden ornament left out in the rain –

A group of holiday-makers walked past, plastic macs hollow against the wind, tracksuits dark with rain, the children dawdling behind, twizzling ice-creams round on their tongues, their hair wet, rain-gear undone.

Ahead of them, half-hidden by sea-steam, loomed the wall of a module for a gas platform, the colour of silvered fog, emerging and fading as the mist about it thinned and thickened. The idea of a building as large as a supermarket and tall as a block of flats being able to appear and disappear appealed to him; then its lights came on, hundreds of internal and external lights for the welders, plumbers, plate-layers –

"Someone's deep in thought," a quiet voice said.

She was wearing an oilskin-yellow top with the hood up. Healthy, attractive, rain droplets on her face. Her tracksuit bottom and gymshoes were soaked. He loved her for not caring about being wet, loved her rain-wet face, her soaking shoes.

"I came here to look for you," he said.

"In the rain?"

She was good-humoured, her voice soft.

"Just on the off-chance."

He indicated the empty raft. "I was a bit disappointed not to see you."

"Only a bit?" she laughed.

"And here you are."

He touched the arm of her oilskin.

"It's marvellous – "

He touched her arm again.

They laughed at the pleasure of it.

"Been for a run?"

He meant her gymshoes.

Been playing squash at the Sports Centre. She asked if he played. No, he said, he didn't know one end of a bat from the other.

"Bat!" she scoffed.

"You'll have to teach me."

"If you get yourself a bat!"

He asked if she'd heard how Richard was, after his accident.

He was back on the rig now. She'd met his mum the other day and she'd said he was as right as rain. She'd known Richard's mum years; the two families used to live next door to each other; she and Richard had grown up together.

"And then he goes and does a thing like that!" she joked.

"If he hadn't, I wouldn't have had to run down the beach. I thought I was in heaven, you being close like that. I could hardly sleep."

Young as she was, she was pleased she excited him.

"So when are you going to teach me to play squash?" he asked.

"I shall have to check my engagement calendar, Alphonse."

She giggled at saying his name.

He asked how she knew it.

"I asked at work. I asked Rita."

The girl on the desk!

"So you knew my name when we were with Richard?"

"Yes, I did, Alphonse!"

Her mischievous eyes watched him, delighted that he was surprised.

"Alphonse Fenley!"

Even her chin seemed amused, dimpled.

"I'll get a racquet," he said. "And some shuttlecocks."

"You don't play with shuttlecocks!"

She thought he was funny.

"You play with balls. You can play with mine. I've got some."

Her eyes were full of the devil. He couldn't imagine why someone hadn't got her living with him.

"Live with your parents?"

They lived back along the esplanade, she said. *Hotel In Concert*. It had been started by her nan and granddad and her mum and dad. They all worked there. She wasn't particularly musical herself though she liked it well enough.

He put his umbrella over her, the nearest thing to putting his arm round her.

"Awful about your job," she said.

He felt the blood rush to his face.

"You know about it?"

"It was all round Head Office. We thought it was dreadful."

It hadn't occurred to him she would know.

"I bet you were shocked when you didn't get it."

"I was, rather."

Failing to get his own job! And Amanda knowing all the time!

"Rita thought you were eccentric. Telling her you'd found some amber!"

"It was seeing you. I felt – totally..."

He daren't tell her he was caressing the tread of her feet on the carpet.

"Eccentric?" she supplied, smiling.

"That was the first time I saw you. You knocked me for six."

He let his arm rest lightly against her, holding the umbrella. Suddenly she tucked her hand round his arm.

"Comfy," she laughed.

They were outside her hotel.

"I'll know where to put up for the night now," he said.

"When you feel like blowing your own trumpet."

He loved the way she took the seriousness out of things.

It was an attractive looking place. The guests better off than many along the sea front. Amanda wouldn't be short of a penny.

"Amanda who?" he asked.

"Amanda Morton," she said. "Alphonse Fenley."

She said it as if the sound of his name was a pleasure.

"So what were you doing on the sea wall just now?" he asked.

"Wondering if I'd see you."

He couldn't tell her he adored her. He was too head over heels for that.

After she'd gone inside he watched the door. It didn't remained closed. Somewhere just beyond, there she'd be. Somewhere wonderful.

His way home lay past the church.

It was the final day of Emilia's exhibition. He decided to go in. He hoped it had gone well. He'd had his glimpse of paradise, didn't begrudge Emilia a little success.

The exhibition was over.

Half the paintings were off the peg-boards, some stacked against a pillar awaiting collection, others were being wrapped and put in bags. Someone was paying cash, counting out ten pound notes – three, four, five, six, seven.

He wandered round. Even the paintings not taken down had a red spot in the corner. But if Emilia was elated she didn't show it.

"Bought it on Thursday," a military-looking man reminded her. "The one of the boozer – people on the bench outside..."

She found his picture, thanked him for buying.

Alphonse guessed she was tired out.

"What do you want done?" he asked.

She looked grateful.

"Take these down?"

She handed him a list of about half a dozen. She had promised she'd deliver them.

"Being a beginner," she said.

"Give us your car keys. I'll put them in the back."

A pleasant little liberty, opening her car, bringing it round to the side street. He took the paintings out, ticked them off the list.

He wheeled the display stands to the back of the church.

The last customers left. She was too drained to smile.

"I've sold fifty. Out of fifty-two."

She closed her eyes and for a moment put her hands to her head. She should have been drinking champagne!

"It's Mum," she said.

They tidied up, too busy to talk. She locked the church door.

"Just got to drop the key back to the caretaker."

"So you did it!"

"I think the wet weather helped – people came in out of the rain and decided to buy a picture. And they kept coming in."

She didn't sound exhilarated.

He asked when she was going to take the paintings round.

They were all local, she said. She hoped to get it done this evening.

He told her to drop him at his flat. He'd take them round for her if she'd got the addresses.

She didn't need much persuading. She was anxious to get back to her mum.

It was late when he got to her house.

"I didn't know how I was going to do it," she confessed.

He'd quite enjoyed it, he said, giving people what they wanted.

"It's funny how they love to recognize what they see every day."

"That's art," she said.

She asked him if he'd like to come in and say hello. Her face said it would be beneficial.

Mrs Connaby was half-sitting, half-lying on a settee. There was somehow less of her. But her spirit was as intense as ever.

"Emilia says you've been so helpful," Jean said. "Such a shame, the exhibition going so well and me going down like this. I tell her she mustn't feel guilty about carrying on with her painting."

He took her hand. This thin little bag of bones gave him comfort. He felt free with her, as if she would eternally approve. She had a force he wished was in himself. Perhaps when he was with her it was in himself.

"It's exasperating joy can't be unalloyed," she said. "Emilia's had such a triumph – and I have to choose that very week to have a set-back."

"I don't feel exasperated, Mum," Emilia said.

"I know, dear. You've too nice a nature. But ointment never comes pure. There's always a fly in it."

Emilia went out with him to the car.

"I don't know anyone who's nicer with Mum than you," she said.

"I just feel – "

His voice tailed off. It seemed ridiculous to talk as though he'd always known the woman.

Funny thing was, he said, she seemed more alert mentally than ever.

She looked as if she wished he'd say more.

But knowing she was Emilia Brainbox, he didn't elaborate.

CHAPTER 14

It wasn't yet time for the pain-killer. Emilia put her arm round her mum's shoulders, all too aware of bones under the blouse.

"So how are you, dear?"

"Nothing untoward."

Jean noted her daughter's dark hair, her strong face, her nice frame. The girl would be all right. She had the possibility of a good life. There was little more one could hand on.

She noted the tired way Emilia was sitting, her back slumped, her head down.

"You'll remember me when you're sitting, Emilia."

Emilia smiled, let her spine straighten, let her sitting bones take her weight. Frail as she was, losing ground as she was, her mum was indomitable.

"I wish I could be like you, Mum."

Jean tapped her daughter's hand with a finger.

"If you're anticipating a painful event, my dear, take the long view."

Emilia heard the words, unable to relate them to what she was feeling. She studied her mother's face, aware that the pain of what was going to happen had already begun to separate them.

"I can only think of the day-to-day."

"Then you must think of the year-to-year. It's only difficult because we don't practise it. Try to anticipate how you'll feel afterwards. Then think of the long term."

"I can't!"

She drew back, afraid it sounded as if she was contradicting.

Her mother took her hand.

"Look at the evidence all around, Emilia. All the people who've been bereaved. They've all suffered. And survived. It's how we cope with what's to come, by absorbing it."

Then, seeing the pain, the intentness of her daughter's face, added, "Perhaps I shouldn't have mentioned it."

"But I *want* you to say it!"

She felt like seizing her mother in her arms and shouting it.

"I want you to say *everything* you think of, Mum. So I can remember. Everything you can!"

The face in front of her, the features she had known all her life – now all so temporary!

Jean touched her face, eased the trouble off the girl's forehead.

"Well, my dear, that's the way the dead live. By their influence. So as I say, you can think of me when you're sitting."

Emilia buried her face against her mother. Her mum was so brave, so matter-of-fact.

"You used to do that when you were young," Jean laughed. "It was a way of wiping your nose."

"Oh, Mum!"

She felt better for being reminded of the comfortable days.

"It's like Dad, you see," she said. "I know hardly anything about him. I don't just mean facts. I didn't really know *Dad*. And I don't think he knew me very well. I don't want it to be like that with you."

"'After you die,'" Jean supplied.

"After you die."

"'After you're dead.'"

"After you're dead."

Jean touched the girl's hair back from her forehead.

Emilia eased herself away.

"I've got something to show you."

When she came back she said, "You're going to think I'm peculiar."

She showed her mother an unframed painting. It was her illustration of D H Lawrence's *The Ship of Death*.

"I've already painted something. Anticipating."

"'Your death.'"

"I wanted to avoid the emptiness I feel about Dad."

Jean studied the painting, the ancient ship riding a crimson wave out of the world's existence.

"It's magnificent."

"It's symbolic, you see. Carrying our thoughts."

"It's what I'm to go on?"

"You've done so much for me, Mum."

She read out part of the poem.

"I want you to know what you mean to me."

Jean studied the painting again, the ship awaiting its call. Every day she had intimations she was approaching the same voyage.

"A royal way to go, Emilia."

The ship riding at anchor, awaiting the signal to cast off, seemed to fascinate.

Emilia put the picture on a chair.

"Shows you how presumptuous I am," she said. "You'll want to remember Dad even more than I do."

"He was a lovely man," Jean agreed. "Quite wonderful, really."

"I loved him. But I can't – I can't see him. I feel he could be near me – but more like a kindly stranger."

She stroked her mother's arm.

"Tell me how he was wonderful."

"People are when you love them – don't you think?"

"I thought you meant something specific," Emilia said. "Something I could remember about him."

Jean gazed at her daughter, a long searching look. Then with a gasp put her hand to her face.

"Mum!"

Emilia was on her knees, trying to cradle her. All her life she had never seen her mother give in, had never seen her less than herself.

It was only momentary.

"Forgive me, Emilia."

Jean sat back. There was something in the look, something different in her face.

"What is it, Mum?"

Jean shook her head, tried to smile. It was meant to be a signal that things were back to normal.

Emilia knew better. Her mother had faced bereavement, physical pain, the certainty of her own imminent death, and had never recoiled. Now a different crisis had come. One that the tired-out mind couldn't deal with.

"No need to bother about it now," Emilia said.

But her mother's eyes held her, wide-open, almost unseeing. As if seeing what was ahead.

The voice was a whisper.

"It's time you knew."

Emilia knelt on the floor in front of her, holding the hands that had once been smooth and unveined.

"I gave you a dishonest answer just now," Jean said. "When you asked me about your dad. I did mean something specific – and then I tried to mislead you."

The eyes were those of a child, in wonder at what its voice was saying.

Emilia knew she had pushed too far, had barged her frail mum into telling what ought not to be told.

"I don't want to pry into private things, Mum."

But the voice, sometimes inaudible, had its agenda, was at its confessional.

"I don't know why it is – but some people, or myself at any rate – can feel that dishonesty is beneficial. It's so foolish."

"Mum, I really don't wish to – "

"It isn't prying, Emilia. You asked me why I thought your dad was wonderful and I should have answered you honestly."

She sat a moment or two, her concentration unweaving the past for her daughter.

"You know," she said, "that he was only forty-seven when he died."

"So young."

"The disease that killed him, Emilia, had already made him infertile. He was incapable of being a father."

Emilia could only stare.

"You mean he wasn't – ?"

"He was your dad, but he wasn't your father."

Jean gave her time. She knew it wasn't the fact itself that needed time. It was her attitude, a lifetime's attitude to be adjusted.

"But you're – my mum?"

"I'm you're mum and your mother. Your dad was your dad, but he wasn't your father."

"Did he know he wasn't?"

"Very much so."

"Did he mind?"

"The opposite. When he realised how much I wanted a baby he advised me what to do. To let another man be the father."

"He knew the man?"

"We both did. It was his brother, your Uncle Kendal."

Emilia had to move, had to walk up and down as though to shake the news down into herself.

"So Kendal's my dad!"

"Not at all. Kendal is your father. Johnson was your dad. And that's what I say is wonderful about him. He loved you – nobody could have loved you more than he did. He watched you, he played with you, he bought you things – he was always talking about you. I think he loved you almost more than I did. He was so pleased when I got pregnant. So *pleased!* Not just for me. For himself."

Jean put a hand on her arm.

"That's why I say he was wonderful. He used to touch my tummy when you were growing. "`In there, Jeanie,'" he'd say. And look so pleased."

"Why didn't you tell me before?"

Jean's face seemed to set.

"Think about it, Emilia. Think it through."

"I've got so many thoughts in my head," she sighed, "I can only guess. Because you didn't want to worry me?"

"I don't think I minded worrying you, dear. If we don't have worries we don't learn how to manage them. I wasn't concerned about *worry*. I knew you could accommodate the idea in time."

"Uncle Kendal, then? Or I suppose he isn't my uncle now?"

"I think he'd still like to be your uncle, Emilia. But it's because of him. It's because he's married, you see. We didn't, by the slightest look or tone of voice – didn't want to give Valerie any suspicion."

"Don't you think she suspects?"

Jean took a moment or two to consider.

"I'm sure she'd like to think we're adulterers. But she knows we're not. At least, she knows there's no evidence that we are. But she hates Kendal – as you know – and would love to believe the worst. Like that cardigan affair she was so full of the other day. But she may have a sixth sense. I don't rule that out – something she can't put her finger on."

"I didn't have a sixth sense about it."

"You've got an unsuspecting mind. Valerie is the opposite. A sixth sense would be second nature to Valerie."

"I suppose it's true you and Kendal were adulterers once."

Jean sat up at once.

"Oh no, Emilia! There was a transfer of seed, that was all. We weren't adulterers, and never have been – even though I'm a widow and Kendal is unhappily married. No, I shouldn't like you to think we were adulterers."

"You must have enjoyed it at the time, presumably?"

"Of course I enjoyed it. I was a young woman, Kendal was a young man, I'd got my husband's permission – more than permission: it was Johnson's idea and he arranged it. And I knew it should lead to having a baby. Of course I enjoyed it."

She smiled. "I'm not a machine, Emilia. But we were certainly not adulterers. As a matter of fact, it was easier for me than for Kendal."

She smiled at her thoughts. "Poor Kendal."

"You've never felt guilty about it?"

"Guilty! Where else was I to get a baby from? If I hadn't done it there'd have been no you. Imagine that! No little Emilia, no big Emilia, no Emilia Brainbox for some nice young man."

She laughed. "I sacrificed myself for you, Emilia!"

Emilia hugged her.

"What an extraordinary mother I've got! An extraordinary mum and dad!"

"It's done you no harm, I hope."

Emilia thought about it.

"Not a bit. I'm the same now as I've always been."

She walked about a little to settle the new order of things down into her mind.

"I'm exactly the same. It's as if I'm a portrait in a picture – and someone has suddenly altered the background."

Jean watched her trying to come to terms with it.

"Though to me," she murmured, "the background looks the same as it's always looked."

"And as it's always looked to Uncle Kendal, I suppose. He's always treated me – like a nice uncle. I'm glad I've always liked him. Did he know you were going to tell me?"

"I didn't know myself, Emilia. I'd always meant to. But lately I've debated whether to take the secret with me. But when you showed me that ship – and told me about its cargo of truth – I couldn't *not* tell you. I couldn't have you look at that picture and not know. It's only a little truth, after all. Done in love. But there was an urge to hide it, I'm afraid."

She looked up at her daughter. "I'm as weak as anyone, you see. It's your dad who was wonderful."

She asked to see the picture again.

"There's a power about it. Something alive."

She studied it, the imminence of its leaving.

It was time for her to have her pain-killer and go to bed. She thought she'd sleep well. Her mind was clear now, clearer than for a long time. Thanks to her dear daughter, she said.

Emilia lay awake. She felt she knew her mother better than before, and her dad less well. And now she had another father. She felt no worse for it. Her beginnings were socially complicated, perhaps; biologically, as simple or as miraculous as everyone else's.

Her thoughts veered towards Alphonse. The way he had attacked that pervert! There was something primitive about it. And attractive, him doing it for her! She doubted if the man's parts would work properly now.

What a phrase – man's parts!

Do you go quick? she had asked.

Do you? he had answered.

Her poor mum, living with that secret all these years! Most women live with one sort of secret or another, it seemed, wondering what's for the best, wondering what's the friendly thing to do for everybody.

Poor Alphonse too! Another friendly thing to do, his trousers soaked through with the rain, taking the pictures round for her – and she'd pretended not to notice. She'd never have got them out on her own... Perhaps she ought to reward him...

But not like that! Letting a man break into her out of gratitude!

Yet her mum and Uncle Kendal... Engendering!

Of course I enjoyed it!

Do you go quick?

Do you?

Until the bell from her mother's room woke her in the early hours she slept heavily.

CHAPTER 15

Her mother lay propped up against the pillows. From time to time she mumbled, her gaze unfocused, attention on some private vision.

The skin on her face had drawn tight, pulling at the eyes, exposing the teeth. Her hands gripped a fold of sheet, the hands like little claws, clinging as though to a comfort. The injection soon took effect. The rattle of words stopped, the hands eased and let go. She would probably sleep now, the doctor said. He stayed till she began to doze.

Emilia went to the door with him. She asked how long her mother had got. There was no telling, he said. Could be days, maybe weeks. The fever didn't particularly signify.

"But I'm sure you make the most of every day with her."

She would have to tell Kendal.

She dreaded it, talking to him, this man who was suddenly her father. But there was a thread of wanting to.

She rang him at work. The secretary answered. It could wait till he was free, Emilia said, but she would appreciate a word sometime this morning.

His niece, she repeated. Emilia.

If only it was true, she thought, if only being a niece was all she was to him! But the adventure of it appealed to her.

He rang back an hour or so later.

"Emilia?"

"Uncle Kendal."

The "uncle" was electric. It was like learning to talk again. And a kind of lie.

Her mother had had to have the doctor in the night, she said.

His voice was so new, this man whose voice she had heard all her life. The way he cleared his throat, the way he asked how she was – all different now he was her father.

He said he'd visit tomorrow. If Emilia thought it appropriate?

She'd get in touch immediately if her mother got worse, she said.

She realised he had always known who she was, had always known he was her father. But she couldn't get over it, that she had spoken to her father.

Jean slept.

And when the doctor visited again she was better, better than she had felt for a long time, she said.

He'd call again the next day, he told Emilia, unless he was needed earlier.

She heard the door of a large car clunk quietly shut, saw him turn and walk briskly up the drive. It was eleven o'clock.

Today's suit was charcoal, with the palest of blue shirts and a mid-green tie. She was glad she'd bothered to wear something different from the painting gear he had seen her in at the church. But another part of her consciousness remarked that if Terry Bracondale didn't like her painting gear he could lump it. Who was Terry Bracondale when he was at home, anyway?

“You’re on the dot,” she said.

Perhaps it was the sort of remark not worth an answer; or perhaps his attention was taken entirely by the girl in front of him. She struck him as being even more impressive than last time, her black hair, green eyes, shapely figure.

“When you’ve been looking forward to something,” he said, “it often turns out disappointing. I’ve been looking forward to this morning and it isn’t the least disappointing.”

His grey eyes were as direct as his voice, yet she had the impression he had rehearsed what to say.

“Like to come in?” she said. “Mum’s not well so I’d better be where I can hear the bell. Though she’s better this morning.”

“Not serious, I hope?”

She told him.

He said nothing. A topic he hadn’t rehearsed for, she thought.

“Here it is.”

She put his painting on the table.

He picked it up, studied it.

“Still like it?”

“Even if I didn’t, it’s paid for.

He put things in an odd way, as if he was slightly quarrelling or taking offence.

“True. You were my first customer. The answer to a maiden’s prayer.”

“Did you manage to shift any more?”

“All bar two.”

“All that – churchful?”

He looked quite sharply at her.

“There were about fifty!”

He began to sound as if she shouldn’t have sold so many.

"People kept coming and answering a maiden's prayer," she said.

"Fifty!"

His smooth forehead furrowed momentarily.

"How do you stand for income tax in a case like that? Or VAT?"

She didn't know.

"You've sold pictures before, presumably?"

"I suppose so. Do you have to pay tax on that sort of thing?"

"If I was into painting, Emilia, I'd know."

What about her income tax forms, he asked. Did she claim all her allowances?

She gave everything like that to her uncle. He knew someone who was an accountant. She'd never paid anything so far as she knew.

Terry asked if many people had paid her by cheque. She couldn't be sure. Some had, she thought.

Because cheques were traceable, he said. Cash wasn't. If she liked – if she hadn't paid his cheque in – he'd give her cash instead.

"I haven't paid any money in. Haven't had time."

"You've all those cheques and cash lying about?"

It was his voice, she decided. His face was calm and composed enough, almost bland except for those ultra sharp eyes; but the voice could sound worried – or irritable. Yet it was pleasant enough as a voice. It didn't grind or squeak.

"If you knew me better I'd pay it in for you," he said. "I can't bear money lying about not doing anything."

"A problem for you is it, things lying about?"

"It shows a lack of concentration."

She couldn't resist a smile – not paying money in, with all the things she'd had to think about lately!

"You laugh," he said. "But it's indicative of what's wrong with the country. Resources scattered instead of concentrated. Thinking scattered instead of concentrated."

"O.K. You can pay it all in for me, then."

It was as if he'd been struck.

"I'm a stranger! I might be a crook!"

He looked so suspicious of her it was amusing.

"Don't look at me like that. I only said O.K."

"You can't entrust your money to someone you don't know," he said. "I wish I'd not mentioned it."

He spoke as if it was thoroughly untrustworthy of her. "But if I knew you well I would. Of course I would. Are you always free and easy like this?"

She laughed. "Mind your own business."

But she liked his concern for her. There was something paternal about it.

"I'd like to commission a picture," he said. "Two hundred and fifty pounds. That's the general going rate. What do you say?"

"A picture of what?"

"One of my restaurants. *La Golondrina*. The one near the church."

"What size?"

He indicated the size with his hands.

It would be a change to have paintings in the restaurants. Could be useful in advertising. It wouldn't do Emilia any harm either – get her name known a bit.

She was interested. When did he want it by?

As soon as she could manage it, he said. If it was satisfactory other commissions might follow.

"Except that my mum's ill and I can't leave her. But in the long term," she said, recalling her mother's words, "I'd like to do it."

"It's a deal then. Two-fifty. This big by this big."

He put his hand out to shake on it. But when she moved to accept he pulled his hand away.

"What does negotiation begin with?"

To spare her answering he said, "It begins with not accepting the first offer. Think of what's involved – your time on site, your time in the studio. And who's to pay for the frame? And you don't even know where the other restaurants are you'd have to visit."

He glanced at his watch.

"I won't pursue it now, with your mother so bad. But I'd be glad if you'd get in touch."

He sounded a shade more gentle. Or less abrasive.

"My offer stands. But always try for a better deal. Negotiation is the name of the game."

He took his picture under his arm.

"About that tax business," he said. "Don't forget your expenses. Materials and so on. Do you keep receipts? And a diary of where you travel to work?"

She found herself walking to his car with him. It looked large and new and as concentrated on money as its owner.

Terry came from a different world. Spoke a language she'd never bothered to learn, that rather repelled her. But it seemed he could use it to find his way to a goldmine.

"I will shake your hand," he said, taking her hand. "Because I'd not like you to think I'd refuse to."

He studied Emilia as if he had met her only just in time to set her straight.

He got in. The car purred, whispered away and was gone.

"One is nearer to God in a garden, Emilia."

Emilia looked at her mother in astonishment.

"I thought you didn't believe in God."

She and Jean were taking a walk round the lawn, arm in arm, stopping every now and then at a shrub or flower.

"I don't know that I do believe in God. But when you're on the way out you tend to explore possibilities. Maybe one is just nearer fresh air in a garden."

Her improvement had continued. She had had a good night and felt she would be better outdoors for a while.

"It would be disconcerting if you were to change your mind about God now," Emilia said. "I shouldn't know where I was."

"That's no hardship. Good for your sense of adventure."

The kind of adventure, Emilia thought, which was all too plentiful at the moment. Another adventure was the imminent arrival of Uncle Kendal. Her father. But she was glad her mother felt well enough to pull her leg. Anything to defer the huge adventure of bereavement.

A car slowed, pulled into the drive.

"Oh, Mum," she murmured.

Jean squeezed her arm. "Leave it to me, dear."

The greying hair was still thick and wavy, the face still broad and strongly lined, the kiss the usual kiss. But the man was a stranger.

She asked him if he'd like tea or fruit juice.

When she came back with the tray she wondered if he sounded too easily satisfied with what her mother was telling him of the relapse – how much better she was now, the whole thing no more than a storm in a tea cup. She and her mother would have probed deeper, would have sensed beyond the placatory words. Perhaps he was too innocent. Or lacked imagination. Yet she loved him more than when he was her uncle.

"Valerie sends her best wishes," he said.

"How is she?"

"I get the feeling she's – receding. Mentally."

"If you think Valerie is getting duller or less alert," Jean said, "you want to think again. There's nothing wrong with Valerie's faculties where you're concerned."

Emilia wondered what sort of a match they'd have made, he so unsuspecting, her mother so intuitive.

"Anything more been said about Pauline's clothes?" Jean asked. "The tale of knickers and cardigans?"

"Not a word. There was only the cardigan, of course. She's probably accepted what I told her."

Emilia supposed it was his legal training that made him sound so even-handed.

"I told her life could be difficult if everything came out. She's probably taken it to heart."

"She's got no heart," Jean said. "Except a stone one."

Trust her mother for common sense, Emilia thought. Kendal's critical faculties sounded undeveloped. Or worn out. Perhaps it was what Valerie wanted to do – wear him out of the marriage. But he'd got another daughter to back him up now. She recalled her feelings when Alphonse had given the pervert a going-over. To have someone in your corner, actively fighting on your side, oh, it ranked high in the satisfaction stakes!

"I think I'd like you to take me indoors now, Kendal," Jean said. "If you wouldn't mind?"

Emilia said she'd stay out and do some weeding. The weeds grew so quickly this damp weather.

She liked being on her knees in the garden. She imagined the plants as towns and villages, neighbours in the earth; and she loved their separate attitudes to organising their displays, some early, some content to wait, others always wanting support. But plants had their agenda too. The leafy caresses that try to smother a neighbour's leaves, their roots in a campaign to undermine the roots of competitors. Plants were as bad as the rest of us. The Garden of Eden had been no paradise. Had been full of cut-throat competitors from the word go. One was no nearer to God in a garden than anywhere else.

The alternative seemed equally unattractive, that we were the result of the survival of the fittest. Maybe those that didn't survive had the nicer characters. Like her dad.

She heard a movement behind her, guessed who it was.

"You look busy, Emilia."

She knew he knew.

CHAPTER 16

She stood up, brushed the earth off her hands.

"Hello."

She felt shy with him, this man who used to be her Uncle Kendal.

Who had given her mum a baby.

They stood apart. Strangers. Who had known each other years.

"Do you mind?" he said.

She did mind. Suddenly she minded a great deal that life should have played this trick on her. Why couldn't her dad have been her father? Why couldn't she be the child of a normal couple?

"All these years – " he said.

She saw he was uneasy. Was glad he was uneasy.

He looked away. Knew she didn't approve.

She knew what he'd meant: that all these years they had kept it a secret.

"Was done for the best," he murmured. "Or so we thought."

Greying, an inch or so shorter than she was. He had aged lately.

She couldn't come to terms – how it was sprung on her.

"Perhaps -" he said. "Needn't let Jean – "

He walked away a little, wouldn't go indoors yet in case Jean guessed how Emilia had taken it.

"I'm glad it was you," Emilia said. Meaning she was glad it wasn't anyone else.

He turned away, went round the back of the house.

Emilia looked down at the patch she had been weeding. Was reminded of earlier thoughts. The Garden of Eden.

Nothing had changed. Plants had wanted their own way then. So had Adam and Eve. Just like nowadays.

Yet she had brought it on herself. She had wanted to know her mother's deepest thoughts, and her mother had told her. Perhaps against her better judgement.

Yet she had a point, she felt: suddenly being inflicted with a situation like this. It might not have been so bad if Kendal had been only a memory. But to see him in flesh and blood, while her real dad was in his grave! If only it had been the other way round!

She found herself on the path to the back of the house. Kendal was in the greenhouse, tapping the earth out of some old flower-pots.

She watched him run a stick round, tap the soil on to a bit of newspaper, wipe the pot with a rag.

The gene-giver, she thought. My biological forebear. As near to me in that respect as Mum.

But *father* wouldn't form on her tongue.

He turned. "Didn't hear you come in."

"I'm glad".

He put the pot down, wiped his hands.

"I think I'm a bit all over the place, emotionally," she said.

She felt his arms round her, was glad of their pressure. "I'm glad, really."

She wanted the smell of him, his hair, his skin, the trace of aftershave, wanted to treasure them. He was new, had been long lost, and now he was here, suddenly, ready-made.

She stood back to look at him.

"I haven't got used to the idea yet," she said. "I suppose I've got a lot of loving to make up."

They walked back to the house. She took his arm.

"What am I to call you?"

"Call me Kendal."

They walked a step or two. He gave her a squeeze and kissed her.

"You feel almost like a boy-friend," she said.

He looked pleased, tickled her as when she had been a child. She laughed. They had always been close when he'd been her uncle.

"I tell him he feels almost like a boy-friend," Emilia said.

He sat on the settee next to Jean. Emilia sat on his knee. She wanted to settle on him and curl up and go to sleep. Wanted to claim a long lost daddyhood back into herself.

Kendal stirred. She felt his unease.

"I'm too heavy for you," she accused, getting up. "Aren't I?"

She dug her fingers round the tendon at the back of his knee, strumming it till it was unbearable.

"Call her off, Jean."

They laughed, and Emilia sat in another chair.

"Dad used to do that to me," she recalled, "till I'd nearly wet myself."

They laughed again, but with the word *Dad* the ghost that lurked at the back of their memories returned.

"Dear Johnson," Jean said, her eye meeting Kendal's.

They sat, pursuing their criss-crossing thoughts: husband, dad, brother.

The recent rains had gone and the skies were broken. Emilia imagined the brightness on the sunlit edges of clouds as her dad.

"I think he'd be pleased the way things have turned out," she said. "I am. And Dad and I nearly always thought the same."

"True," Jean said.

"So I want to say," she took Jean's and Kendal's hands, "I want to say thank you to both of you. I'm glad Dad suggested it. And I hope you're as pleased at the way it's turned out as I am."

Her mother and Kendal looked at each other.

"And I hope you both enjoyed it," she said.

"I've told you all I'm going to tell you about that, young lady," her mother smiled.

She looked tired.

Emilia asked her when she would like her tea.

She'd have a rest first, she said. Emilia and Kendal could have a chat.

"The exhibition went well?" he asked.

They were wandering round the garden, happy to be close to each other.

Very well, she said. And one person had subsequently commissioned a painting.

"Which reminds me, someone mentioned income tax."

He looked vague, seemed to know little about it. He always passed such matters to his accountant, he said.

"And what about the accountant's charges?"

"Charges?"

He wasn't clear what she had in mind.

It wasn't convincing.

"You've been paying him on my behalf, haven't you!"

And so it might have gone on, she realized, if she hadn't met Terry.

"You never said a word."

"The least I could do – for my daughter."

All these years, she thought. Looking after my affairs from a distance.

"Did you use to think of me as a daughter?"

It varied, he said. While Johnson was alive he had done his best to shut out thoughts of being her father, and had continued to do so after Johnson died, as best he could. It was the safest thing. He wanted to keep all suspicion of it from his wife.

"Sometimes, seeing you as a littl'un – - but Jean and I never spoke of it. I did my best to repress any fatherly thoughts. I fell into the role – most of the time."

"You were always my favourite uncle."

"I didn't have the difficult times," he said. "I didn't have to tell you it was bed-time, so I got the smiles, whereas your mum and dad got the screams and tantrums."

He had to smile. She had been an amenable youngster.

"You sound like Dad," she said. "He was lovely."

She thought how little she had known her dad. His work had absorbed him. He'd be in the room and not be in the room, would be thinking of his patients, the calls he had to make. She had grown from babyhood almost to puberty, had been, it seemed to her, a background to his life, a little thing wanting to climb on his knee to show him some treasure – and then he had gone.

There had been weeks of thinking he was out on a call, hoping she would hear the car, his footstep – but it was never her dad came back through the door.

"It's all your fault!" she exclaimed.

She closed her eyes, aghast.

Bursting out! Like a fool!

"I mean I'm your fault."

She took his hand, held it to her.

"No, I didn't mean that. I really didn't mean that."

She stroked his hand, placatingly, as a child might.

"I think I've gone haywire."

Her fingers traced the contours of his knuckles.

"There's half a dozen girls all mixed up inside me, and they can't remember if you're my uncle or my father or Kendal or – "

She stood away, heard the whisper of some outrageous relationship.

"It won't last," she murmured. "I promise."

She turned away.

"It isn't your fault. And it isn't Dad's fault or Mum's that people go away and don't come back. It's a habit they have."

She was glad he didn't try to comfort her.

"Can you forgive me?"

"None needed, my dear."

She knew he was unoffended.

"I love being close to you," she said, turning back to him. "You don't think I'm bent, do you?"

"A moment's distress. It's fleeting enough."

They walked over to the herbaceous border. For a while the talk was of plants, of what grew best in this or that position.

Then she said, "I'm glad Mum told me. And that it turned out to be you."

"Whatever Jean does turns out for the best," he said.

"And Valerie?" she asked.

She felt his hesitation.

Those tales of knickers and cardigans, she said. Were they all for the best?

"I don't think she's well. I can't think a well person could invent such tales."

"Tales?" she said. "Finding a schoolgirl's knickers in your bedroom? Is that all they are? Tales?"

"Maybe," he said, "when she gets a silly idea into her head she hasn't the brain energy to discard it."

She realized he was afraid of the woman. Knew what she was up to, and afraid to face her down. A rabbit petrified by a weasel.

She put it to him in so many words.

"I've never thought I'm afraid of her."

"She's dominated you for years."

"She's a woman."

"So am I." She put her arm round him. "I stood up to her when she came round to bully Mum, and I shall do the same for you."

He seemed uneasy at the prospect. But Emilia was sure of herself. He wasn't going to have feet of clay if she could help it.

A car door slammed. A woman had got out of a new yellow hatchback, was crossing the road towards them.

CHAPTER 17

Emilia hurried across to confront her. She had mother and a father to protect now.

"I trust I'm not interrupting anything, Emilia."

Valerie's attention strayed from Emilia's waist across to Kendal who was folding the deckchairs on the lawn.

"I saw how much you were enjoying each other's company."

Emilia stood in front of her on the drive.

"I heard your mother was poorly, Emilia. I came to ask how she is."

"She's having a sleep at the moment. Did you want a word with Uncle Kendal?"

She eyed the little stick of a woman in front of her. That her father should have married – should have been to bed with – such a harridan!"

"You've got a nurse with her, of course," Valerie said.

"I'm Mum's nurse."

"I expect you've offered up many a little prayer, Emilia?"

"I don't believe in all that."

"Ah, yes." Valerie seemed amused. "You told me." She looked across at her husband, back to Emilia. "The modern young woman."

Emilia wanted to reply, defeat her. Was dried up by her.

"I seem to recall," Valerie said, "you dismissing any notion that green could be unlucky. I expect prayer is an old wives' tale too, isn't it, Emilia?"

"Some believe in it. And some don't."

"Though if it was my mother," Valerie said, "I'd believe in anything that stood a chance of helping her get better."

"If I'd known you were coming, Valerie," Kendal said, joining them, "I could have given you a lift. I understood you were going to see Freda."

Valerie didn't look at him.

"I've seen Freda."

She spoke as if he was scarcely worth speaking to.

"Pauline back from France yet?" Emilia asked.

She wanted it out in the open. She wanted to discuss the business of the cardigan so it could revert to being what it was in fact, a few pounds of navy blue wool, not something dreadful talked about in secret.

"She came back last night."

"She have a nice time?"

"Pauline had a nice time in France. What sort of time Pauline had before she went, or what sort of time she'll have now she's back, is a different question, poor girl."

"What's poor about Pauline?"

"What's poor about Pauline is that now she's back in England there are those who won't leave her alone. She's ill from worrying about it."

"Does her mother know what she's worried about?"

Valerie stared at her.

"I came here to ask about your mother," she said. "Not to be quizzed about my niece and a person who can't keep his hands to himself. No matter what female he's with, it seems."

Emilia stared back, angry, ushered the woman towards the gate. "Thank you for asking about Mum. When she wakes up I'll tell her you called."

At the end of the drive Valerie paused and cast an eye over the garden.

"Might pay you to grow a taller hedge in front here, Emilia. Neighbours and passers-by – seeing a man and his niece like that! Unless that's something else you don't mind about?"

Emilia stood there, waited till the woman crossed over to her car. Wished she'd been able to say, *But Kendal's my father!*

And see the look on her face.

"Just going to see Mum," she called.

Kendal closed the garage doors.

The visit worried him. Years of dealing with the public had convinced him it was often a mistake to be open. Revealing a secret was easy; making it secret again impossible. But it was out now. Emilia and he were hostages to fortune. What Emilia hadn't seemed to notice was that before getting out of the car Valerie had been busy with her camera.

The concept of evidence began to emerge. For whom, he wondered.

It was an item he wasn't going to burden Emilia with. His wife had often called him secretive. So be it, he thought, and secretive he would remain.

"Kendal!"

Emilia was at the doorway. He knew by her voice something was wrong.

CHAPTER 18

She was in hospital.

Remembered something had been on her face – a mask perhaps, oxygen -

Voices. Close by.

Hadn't wanted to die in hospital. Wanted to die at home. In her own bed.

Selfish wish. She didn't mind dying here. Would be better for Emilia.

Be upset to think her mother had gone and no-one with her.

Gone! she chided herself. *Passed away! Passed over!* Would try not to *drop off her perch* till Emilia came.

Knew she wasn't going to die. Mind too active. The mind could never make such connections at the point of death.

Too soon to die. She'd barely begun the process of being a better person. Always been a struggle, to do the right thing, become what one hoped. Extinction couldn't come yet.

Surprised she wasn't frightened. Or appalled.

"My mind doesn't believe it's to be switched off. No experience of being switched off."

Wasn't a waste, dying. Leaves fall from trees. Earth is renewed. When we're dead, no longer mankind, more part of what mankind wonders at.

My mind is part of other minds.

What shall I see when the boat slips away?

I need no house now, nor my body.

The boat is ready. Will I take my thinking with me?

Was there no reason before the human brain? The world is full of human heads – is it more full of reason than when there were no human heads?

Boat slips away. Sounds recede. I am not as I was -

didn't plan this journey – stages laid down – pre-planned route – beginning of things?

It had got to her heart, the sister whispered. Was better this way. Wouldn't be long.

Emilia squeezed her hand. No answering squeeze.

Jean lay still, eyes closed, head to one side, the room filled with the noise of her breathing.

Her mother, who she'd never made the most of, never quite got to know –

The breathing lumbered on, as if air was hardly needed, now desperately needed, poor frame gasping – this peculiar rhythm – at least she was still here, still her dear mother – still the two of us together – me and my mum. If she wanted to – if she really wanted to – she could call her back. Her mum would respond – as she'd always responded -

She took a flannel, soothed her mother's face. Then dried her.

Breath leap-frogging in – out of her throat – face folding. What had been human in her – individual, what had been Jean Connaby – these had gone somewhere private. What remained was a shape in the bed – no longer her mum – her mum –

"Oh, mum," she whispered.

She smoothed a few wisps of hair stuck to the forehead – wanted to whisper, "Don't die!"

But her mum might have heard, might have deferred her dying as a kindness, only to face it later. For whose benefit would an extra hour of torment be? Yet every fought-for breath was a treasure, a sign she was still on earth.

Time passed. Emilia remained at the bedside, sometimes close, sometimes on her knees beside the bed. From time to time she wiped the sweat away, the dribble from the unclosed mouth.

The sister came, looked at the raw-pastry coloured face, the neck beginning to purple. She lifted the covers at the foot of the bed, felt Jean's feet.

Shook her head.

Emilia felt them. Cold, like the feet of a statue, like cold clay. The legs cold too.

The sister said she'd bring a hot bottle.

When she returned she put it under the feet.

The desperate rip-saw breathing had stopped. Around the bed only the background sounds of the hospital.

No terror.

She'd slipped away, had folded her gifts and gone. No trouble to anyone.

Emilia in a kind of wonder.

Her mother lay still, bright spirit all gone. Instead of her face, only the stuff faces are made of, hanging, a wrinkled bag on its frame.

What she had feared for months had happened. Her mother was dead.

She informed the duty nurse. She went back to the bedside to see her mother in death. Scarcely dared acknowledge the feeling, but she felt relieved. Not because her mother had died. Not because the days and nights of watching and wondering were over, nor even because her mum's pain and suffering were over too. She was relieved that death was natural. Wrenching, grief-stricken, empty as death was, in the end it was natural.

She whispered her love. She said good-bye, said it was not good-bye. All was numbness.

A couple of nurses came, drew the curtains round the bed. They were young, chatty, had seen death before. Her mum would have liked them, would be glad they were seeing to her.

CHAPTER 19

Cecily called round morning and night.

"You'll be getting fed up with me."

"Don't know what I'd do without you," Emilia said.

One day Emilia said, "There could be a reason why we get on so well."

They were looking out on to the garden. Across to the left was the flower border she had been weeding that last afternoon, the lupin spikes spilling their crimson against her skin, the canterbury bells – and then had heard him behind her, had stood up, brushed the earth off her hands, wondering how he had taken it.

"We've always got on well," Cecily said. "You and I."

"The thing is, we're sisters."

"Best news I've had since I was pregnant," Cecily said.

She wiped her eyes. Felt she was listening to a fairy tale. As if she was living a fairy tale.

"I've had a little sister all these years!"

She gazed at Emilia and flung her arms round her, didn't want good news to disappear.

"My mother is enough to make anyone discreet," she said. "Dad's life wouldn't be worth living if she found out. I shouldn't think it's worth living now, so far as married life is concerned."

"I asked Mum if she enjoyed conceiving me," Emilia said. "She said she sacrificed herself for my sake."

Cecily laughed.

"When I think what you could say your mum," she said. "And the little mine says to me! Your mum gave you love. Mine gives me advice."

Emilia caught herself observing Cecily as if she was a subject for a picture. But doubted if a painting could convey it, the niceness, the lack of any trace of envy. And under it all, that mist of unhappiness.

"One thing bothers me," she said.

It was whether Cecily thought Valerie had been wronged by what her father did.

"Wronged?" Cecily said. "Right and wrong! You do bother your little head about such things!"

"What do you bother your little head about?"

Cecily said she bothered as little as possible.

"I suppose all I ask is whether it's kind."

Otherwise, she said, it was like asking if a cow had been wronged because the bull had given another cow a calf too.

"Have to be a pretty mean cow," she said.

The evenings that week were long, full of sunsets. Clouds were hung with colour, and where the sky was clear its nakedness glowed blue and green and gold beyond any brilliance from a palette.

In honour of her mother, she told herself.

Cecily's company was more than ever welcome.

"Robert can manage," Cecily assured her. "He loves being with the kids."

One day Emilia said, "There's something I want to tell you."

"I'll sit down," Cecily said. "I'm beginning to recognize that tone of voice."

"It's more of a confession," Emilia said.

"You've got a confession?"

Cecily almost laughed.

"Tell me if you want to, dear," she said. "But I hardly think a saint need confess to a sinner."

It was to do with how she felt about Kendal, Emilia said. That afternoon he knew she knew he was her father.

"I hated him then. Seeing him, and him not being Uncle Kendal any more. And then he seemed – vulnerable. And suddenly I loved him!"

Cecily waited. Thought by the trouble in Emilia's face that there must be more to follow.

"Well, he is your father," she said.

"But it wasn't as if he was my father."

Emilia felt the words bursting out of her, couldn't stop them spurting out.

"It was as if he was my lover!"

Cecily sat back, amused.

Emilia didn't mind her being non-judgemental as long as she understood. But could anyone understand the near-incestuousness, the nakedness of what had passed through her?

"Only momentary, of course. I'm not like it now."

Cecily went over to the window to look at the last of the evening.

"But I'm still not easy with him," Emilia said. "Not like it used to be."

"Still feel peculiar?" Cecily asked, her back to her.

"A bit."

Cecily turned, her face and shoulders almost a silhouette against the evening light.

“So what’s peculiar about feeling peculiar? We’re all peculiar.”

CHAPTER 20

"I thought I ought to let you know, Freda," Valerie said. "Jean Connaby died. Last night."

"So you told me this morning."

Valerie glared at the handset.

"You won't be going to the funeral?"

"Why not?"

"Because now's the time you must tell the police."

She knew by the tortured breath the other end what the reaction was going to be.

"I can't. Paul isn't here," her mind mimicked.

"What does that matter!" she demanded. "Pauline's your daughter as well as his."

More sounds of pain the other end. Soon be raindrops.

"Don't know what I'm going to do with the girl."

"Yes, you do. Tell the police."

Freda seemed to think it over; asked when the funeral was.

Eleven o'clock, Saturday. At the crematorium.

As to telling the police, Freda said, she couldn't make her mind up about that.

Valerie sniffed. "Sounds to me you've got something to hide."

What people didn't understand, Freda said, was how quick Pauline and her dad could go over the edge. Paul couldn't stand pressure. Pauline took after him. She herself couldn't sleep, she said, worrying about the girl.

"Shouldn't think you can," Valerie said. "You'd be a poor sort of mother if you could."

Perhaps Valerie could come over, Freda said. Help her sort out what to do. What to say to Paul.

"I don't want to do the wrong thing."

"You've already done the wrong thing," Valerie told her. "You've kept quiet about something you should have done something about weeks ago."

By the time she rang off her sister was sobbing.

"That's that over for another night, thank God!"

Pauline came in, threw her homework book on the floor, flopped down on the settee.

"What was it tonight, Pauline? French?"

Her aunt's voice.

"Oh, it's you!"

Pauline zapped the telly on, zapped over to a pop show.

"That noise!" her mother said.

"Got to have something," the girl snapped. "I should go crazy else."

"You don't look well to me, my dear," Valerie said. "Anything the matter?"

Pauline kept her eyes on the set, huddled deeper into the settee.

"Only a friend of mine's got a daughter about your age," Valerie insisted. "She's been off colour for ages. Her mother kept taking her to the doctor's – "

Pauline pressed the zapper. The room throbbed to screen music, screen voices.

Her mother switched the set off.

"You can turn it on again in a minute, Pauline. Your aunt is talking to you."

"She's always talking to someone! I wish we'd never moved here."

"Nevertheless, it turned out this young girl was being abused," Valerie said. "By a relation of hers, I'm afraid. Who should have known better."

Pauline looked her aunt up and down.

"So that's why you're here. I was sure it wouldn't be good news."

"Pauline!"

"It's all right, Freda. It's always the messenger, never the perpetrator."

She turned to her niece. "I notice you don't deny it, Pauline."

"Haven't got anything to deny."

She was up out of the settee, across to the door. But Valerie was there first.

"Let me out! Let me – out!"

She beat her fists on Valerie's arms.

"Pauline!"

Her mother held the girl till she stopped. Then the tears came, the heartbreak. Unstoppable waves of heartbreak.

"She's only crying for attention, Freda," Valerie said. "Like you used to."

Pauline clung to her mother, catching her breath, unable to talk. Freda helped her over to the settee, sat with her.

"So it's true," Valerie said. "Isn't it!"

"Send that – old bitch – home, Mum."

"Who is it, dear?" Freda murmured. "Tell me who it is."

Pauline shook her head.

"Is it still going on?"

Pauline glared at her mother, eyes red-rimmed.

"You know who it is. Don't pretend."

"I! Of course I don't know who it is! How should I know?"

"The only one," Valerie chipped in, "who can tell us who it is is you, Pauline. Apart from the abuser himself, that is."

Pauline sat round and glared at her.

"You're the one who knows everything, you old hen. You're going to have a terrible surprise!"

And there she sits, Valerie thought, a shapeless lump a filthy pervert has tried to have sex with. Probably has had sex with.

"I could mention a name," she said, "but it's not my place to. I'll just ask you a question you can answer how you like: is it your uncle?"

Pauline shot her arm out, tried to scratch the face that wouldn't leave her alone. Then sank back, defeated.

Valerie moved away, pleased the question had struck home.

Suddenly Pauline sat up, faced her aunt.

"You know it's my uncle. Don't you!"

She grinned, mouth sticky from crying.

"I can't help it if he fancies me, Mrs Clever-Britches."

The television was switched on. The room jolted with voices, music, colour. Pauline was a young girl again, absorbed. Even to Valerie it seemed unreal she was being abused.

The sisters went into the hall, one vindicated, the other in despair.

"At least I know what's got to be done now," Freda murmured. "I've got no choice."

CHAPTER 21

Shirley Fanshawe was a trained social worker with experience of child abuse cases.

Her report on the Pauline Southwell case stated that the preliminary meeting with the mother and daughter, Freda and Pauline Southwell, had been satisfactory. The mother had been cooperative; the father, Paul Southwell, worked all week in London as a street trader and was not present at the interview. So far as Ms Fanshawe could ascertain he was both unaware of and uninvolved in the alleged abuse, but likely to react violently when he became aware of it. He had had an eighteen month custodial sentence for malicious wounding two years earlier. It was concern at his reaction which had been the reason mother and daughter had been reluctant to make the alleged abuse known.

Nevertheless from the initial interview Ms Fanshawe was of the opinion that Pauline was in a secure family unit, that there was no abuse in the home, and the mother would raise no objection to the girl being interviewed separately. Pauline herself seemed to display some of the psychological effects of abuse and could be expected to be in need of therapy. It was therefore Ms Fanshawe's recommendation that the usual network procedures be implemented as soon as practicable, and an information-gathering interview with Pauline be conducted by herself and a member of the police special offences team, the interview to be videoed in accordance with the team's usual practice. It was her view that the interview should take place if possible on Monday the 14th July, and the family be notified to that effect and asked for their consent.

In view of the reported attitude of the father Ms Fanshawe recommended that either she herself or a member of the police special offences team should contact Mr Southwell to make it clear that the over-riding object of all concerned must be the well-being and protection of the child. It should also be represented to him that any violence on his part could not only result in prosecution but also affect the mental state of his daughter.

The report was considered by the team as a matter of urgency. Matters should be put in hand forthwith.

CHAPTER 22

He sensed something was wrong as soon as he opened the door.

The look on Freda's face was enough.

"What's up?"

"Everything's up."

"Pauline all right?"

"Keep your voice down. She is and she isn't."

She had weathered him for years. Knew all about storms.

"Where is she?"

"Don't talk to me like that. I've had it up to here. Police and everything."

"Police?"

"And social workers. She's been abused."

He was on the brink, absolutely on the edge. She was glad she'd got it in about the police. It was the only thing stopped him going berserk.

"Abused? Who? Where is she?"

"Look at yourself," she said. "Just look at yourself. Do you think that's the way to help her?"

He was striding about, thumping his fists, hardly able to breathe.

"Pauline said, `If Dad loses his temper I don't want to see him.'"

"She in her room?"

He made for the door. Freda got in front of it.

"It's her that's been abused. Not you. She needs help, not someone stomping about in a temper."

He glared at her. At everything.

"If I get my hands on him I'll pull his bloody balls off – "

"Listen to him! How's that going to help Pauline?"

"Do you know who done it?"

"I know no more than you."

"When did all this come out?"

"I've had my suspicions for weeks – "

"Weeks! You've said nothing!"

"Said! Who have I got to say anything to? I can't say a word to you or you burst into flames. Of course I've said nothing. The only person I've said anything to is Valerie."

"You told that bitch! And said nothing to me?"

"I know she's a bitch. She's a total bloody bitch. But she's all I've got. If you didn't go off the rails at the least thing, I could tell you. That's why Pauline's scared to say anything – knows how you go. Specially since you came out of prison."

She thought *If looks could kill...*

"And who does precious Valerie think it is?"

"Come and sit down," she said, sitting on the settee herself, "and I'll tell you."

"I don't want to sit down."

"Then I don't want to tell you."

"Christ!"

"No, I don't want you going berserk."

"Look," she said, aware of ears in the bedroom, "You know the bottom line of all this, don't you?"

He waited, clenching and working his hands.

"What is?"

"If they thought this home was unsatisfactory they could take her into care – "

"Jesus Christ!"

"And there's nothing you or I or Jesus Christ could do about it."

"Oh, isn't there!"

She attempted to restrain him but he pushed her away.

"I'll bloody see about that! I'll ring the bloody social worker now. What's her number?"

Freda looked at him. Sat back and looked at him.

"I give up. You're mad!"

"What's her number, I tell you!"

"Look at yourself," she said. "Look in the mirror. It isn't Pauline! We can sort that out. It's you! You're the problem in this house"

"Do I have to ask you again?"

"Don't you threaten me, Paul Southwell. Lay a finger on me and I'll be gone. I've had it up to here in this house."

The door opened. Pauline burst in.

"Stop it! If Mum goes I'll kill myself!"

"I won't let them take you into care, dear!"

Pauline stared at him. Stared from one to the other.

"They're going to take me away?"

She ran to her mother, put her arms round her like the child she was.

"Mum! I don't want to be taken away!"

Freda stared up at her husband. Laughed in his face.

"You don't act like a man! You act like a prat! You haven't been home here ten minutes – you've threatened me, made Pauline talk of killing herself."

She eased herself away from her daughter.

"It depends how your dad behaves whether they take you into care, Pauline. If they think he's violent they will."

"I don't want to be taken away. It wasn't my fault – "

"What wasn't?" her father asked. "What wasn't your fault, Pauline? Tell me."

Sobs made the girl all but inaudible.

"What – the man did."

"What man? What man was it?"

Pauline raised her blotched face, looked at her mother for help.

"Tell him what you like," Freda said. "I've had it up to here with him."

"I don't want to talk about it, Dad."

"Just tell me who it was, Pauline. I shan't do anything."

Again the child inquired with a look.

"Please yourself," Freda said. "I've done my best to keep the family together. You two must get on with it."

Pauline turned to her father, tears, mucus down her chin.

"You can tell me, Pauline," he said. "Just give me a name. It'll be all right. I promise."

She looked away.

"Uncle Kendal," she said. "Kendal Connaby."

CHAPTER 23

It had come.

The day her mother was to be committed to the flames, burnt away into the elements. It was what she had wanted, to be given back to the elements. No burial for her. No slow decomposition in the dark.

Once, when Emilia asked her if she was sure, she'd said, "It began in fire, it'll end in fire, so it'll do for me."

On Guy Fawkes' night she'd have a bonfire of remembrance, colour and heat flaring up into the night. Fire would be her reminder. When lightning crackled across the sky it would be her mother's spirit, long-lasting as the universe.

"When I see fire," she whispered, "I know you'll be near me."

She felt exalted. Had thought too much about her mother's going. Had seen her go to that last incineration.

"Go," she whispered. "Go in your ship of death. Like the adventurer you are."

She felt she could almost go with her, to be with her. But when her dad had died her mother had been brave enough to let him go. They were together now, her mum and dad. Who was she to interpose?

Let them have their years together, she told herself. Sometimes an image came, a child arriving , calling, "Mu-um!" And her mum saying to her dad, "Little bugger's here already!"

It was the coming together at the chapel. Everyone full of sadness and pity.

"Don't be sad," she wanted to tell them. "All this black, these tears. She's going to celebrate in flame, going to join the sun and the sky and the stars."

The hearse. The coffin. The drawn-in silence. Wasn't just herself. So many heart-aches.

"You've left a bloody hole here, by the looks of it, Mum," she thought.

Men in black brought the coffin in. Her mother, alone in that blackness. Soon the flames, the bright extinction.

She hadn't wanted flowers.

"All those poor blooms," her mum used to say, "lying about with messages on. A funeral's no place for flowers."

But there were chapel flowers round the roller apparatus, brightly-coloured pot plants, busy lizzies, geraniums, lobelia, cheerful as a municipal roundabout.

The service proceeded. Ancient words spoken. The green curtain parted, the coffin slid noiselessly behind it, the curtain closed.

The busy lizzies, the geraniums and lobelia were as bright as ever. The organ spoke its soothing music.

Emilia studied the curtain. It remained quite still.

Robert reminded them they were invited to a buffet lunch over at The Warren.

People hugged her, kissed her, wiped their eyes. The next funeral was due, mourners gathered outside. Soon the organ would play for them, the flowers glow, the priest say comforting words.

She didn't want to look round the crematorium garden, inspect the congregation of plaques and name plates. Didn't want to think of her mother as a rose bush, ornamental tree, part of the crematorium gardener's art.

A boat was moving out of the reeds, away on its voyage to the unknown.

Someone touched her hand.

"Emilia B."

He looked cut up. Stood with her a few moments. Neither had anything to say. Then he went.

Robert had borrowed chairs and tables, light wood furniture that stacked and carried easily. He'd organized disposable plates, cutlery, the buffet lunch of cold meats, salads, rolls, the sponges, trifles, fresh fruit salad, the napkins, glasses, drinks. Had organized the disposal, the plastic sacks, the van for transport.

"Born organizer, Robert," Cecily said.

Cars pulled into the Warren driveway. Mourners made their way through the open security gates round to the back of the house. Robert and Gerald were checking the placing of music stands for later.

"Must help the wheels go round," Emilia said, "having a man like that."

"But that's all there is," Cecily said. "If he isn't organizing something, Robert isn't there! It's like when we go on holiday – he enjoys organizing how to get there, and what we'll do, and where we'll go on trips – and then he'll be organizing how to come home. But as for the holiday – he doesn't seem to notice it."

To Emilia the occasion was a kind of magic. It hadn't been conjured out of nothing; it had needed work and thought and money; and she was grateful and wondered if she hadn't misjudged the man.

"You try living with him," Cecily said.

Her children came over to find her. They were hungry. When she told them they could have helped themselves Zoe murmured, "But we wanted to have it with you!"

Emilia watched them go, three girls gravely pleased to be having a picnic with their mum.

"I'm so sorry for you, Emilia."

Emilia tightened at the voice.

"Must be the most awful day of your life!"

Valerie sat herself at the table, her made-up face not particularly unhappy.

"You'll never forget it, of course. No-one forgets it when it's their mother."

"I can't bear to talk to you," Emilia said. "I wish you hadn't come."

"It isn't my idea of a day out either," Valerie said. "My life isn't so wonderful I want to fill it with more funerals than I have to. But your mother was my sister-in-law and I've come for her sake. Not yours."

"You've come to gloat. You aren't worth so much as a roll of her lavatory paper!"

Valerie sat back, affronted, her hand at the gold and black necklace on her blouse.

Emilia noted the well-cut jacket and skirt, the expensive hair-do. The funeral was no more than an outing to the woman.

She stood up.

"I can't bear to be near you. I'm sure you can't be all bad – but I can't think a good thought about you."

Valerie's annoyance seemed short-lived.

"It started before you were born, Emilia. I was a hundred words a minute girl. With prospects. Thrown away because of the Connabys. You don't know the half of it."

When Emilia later re-lived the events of the occasion it was that curiously persuaded look of her aunt's that haunted her.

"One day the Connabys will see – what they'll see."

Valerie spoke as if it was an attractive prospect.

People were eating, chatting. Gerald, two or three other musicians and some of the choir were grouped on a low platform, looking through music Emilia had asked to be played. Cecily was at the table nearest them. Emilia wondered what Robert made of it, his wife so open in her feelings for Gerald.

The children were with her, one on her lap, one pulling Cecily's arm round her. Valerie joined them. The children sat away, had to be told to sit with their nan; did so, politely.

The late afternoon grass not yet browned by the summer; groups of mourners, eating, drinking, chatting; newly-leaved oaks massed behind the pond; quiet music; singing. Realised she was looking at the scene as if for a sketch.

And why not? she thought. This is the world my mum was in. It's right to celebrate it.

An Die Musik. She closed her eyes, let the music do as it would. When the last notes died she knew she had been in good hands.

It was Gerald at his best. Cantankerous, eccentric, master of his craft.

Kendal joined her. She hadn't seen much of him lately. She read his loss in his face.

Les Millions D'Harlequins. He gripped her hand, entranced. When it was over he told her.

Years ago the four of them, Jean and Johnson, Valerie and himself, had been to the theatre in London. Making their way down the underground afterwards they'd heard this zither echoing through the tunnels under London Bridge station. Jean had been enchanted, had tracked it down, this tune, echoing round those underground vaults – to your typical grey-haired musician in a black overcoat.

"Corny?" Kendal was back in the underground, in the land of years ago. "If you'd seen her down there! She was in love!"

"We missed the last train," he said. "We knew it was worth it. Except poor Valerie."

Footsteps crunched the gravel. Irregularly. Towards the mourners.

Paul Southwell, Pauline's father. Brandishing a loud-hailer.

Unsteady. His eyes everywhere.

"I know the man!"

Swaying round, his voice slurred.

Then he saw him.

"Kendal Connaby! Abusing – my daughter."

His feet were rooted, defying these friends of his enemy.

The loud-hailer brayed: "Thirteen years old! That's all she is. She named – HIM!"

His fist and stubby finger shook. But there was no mistaking.

"Kendal Connaby!"

The object of everyone's attention stared back, as concentrated as his accuser.

"The respectable Mr Connaby! Child abuser!"

There was a movement, another energy in the stillness.

Gerald snatched the loud-hailer away, hurled it into the pond. It hit the surface, remained afloat, water poured into the horn and took it down. A cluster of bubbles effervesced to the top.

"Coming here with that thing!"

The two faced each other, Southwell broad as a barrel, Gerald long-necked, willowy.

"This is a funeral! Not a market place!"

Southwell reeled back, swayed to deliver the blow.

"You lay a finger on me!"

Gerald, angry as the intruder.

Southwell let his arm fall.

He tried to speak, seemed choked, as if Gerald too had betrayed him. It was the last straw.

He looked about him, suddenly out of place. Made his way up the drive.

Her aunt, Emilia noted, was enjoying it. Seemed uplifted, as if Southwell was some kind of hero.

When Kendal got as far as their table with his list for their signatures she said, "What do you want me to sign for, my darling?"

"To say you heard what he said," Kendal said.

"I should think I did!" she said. "What will you do? Sue him? Oh, I think you should."

Valerie eyed him almost tenderly, as a hunter might eye a caught creature.

Using her own pen she signed, her signature twice the size of the others. The word CONNABY was underlined.

"The least I can do for you," she said.

CHAPTER 24

Amanda had already seen him, was at the lay-by, waving. "Couldn't wait any longer."

She got in as he pulled up. "Had to come and meet Alphy."

She threw her sports bag in the back, settled into her seat.

"I've told Mum and Dad you're coming."

She was so new, so utterly the person he had dreamed of. He could only look at her, her face, her hair, the shape of her.

"Your face!" she laughed.

But it pleased her, how he looked at her.

"Been waiting long?" he asked.

"Two or three days."

Every word she said was like a fever.

"Thanks for taking me," she said. "I'm really looking forward to it."

"My pleasure." And thought what a dull word *pleasure* was, to have a girl like this. Beside him. In his car.

She pointed him down a side street. He pulled into the *Hotel In Concert* car park.

Jack Morton was a greying, stockily-built man.

"Saved me a job, Alphy. Now she's got someone else to cart her over to Northaven."

"Make me sound like someone's luggage," she laughed.

"Just a little baggage," her dad said.

Alphonse sensed a business mind under the kindly exterior, weighing the advantages and disadvantages of not taking her himself.

Strange, seeing her in her home. Had wanted to believe she had emerged from the mists of magic, no past, no allegiances. Yet here she was with a father who spoke with a Midland accent, living in a money-making outfit known as a seaside hotel.

Mrs Morton came in. Aproned. Kindly. Not a young woman, probably overworked.

"Mum's packed us a picnic."

"Mandy's idea," Mrs Morton said. "So you could stop at a romantic spot somewhere."

She looked fondly at her daughter.

"Poor little fool."

He guessed she knew what was what. A woman probably too bright for the work she was doing. But he sensed they liked him.

"No more a fool than I am," he said.

He felt younger than his years when he was with Amanda. More open. Life had come right at last.

"If you get back in time, Alphy," Mrs Morton said, "perhaps you'll stay and have dinner with us?"

He was taking her up the coast to Northaven. She was in the Kirkhaven diving team competing with teams from Kings Lacton and Northaven as part of a charity event to raise funds for the local hospital. Each team had four men and four women, each of whom was to have three dives.

After that the water sports, but Amanda wasn't going to stay for the water sports.

"Specially now I've met you," she said.

He got the impression Amanda's time was generally put to use.

She cleared her throat. Unobtrusive little sound.

She was looking at hay meadows the other side of the hedges.

He caught her eye, drew in at a gateway. It was a rickety old gate, grey and veiny. She was as agile at getting over it as he was. Then they were walking through headland hay to the shade of a beech tree.

"Come and make yourself comfy."

He was glad she was so natural. Let alone her being a girl, he thought, and a pretty girl too who seemed to like him, as well as all that, he thought, she was someone who enjoyed life, a young pup enjoying every sight and sound and smell it scampered up to. He wished he was the same, wished he could make the most of life. It was easy when he was with her. Everything was possible when he was with her.

Yet it was too new, too perfect, this wonderworld. He felt he couldn't trust it.

"Alphy Milesaway," she laughed.

He laughed too. He said he'd been remembering that time on the beach when Richard had his accident, and this gorgeous girl had come and brushed against him -

He shivered, and she slapped his arm, enjoying the effect she had on him.

"Stop it," she said. "I like it."

She leaned back, munched a sandwich, a picture of comfort, her shirt loose, jeaned legs relaxed as if she'd known him ages.

"Eat up," she said. "Got to keep your strength up for all those thoughts."

He liked her voice. It was small and light. As leaves when the wind fell, he told her.

He could see she was pleased. Perhaps it was something she hadn't been told before.

"I bet you've had lots of girls," she said.

"Pourquoi?"

"The way you sweet-talk."

Her eyes drifted over him. Her voice was little more than a murmur.

"I bet you can get them to do anything you want."

It was like a dream, he said, being with her.

"I'm just afraid when I wake up you'll be gone,"

Her eyes were gentle.

"I won't be gone."

"Be the worst thing in the world," he said.

She leaned over to him. Without brushing the crumbs from her mouth she kissed him.

"Now do you believe it?"

He noticed them again on the way out, exposed ridges of wood like grey veins on the bars of the gate. Barely half an hour since they climbed in – but they were different worlds, the worlds before and after a kiss.

A farm tractor rattled past. The driver grinned, as if to say he knew all about hay in the sunshine. Amanda laughed, waved after him into his mirror. His hand acknowledged her.

A shriek of rubber soles, the thud of cannonading squash balls; then the air spiced with chlorinated water and wet bodies; and then the public pools, and the diving pool where the competition was going to take place.

Most of the team were there already along by the pool.

"Here she is!"

"Flirting again!"

"Hurry up, Amanda."

She didn't hurry. Merely waved, laughed, took it all in good part.

"Sure you won't be bored?" she asked Alphonse.

"With you to look at?"

"That's what I mean. Don't expect too much."

Then she had gone.

He found a seat high up at the back with a good view of the pool.

He imagined himself climbing that white circular stairway, his fingers tight on the handrail, up and up to the top board – and seeing its narrowness rearing out over the pool – and walking – nothing either side – to the end that was barely wider than his feet.

It might be Amanda's world. Could never be his.

He tried to think what he could claim as his world. Nothing came to mind. He felt he'd been born rather outside the world. Hardly at home in any of it.

The pool like polished green glass. High above, the board stretched out, a lath.

The teams came out, sat around. He recognised Richard, well-built as ever, bronzed. Amanda was nearby, chatting, laughing. She shaded her eyes, scanning the spectators for him. She didn't pick him out. Alphonse stood up and waved like she would have done, spontaneously. It was a symbol of the way things were between them, he thought, she the doer, he the viewer. He wished it wasn't so, but he couldn't think of anything he did that could be of interest to others. Made it all the more a miracle she should be fond of him.

The diving began. One competitor after another climbed the stairway, walked to the end of the board, paused, concentrated mind and body, dived, the commentator remarking on pikes and tucks and swallows.

Then it was her turn – to take off her navy-blue top, climb up and walk along the top board, shapely, in a blue one-piece, at ease with the height, with the crowd.

She turned, her back to the pool, heels over the edge of the board. She paused a second or two, took her weight on the balls of her feet. How she could dare, relax, and think of plunging down and down headfirst through the air!

An instant later she sprang backwards and upwards, dropped her jack-knife of a body forwards, straightened out from finger-tips to toes, slid into the water like a dart.

She surfaced, pressed the water off her face, looked for him. He stood up and waved. Got a wave back. He felt like a king. And like someone inferior.

He watched her other dives, watched all the dives. Saw the beauty of the human body pitting itself against danger. Wished there was something he could pit himself against. If the time ever came, he wondered, would he be prepared to pit himself against the odds?

Her dampness smelt warm and animal. She had put a tracksuit on for warmth, blue, against which her hair lay like sunshine. Everything she wore made her irresistible.

"You were brilliant," he said. "You all were."

"Yes," Richard agreed.

Amanda turned on him, warning him. It made Richard laugh, all the more determined to say it.

"Specially her swallow. She's got a brilliant swallow, Mandy has."

She hit him across the arm with her gear.

"You should have seen her, Christmas," Richard laughed. "Legless as a snake."

"Oh!" she exclaimed. "Only because I wasn't used to it!"

Everyone laughed. They were a humorous crowd, jokers, leg-pullers.

They took it as a matter of course that Amanda should leave with him, girl-friend and boy-friend; as Amanda did too. To Alphonse it was like a dream.

They were in the car on the way home.

He asked if she had enjoyed the afternoon. She had on the whole, she said.

"Except for that Richard!"

He didn't press. She seemed half humorous, half cross. He guessed she was the sort who'd always liked boys.

He asked if she had been nervous up there on the board.

She'd had to concentrate too much, she said, to think about nerves. It was only a matter of thinking what you were doing. "You'll have to have a go, Alphy."

He could have a go on the raft, she said. Sunday morning. Early. Before the breeze got up.

"Be a laugh," she said.

The *In Concert* was quite a place, now that he looked at it. Detached, large, woodwork newly painted black and white, the music motif on the signboard, on the doors, everywhere.

"Have a chat with Dad," she said, "while I go and have a bath."

Jack Morton was behind the bar, a mahogany quadrant around a corner of well-stocked shelves.

"They didn't win, then, Alphy?"

A well built chap, trim moustache, greying hair combed back.

"Only a few points in it. Amanda was brilliant."

Jack passed the gin and tonic over, got himself another whisky.

"Gives it her best shot, does Amanda. Gives everythin' her best shot."

He leaned across to him, confidential.

"When she knew you were going to watch, she's been down that pool by seven o'clock. Every morning. Before work!"

Easy-going chap; proud as hell of Amanda. Alphonse wondered how he would feel in Jack's place, having a young chap nosing round a daughter like that.

He told him how he had first seen her. At Head Office. Going from one office to another.

"That was enough for me."

"Once seen, never forgotten, eh?"

He looked pleased, his girl able to crack a chap's heart open like that.

"When she sets her mind to anythin'..."

He indicated Alphonse's glass, got himself one nevertheless.

"I didn't get what I set my mind to," Alphonse said. "That job. I don't know whether Amanda told you?"

She was surprised, Jack said.

He held the raw whisky in his mouth, seemed to let it vanish without swallowing it.

Alphonse said he'd apply again. If anything came up.

"I daresay you gave it your best shot," Jack said.

They talked a bit about Head Office. Amanda liked being there, liked the staff.

"Been noticed by the powers that be, you know," Jack said.

"I'm not surprised."

"Oh, ay. Not that she's got much longer to go now."

"She got another job?"

Jack swallowed before he was ready, choked a bit.

"Hasn't she said? She's off to university."

Alphonse could hardly take it in.

September. Jack couldn't remember whether it was the end of the month or the middle. But definitely September.

"She'll have a week or two before she goes. Get her things together, see a few people."

In the next room a group of guests were going over a Gilbert and Sullivan score.

In for a penny, in for a pound,

It's love that makes the world go round...

"She'll not be gone for ever, you know," Jack said, seeing his face.

It was like a blow in the stomach.

"Which university?"

Jack thought it was Thrunes. Bit of step from Kirkhaven. But it had the courses she wanted.

"Maybe you'll be able to pop up and see her."

Sometimes Amanda didn't get round to telling you things, Jack said.

"Other times she'll tell you anything. Tell you what you don't want to know, sometimes."

Some way off the dinner gong sounded.

Jack got himself a whisky, knocked it back and rinsed the glass. Seemed there weren't many pit stops round the dinner table.

Nothing venture, nothing win,

Blood is thick but water's thin.

A young man came in to tend the bar for an hour. Jack told him which taps were on, which bottles to use.

"Time to face the music, Alphy."

He led the way. Doors bore names like BACH, SCHUBERT, SOUSA. Eventually one was marked PRIVATE.

"Mustn't show up on the breathalyser here, Alphy."

He drew a finger across his throat.

Alphonse liked him. Unpossessive. Someone he didn't mind sharing Amanda with.

She was laying the table in the dining-room. Wearing a short flowered dress, her legs bare down to her trainers, hair damp from being washed. Tied back with a ribbon.

"I've kept him out of trouble, Amanda," her dad said. "I'll leave you to sort out who sits next to each other."

He went through to help in the kitchen.

"Nice bloke, your dad."

"I'm glad you like him."

As if approval was unexpected.

It was a pleasant room, overlooking the inland side of the town. The sun flamed her skin, the tablecloth, surfaces in the room.

"Mum says this is too short," she said, referring to the dress. "I thought you'd like it."

He loved her for it, dressing to please him.

"So you're off to Thrunes."

She paused, plate in hand.

"Do you mind?"

"If Thrunes is what you want, Thrunes is what I want."

She came and stood close, grateful.

"You're like my dad. Letting me go."

She reached up and kissed him.

"Excuse me, Amanda."

Her mother wanted her to go and find her grandmother. She was just going to serve up.

"If you can manage to tear yourself away."

"Alphy says he doesn't mind me going, Mum."

"Oh, good."

Alphonse liked Mrs Morton, her dry style.

"I'll introduce him to Nan while you're gone."

He went through to the kitchen with her. The grandmother was standing at a worktop, busy. Was one of the singers at the choir. Called Irene. One of Gerald's loyal band. Had a feeling she'd seen Alphonse there.

Alphonse was equally hazy. Was glad to be introduced as Mandy's friend.

"They've already met," Mrs Morton told her later. "He's in the choir."

Amanda smiled. "Told you he was wonderful".

The sun was low. Irene wanted one of the curtains pulled in the dining-room.

"Guests like to see what's going on."

They brought in lasagne, bowls of salad, baguettes. The handles of the salad spoon and fork were decorated with the treble clef, knives with the bass.

Mrs Morton said, "We're busy all year round here."

"Which is why," Irene cut in, "a certain young lady would be better staying here learning how to run a hotel rather than gallivanting off to university."

"I suppose she could remain at Head Office if she wished?" she asked Jack.

"Dickson said he'd be happy for her to keep there. But she'll be best to go to university if it's what she wants."

"Dickson?"

The name was too hot to pass unremarked.

Jack winked. He'd pulled a string or two, he said.

"At Lodge. Strictly between you, me and the gatepost, Alphy."

Pete Dickson had owed him one. So when Jack told him Amanda was looking for something for a year before going to university – bingo! All fixed up in no time.

It was dusk. They were standing on the beach. The sea was blue-grey, the waves falling in curls along the shore, the air cool, seaweedy.

"So what was the funeral like?"

She spoke quietly, shy of asking.

He tried to tell her how fond he was of the woman – whom he hardly knew.

"Emilia and I knew each other when we were kids. Then my family moved away – when I was eleven. But I always liked Mrs Connaby."

He suddenly felt moved for her: Jean Connaby, dead and alone.

"Anyway, she was ill. Didn't last long."

A remnant of twilight hung in the sky. Over the sea a sense of stars. "That's what happens, you see."

She stood close to him.

"Would you rather I didn't go to university?"

He studied the arch of darkness. It pleased him to think Jean was there.

"When I met you," he said, "you were a girl with a future. I'm not here to take it away. I want you to go."

He knew he didn't believe what he said. But felt better for saying it.

They walked up the beach towards the esplanade, its loops of light and neon signs, chip stalls and dough-nut parlours.

"Alphy Milesaway."

She took his arm, wanting him to feel comfy.

They found a stretch of clean sand in the shadow under the sea wall.

"This Dickson – " he said.

"He's someone my dad knows. He put a word in for me."

"He used to be in my office at SBA, you see," he said. "One of my juniors."

She was suitably appalled. Young as she was. He didn't have to spell it out.

"I think he goes to Dad's lodge."

She sounded apologetic, as though it was her fault that things happened behind the scenes.

"Must have been awful for you," she said, "how that interview turned out."

Things began to fall into place. Big Dick wasn't one of the brightest. And what of Evans? A mystery indeed why Evans had been appointed. Unless he too – ?

She'd heard the name, she said.

He felt a cloud had lifted.

"So that's how Big Dick did it!"

"Who's Big Dick?" she laughed.

"What we call him at Audley House – Big Dick Dickson."

"Has he got a big dick?"

It was because he was a big dick, he said; not because he had a big dick. Loved the innocence that said what it thought.

They leaned close. She twisted down and lay so that he was over her.

"Might as well get comfy," she said.

Her body was soft, shapely. Her hair lay over the sand.

He had a momentary concern for her clothes, that her dress would get crumpled.

Her arms were round him, holding him down to her, loving him kissing her throat, her mouth, his hand on her breast.

She lay still, her face knowing and not knowing.

"There," she said.

It was time she went home.

It was only ten thirty.

He helped her smooth her clothes. She shook the sand out of her hair.

"How do I look?"

He checked her back, patted her coat down.

"Good as new."

They walked up the sea front towards the hotel. After a while he drew her close for a kiss. She turned away.

"Don't make it hard for me."

But she held his arm all the way back to the hotel gate.

"Be there in good time in the morning," she said. "I shan't be happy till I see you."

She went round to the side door, let herself in.

He stayed around a while. A few guests came and went through the main entrance. No sign of Amanda.

He got in his car and left.

CHAPTER 25

Sunshine hung over the sea, glowed on the bathing chalets, the concrete walls of the changing rooms.

Amanda was sitting on the parapet of the sea wall, green towelling robe open over her swimwear. "I'm glad you're early."

"I've got so I can't bear not to be near you."

"Richard could. He was nearly always late."

"Go out together much?"

"About a month."

He recalled her concern at the time of the accident.

"The times I could have strangled him! Used to call me Man. Knew I couldn't stand it. 'Have a coffee, Man?' he'd say. People used to look. And I'd say, 'No, thank you!'"

"Was it him who got you squiffy last Christmas?"

They'd all been out for a meal, she said, the diving club members. Richard had got her to try various drinks.

"Till I was sick in the street!"

He asked if Richard had been her first boy-friend.

"Friend!" she said. "I didn't think that was very friendly."

A satisfactory conclusion, Alphonse thought.

They sat and chatted, waited for Joan to come and open the club chalet.

Across the sea a track of sun-dance brillianced out to the horizon, imaging a path to somewhere wonderful.

He noticed how far out the raft was, further than when he'd watched her in the sunset.

"Isn't far," she said.

He wasn't so sure.

"I haven't swum for years. Since I was a kid."

"We'll swim with you," she smiled. "You'll be all right."

He believed her, made up his mind to be unworried. It looked inviting, the calm sea, the raft barely moving, small waves unfolding into the shingle with a slight fizz.

"Be a laugh," she said.

Joan Bedford strode up with the keys, a chunk of a woman, tall as he was and three times as hefty. He could smell the heat of her powerful limbs through the track suit.

"New recruit?"

"Not really," Alphonse said. "Haven't swum for years."

"Shame on you. You want to get in every day."

She looked him up and down.

"Make a man of you."

They went in to change. Outside, waiting for them, he was aware of his white skin, his non-swimmer physique.

Then they came out, Joan the battleship, great thighs and upper arms bronzed and red, used to crushing and cruising the seas, Amanda a quarter the size, shapely, the colour of sunlight.

"Come on, Adolphus," Joan said. "Let's get you out there before the others turn up."

Amanda checked the tide clock on the front of the lifeguard station. It was just past high tide.

They made their way down the beach to the sea, the pebbles bitter under his feet. The girls dived under, surfaced, shook the water from their heads like birds in a birdbath. Alphonse took the shock of the cold water on his legs, his privates, his belly. Deep under the surface his toes clutched at cold shingle.

The raft seemed a long way out, smaller than ever at surface level. But Amanda was circling him, lying back on the water, legs occasionally stretching and closing, every movement shooting her through the water.

He leaned forwards, took his first strokes out to the raft. He was less aware of the cold now he was swimming, his hands and arms breast-stroking forwards, his legs opening, squeezing together.

He was getting nowhere. He felt confident enough, didn't feel in danger of going down. But he was like a fly in treacle.

He remembered how he ought to relax on the sea, let it take his weight. Ought to lengthen his body and synchronise his breathing with the strokes. Then his chin dipped under when he was breathing in and he swallowed water.

He coughed, choked, his legs went down, his feet fighting to stand on water. He tightened and sank a little, had to struggle to keep his mouth above the surface.

A great hand reached down, seized the back of his trunks and lifted him clear, pitching him forwards into the swimline.

"Carry on, Adolphus. You'll be all right. Aim for the raft."

Joan was alongside, swimming on her back, the thrust of her great legs and right arm enough to propel herself and him so that he fairly felt the water ripple under him.

Just before they reached the raft she let go and swam ahead and joined Amanda waiting to help him up, one hand on the raft, the other under his armpit.

"A-hee-e-e!"

He shot up and aboard, and Joan gave his trunks a heave down, exposing half his bum. Laughed like a drain.

He sat down on the matting, leaned against a post and recovered. Amanda let him get his breath back, bending and stretching her limbs, her body.

She walked to the edge of the raft and stood there, mentally preparing. When it came to diving it seemed she had an agenda, intent on doing it well. When it came to doing anything, he believed, she had an agenda, in spite of her easy-going nature.

She stood still, poised. He realised again what a beautifully shaped girl she was; and wondered at the chance that brought them together.

She sprang, curled over and entered the water head first, her arms in the swallow dive position, gone with merest plip.

"Follow that, anyone," Joan muttered.

Amanda surfaced, swam to the side and was aboard again.

"Come on, Adolphus," Joan said. "Your go."

She got him to touch his toes a few times and twist his body this way and that. He was to stand at the edge as Amanda had done. And then bend forwards and give a spring.

"Let your legs follow you in."

He took a breath, gave a spring – and hands and feet entered the water together.

Green water stifled him, in his ears, his mouth, stinging his eyes.

He surfaced, gasped for air. Gasped again, salt in his nose, his saliva. Made his way back to the raft. The noise was Joan laughing.

"He went off like a rabbit! Hop! Then vanished."

He had to smile to see her, hopping round like a kangaroo, the raft shuddering.

"Hop! And he'd gone!"

She wiped her eyes. "Have another go! Before Richard gets here."

A couple of swimmers had set off from the beach, heads dipping, rising briefly, dipping again, steadily decreasing the distance between themselves and the raft.

He recovered himself and stood ready. He planned to let himself fall forward and push away with his feet.

He tried it. Entered. Surfaced.

Joan said, "Now you're talking, Adolphus!"

"Try one off the board," Amanda suggested. "You're good enough."

He felt a bravado about it, climbing the white pimple-surfaced steps, the board projecting like a lath out over the sea.

He glanced down. There was scarcely the length of his body between his feet and the water but it seemed like an abyss. Amanda was floating nearby, toes up, her hair waving in the motion of the sea. He stood tall, thought of the flight of his body – out of the old life into the new –

He sprang.

There was time to close his feet, extend his arms and legs – and he was under, deep and deeper into the suffocating wetness, sliding down to darkness, to the edge of panic. Then he had stopped descending, was a coiled creature under the depths, trapped away from air and light, struggling to come up, a black crushing sound in his head, his lungs tight, the water tugging at his nose and mouth, and still no surface, no air, his arms pushing round and down, round and down, his feet kicking and pulling deep below, the water impeding their movement like treacle, then the sea lighter, green, pale green, his head still ringing – then air and sunshine at last, gasp after gasp, water in his eyes, up his nose, on his mouth, but air at last.

He felt exhausted.

"Brilliant!"

Amanda was beside him, delighted.

It was his reward.

He wiped the water off his face as swimmers did. He knew it was first time lucky.

"I thought you were never coming up."

"I thought I was never coming up."

"I knew you could do it."

He noticed how far they had drifted from the raft.

"Shall we go back?"

They set off towards it. After a few strokes Amanda was way ahead.

He swam harder. The raft was no closer. He hadn't enough breath, couldn't get enough breath to make his arms and legs work. She looked back, surprised how little progress he was making.

"I can't make it!"

She was back with him in a few strokes.

"I'll get help. Can you tread water?"

He was still panting from the dive.

"Don't try and swim. Just tread water."

She tickled his chin, unconcerned.

"Keep calm. Shan't be a minute."

She was going away like a torpedo.

He remembered how to tread water from childhood days, let his legs move to and fro, feet quivering against the water, backwards and forwards, back and forth, forward and back, to and fro, hither and thither – any phrase, he thought, anything to keep the mind from panicking.

Amanda had reached the raft, was aboard, was strapping on a kind of harness with a wide strap round the body, a narrower one under the crotch.

The raft was already further away. He could see himself gliding past objects on the beach, past the end of a groyne and the post that warned people it was dangerous to climb on the groyne. He noticed how distant sounds of the beach were almost more clear by being further off. He looked at the water around him, its blue-grey sunlit surface, tried not to think of its colour under the surface. This sparkle could be the last daylight he ever saw. He kicked against the thought. Keep calm. Like Jean Connaby. Relax, lengthen the body -

He made a point of observing the beach scene: a red-faced holiday-maker in a deckchair, knotted handkerchief on his head, trousers rolled up over his calves, reading the Sunday paper; a little boy with a red and green ball – the ball set up on a small mound ready to be kicked. The boy tried a kick, missed, fell down...

The water was cold. A body had only so much heat. Soon movement would be impossible. He tried to remember whether it was the flood tide or the ebb that was taking him northwards along the coast...

Amanda had started out towards him.

She was low in the water, head buried, arms whirling over and over; on the diving-board Richard was paying out arm-lengths of orange cord behind her.

He knew she would save him.

She came on, tireless, Richard paying out loop after loop of cord.

"You're still here, then?"

It was as if the water had turned warmer.

She turned her back to him. She had a kind of harness and float attached to her.

"Get your arms through the loops. See them?"

He put his arms through two canvas loops attached to the back of the harness below the float.

"O.K."

She raised her arm, Richard and his friend started to haul, Amanda was pulled along by the cord attached to the harness.

"Kick with your legs," she said.

Like a frog on the back of a female, he was aware of her legs opening and closing under him.

He was cold, had swallowed water, was close to panic. It occurred to him he was an object, a something supported by Amanda and being drawn to safety by Richard; it was Richard and Amanda who were the pair, he the misfit.

The raft loomed. The diving-board reared out over the sea, wisps of seaweed glistening on its underside.

He took his arms out of the loops and clung to the flooring of the raft with his fingers, the tide trying to tear him away. Richard and Barry gave him a heave up.

He had strength enough to crawl out of their way. A moment later he was retching. A subject for one of your paintings, Emilia, he thought: lung froth and sea water.

The sun was higher now, its warmth reflecting off the white rubbery surface. After a while he rubbed his limbs, restored them to life. Joan and the men got on with their diving; Amanda was seeing to the rescue gear. He looked back to the north to see how far he had drifted. The sea was calm and blue, apparently a harmless expanse of water. He knew better now. Knew what nightmares looked like.

"Want a hand, Man?"

She was unfastening the straps of the harness. Richard meant the one under the crotch.

"No, thank you," she said. Severely.

Then had to laugh.

Beautifully built, the pair of them, at ease in the water and with each other. And both content to ignore him, for which he was grateful. They were experienced in a world to which he was a newcomer.

"Better get you ashore," Joan told him. "You look like something the cat's brought in."

"Say 'Thank you, Joan,'" Amanda laughed.

Joan dived in, was ashore in minutes, persuading the lifeguard to let her take one of the rescue skiffs. Then she was back, paddling him to the beach. Amanda swam alongside, the slightest movement of her body propelling her through the water. Then she was wading ashore, helping Joan steady the skiff.

"Get dressed quick, Adolphus, and get yourself warm," Joan told him. "Your dive weren't at all bad. But I preferred your little rabbit hop."

They were drinking hot chocolate in the cafe on the sea front.

"Joan said she's never seen anyone swim as well as you," he said. "She reckons you could try for the national team."

He pressed the point. Wasn't it a talent she ought to make the most of?

No it wasn't, she said. The national team wasn't for her.

What about diving, he asked. Surely she could make the national team, diving like that?

Her attitude intrigued him. There was nothing idle about her. She was obviously talented, had worked at both sports.

Had she got some other agenda?

"If I have," she said, "it doesn't include competing for fractions of seconds."

"So what do you want to do?"

She glanced out at the beach scene, the wide sea beyond.

"What's best for me," she laughed.

"This afternoon," she said, "you can show me where you live."

They were walking back along the sea front to the hotel.

"Maybe."

She felt the hesitation.

"What's up? Is it grotty?"

"After your hotel – very grotty."

"Pish and tush, young man! After the hotel, indeed!"

She laughed at the words.

"Pish and tush, I say!"

He loved her. She was so young, so full of it.

He wanted to ask her if she used to walk along here hand in hand with Richard. He didn't feel jealous of the chap. Richard would have held her hand as the natural thing to do, wouldn't have regarded it as such a miracle.

A beach ball bounced over the parapet along the edge of the sea wall.

Alphonse tapped it back to the child.

"Thank you," the mother called.

Cecily called.

She was the other side of the parapet, on the beach with her children.

"Enjoying yourself, Alphonse?"

"He's been swimming," Amanda joked.

"Not out of his depth, I hope?"

She looked plump and pleasant in her swimsuit.

She and Emilia were off to France, she said. So they'd have to miss the promenade concert.

"She needs a bit of a break."

"Give her my regards," he said.

He didn't ask her to elaborate. He wanted to get away, back to Amanda.

"Gerald'll miss you."

He meant so far as the choir was concerned.

Then he realised what he was seeing. Gerald was by the sea, paddling with Cecily's little girls.

Cecily watched it register with him, amused. He liked Cecily, the way she pitched for love. He liked her eyes. When you looked into them they were endlessly feminine.

Amanda was amused. Took his arm as they walked.

"Another of your girl friends, Alphy?"

CHAPTER 26

"This where you sleep, Alphy? All alone?"

She sat herself down on his bed. He hoped she didn't associate him with the dreariness of this grey box of a room.

"No Emilia?"

"She didn't like the look of it."

"You asked her, then," she joked.

"We aren't each other's cup of tea, me and Emilia."

He loved the light way she spoke, the absence of jealousy.

"Not like you and me," he said.

She considered the remark, seemed to be considering a number of things.

"Am I really your cup of tea?"

"The moment I saw you the water boiled."

"I see."

Quiet, as if her attention had dived away to look at something else.

After a while she said, "Cecily's nice. Is Emilia like her?"

Cecily was nice, he agreed. And Emilia wasn't like her.

"Don't get me wrong. Emilia's had a lot of hard luck. But – – "

He hoped she knew what he meant. He didn't want to say anything against Emilia.

"It was Mrs Connaby I got on well with."

Amanda gave no indication that she'd heard. It was an attractive side of her, this dolphin-mood coming and going.

"Poor old Mum!"

Quiet, as if the remark had escaped from some internal discussion.

"Why `poor'?"

She tried to make it nice for everyone, Amanda said.

"I told her once she was trapped, living in the hotel with her mother and father."

"What did she say to that?"

"Said I was too young to know what I was talking about."

That was what worried her. Her mother had started to think like Gran and Grandpa.

"She doesn't have to think like them – hotel chores are all there is."

So how was she trapped, he asked.

"She's starting to think that's all she deserves. Hotel chores. Ought to be a chance for Mum to be -"

The thought took her away.

He watched the absence in her features, the stillness on her. Mothers and daughters, he thought, daughters and mothers. No bond so strong.

After a while she was aware of him, how quiet he was, waiting for her.

"Your flat's not too bad," she said. "Just needs cheering up a bit."

She swung her legs up on the bed, her eyes mischievous. Her golden-bronze hair lay over the curve of the pillow.

"Like its owner."

She sat up and pulled her top off over her head. She was wearing a small black bra. She unfastened the back and took it off.

She pulled at his tee-shirt.

"Get it off."

She moved herself under him.

"So your heart's next to mine."

He felt her arms round him, pulling him to her.

"Two hearts beating as one," she whispered.

She drew him down tight and kissed him.

After a while she said, "We might as well get properly comfy."

She sat up and took off her jeans, and then her knickers.

Her swimsuit shape hadn't prepared him for her nakedness. "Exquisite" was in his mind, though later he couldn't decide whether he had spoken the word or only thought it.

They lay close. He felt honoured she entrusted her nakedness to him.

"You don't think I'm cheap?"

She was momentarily troubled, anxious for his opinion.

He put his ear to her breast, heard the light regularity of her heart. He kissed her breasts, her nipples.

She moved under him. He took it that she wanted him to stop and lifted away from her.

When she was comfortable she drew him down again.

"Will it go in?" she whispered.

"I'm not sure."

He knew it wouldn't. He was nowhere near hard enough.

Every sign of her body said she was ready for him. But the notion of protecting her was too strong in him. It was impossible to penetrate her.

"Have I put you off me?"

He supposed he had thought of her as a work of art, spoilable. Yet it was the most natural thing in the world for young lovers to make love.

"Must have been this morning," he said. "I think the shock has got into my works."

She cuddled him to her. His hands traced her body, became aware of the curve after curve of her. He remembered the moment he saw her walking by in Head Office and wondered that here she was in her nakedness, in bed in his flat, her hair spread like gold over the pillow.

He kissed her neck, her hair, her body. And as he adjusted to the idea of losing his virginity with her the thought came: How long will our love last?

She shuddered, had to ease away because of the thrill.

"Were you like this with Emilia?"

"I never even took my shoes off with Emilia."

Didn't want to talk about Emilia. He knew Emilia wouldn't talk about him behind his back.

Later, when he was walking her back to the In Concert, he asked, "What if we had done it? I hadn't got a condom."

She squeezed his arm.

"I knew you'd be careful. I'm a bit too young to have a son yet."

"You think you'll have a son?" he asked.

"One day."

She was so confident, so trusting that the future would bring her good things.

He couldn't tell why it made him feel sad.

CHAPTER 27

What WPC Jennifer Lancaster didn't reveal when she applied to join the police Special Offences team, a recently created section which worked in tandem with the Social Services department on child abuse cases, was that she herself had been abused as a child.

Had concealed it all her life, often from herself. But sometimes she was back in the house of her mother's new husband, the box room next to her bedroom with a door that swung open as quiet as her step-father when he stole up behind her and whispered the things he always told her in whispers. At first she'd liked him, his jokes, his attention, especially after the nastiness of her first dad. Then it was attentions she hated – but hadn't wanted to hurt his feelings. Could scarcely credit it now, what she had put up with – out of politeness, his insistence it was secret, she mustn't say a word or there'd be trouble.

Had been a web, she the victim, feeling the soft step of his approach, his groping, probing, amazed this grown up man with a collar and tie – worse than a dirty-minded schoolboy.

The sense that she had colluded, encouraged him almost, still emerged to haunt her. But with it was left a determination that if ever there was a chance to save a child from similar suffering it was a chance she'd take and not be over-fussy about the means. Might not be able to rescue Jenny Lancaster, but she'd move whatever needed to be moved to rescue another child.

Seeing Kendal Connaby brought it all back.

She was interviewing him in the first instance in his office. Her hopes of a confession were high. Professional people, it was well known in abuse cases, had more skills of evasion than most, more knowledge of police powers, more awareness of their own rights, but in the end these were no more than delaying tactics. Child abuse was a headline crime; the instinct of society was against it. Kendal Connaby might be one the top lawyers in Kirkhaven but an investigation in the hands of someone of her experience was pretty sure to yield results. The least crack in his defences and she'd be in for the kill.

"You don't need me to tell you, Mr Connaby, this is a serious charge against you."

He didn't respond, merely watched her.

Did he know the child, Pauline Southwell, the subject of this inquiry?

He did.

Was he aware that allegations had been made to the effect that he, Kendal Connaby, had committed the abuse?

Perfectly aware.

Was it the case that he had had some form of contact with the girl recently?

It was the case.

And would he now be prepared to say where that contact had taken place?

The pause that now occurred, WPC Lancaster noted, was longer than had been the case so far.

No, he was not prepared to say where the contact had taken place. Neither was he prepared to continue this interview until a more precise charge was put to him. So far he had answered questions of a rather vague nature, had answered them truthfully as best he could, but it must be obvious that the term "contact", for example, was ambiguous. He was a professional man who had professional "contact" with many clients to whom he had a duty of confidentiality. Would the officer therefore be so kind as to explain exactly what the charge was, or indicate the nature, time and place of any incident under investigation?

Jenny Lancaster had dealt with this tactic before. If there was one type she disliked more than another it was the clever-clever professional who thought he knew a way round everything.

"It's an allegation, Mr Connaby, that you sexually abused the girl in question on the afternoon of Wednesday the eighteenth of June this year, and that you have repeatedly abused the girl over a period of time. Do you deny the allegation?"

Insofar as the allegation related to him, he said, he denied it absolutely.

"Insofar as it relates to you?"

She wondered if she was on the brink of something more horrible. The papers lately had been full of stories of paedophile rings.

Any allegation of abuse, he said, sexual or otherwise, of anyone in any circumstance he denied absolutely so far as the allegation related to himself.

Web-spinning. Not the most widely used technique to deter investigation, but she had come across it a time or two. It was the term investigators used when they realised the interviewee was creating lines of supposition at right angles, so to speak, to the line of enquiry. Connaby was engaged in creating diversions. Mostly the interviewee tried to trivialize the allegation, or attribute other meanings to what the child had said, but given the devious nature of paedophiles she knew she had to be patient.

She would give him enough rope to hang himself.

She referred to his relationship with his wife. Would he describe it as a good relationship?

She floated the question as if it was something to say while she glanced through a couple of papers.

"Mr Connaby?"

The lawyer let his hands lie open on the desk, let his face lose any trace of anger.

"If you're clear as to your brief..." he said, meaning her papers. He waited for her to resume.

WPC Lancaster was reasonably pleased with the way the skirmishing had gone. She made a note to refer to Mrs Connaby again later.

"A representative of the Social Services and I," she said, "interviewed Pauline yesterday at her home. Her mother was present and gave the team full cooperation."

The police officer was in no hurry, preferring to see if he would volunteer information. None came.

"The gist of it was that Pauline named you as her abuser."

"Gist?" Kendal said. "We don't deal in gists in a case like this, constable."

The constable read from her notes, irritated at having to be precise when it was obvious the man was stalling.

"Very well. We asked Pauline who it was that had abused her. 'It was Uncle Kendal,' she said. 'In his office.' Her mother tells us that Pauline had already told her and her dad it was you who had been abusing her. I take it that this is the office she referred to, Mr Kendal?"

She looked about her, noting its lay-out and furniture.

"This is my office. It has no relation to any office child abuse took place in."

"Did Pauline Southwell ever come to this office?"

Again, the constable noted, the time taken to reply was over-long.

"Pauline is my wife's niece. She may have visited it because of that relationship."

"Did Pauline come to this office on the afternoon of Wednesday the eighteenth of June this year?"

"She did."

She could tell the veneer was beginning to crack.

"Did you see her?"

He did.

"Did you speak to her?"

He did.

"How long was she in the office with you?"

About twenty minutes, he believed.

"Were you and she alone together in the office?"

"There was no-one else in the office."

"Why did she come to see you?"

This time there was only the usual pause.

"I'm not at liberty to tell you."

"What did you talk about?"

He was not at liberty to say.

"Why aren't you at liberty to say?"

"Because she came as a client."

"Will she be paying you – as a client?"

She was a non-paying client.

"So if she was a client of yours why did she tell her parents and then tell us, 'It was Uncle Kendal. In his office.'?"

Jenny Lancaster was used to out-facing perverts. She had fought the childhood battle again and again since her first disastrous encounter with men. Now she was not to be out-talked or out-thought, let them use what tricks or threats they liked. She was here to help the innocent child, to get her free from the fingers of abusers.

"Why was it, Mr Connaby?"

"Perhaps she was under pressure."

"From whom?"

Again the long gaze, as if he was trying to find a way of escape.

"Perhaps – from herself."

"Under pressure from herself?"

WPC Lancaster allowed herself a touch of sarcasm. It wouldn't be long before he broke.

"Pressure is usually to get a child to retract. So it can all be hushed up. That's what pressure usually amounts to. There'll be no hushing anything up in this case, Mr Connaby."

And stab you I will, she thought, and stab again till you break.

There was no response.

"Are you aware the girl kept a diary?"

This was the one! The man sat back, surprised.

She had the coup de grace ready.

"So would you like to make a statement about your relationship with the girl?"

She willed him to pick up a pen. Or speak while the shock was still in him.

But he did nothing.

"Have you read the diary?" he asked.

She had read the relevant entries. They all tended the same way.

"Did you read it with the girl's permission?"

"Her mother handed the diary over to me."

"Without her permission, then."

The constable reddened.

"I've read an account of a child's mental and physical torment, Mr Connaby. In the child's own words – "

"Does it name names?"

"It names relationships and it names places. Anyone can put two and two together."

He shook his head. Almost smiled.

"You know better than that, constable."

Suddenly he rubbed a hand over his mouth. His eyes darted from object to object, the mind elsewhere. *Anyone can put two and two together!*

"My God!"

He glanced at his watch.

"We'll take as long as it needs, Mr Connaby."

He settled back against his chair, his attention still inward.

"Did it ever occur to you that Pauline Southwell might be distressed?" the constable asked.

It took a moment for the question to register.

"I was aware of it."

"Were you aware of the cause of her distress?"

"I was aware – she was being abused."

They both knew what the next question must be, and its significance.

"You knew she was being sexually abused?"

"Yes."

"So knowing the girl was being sexually abused, Mr Connaby, what steps did you take to end the abuse?"

She'd got him. They were both aware there was no way back. From the interviewer's point of view the question was one to which a court would pay the gravest attention. For any person to know abuse was taking place and do nothing to stop it the implication was collusion – or worse; but for a professional man who by his own admission had been alone with the girl and had been named by the girl as her abuser, for such a man to have to state that he did nothing to alert the authorities the outlook was bleak. No authority had been alerted by him, neither had the parents nor any relative. Kendal Connaby had known of the abuse – to put it no stronger – and had kept it quiet.

Of all this Kendal Connaby was well aware. But *anyone can put two and two together!*

That was the remark! Someone was intending that people should *put two and two together!*

His wife!

"I asked you a question, Mr Connaby. What steps did you take to end an abuse you knew was taking place?"

The lawyer considered the face in front of him, the expression almost truculent, the eyes bright with the expectation of victory. Any offer of compromise would be seen as evasion.

He had known his wife was behind the allegations. Theoretically. But had never quite believed it. Despite all the straws in the wind, all the efforts of Jean and Emilia to alert him. But now he knew!

His hands momentarily lifted apart as if to say, "You win, constable."

"Pauline Southwell came to see me at four thirty-five on Wednesday the eighteenth of June."

"Where?"

"At this office. She sat in the chair you're sitting in now."

"She makes a habit of calling in to see you, does she?"

The tone of voice annoyed him.

It was the first and only time Pauline had called to see him, he said. She came on the off-chance of seeing him because she was desperate to talk privately and in confidence.

"Did her parents know of the visit?"

"Hardly. Since she wanted to talk in confidence."

"What took place?"

That wording again! The assumption of abuse!

"Conversation took place! The girl was desperate. Frightened. She was in a situation she didn't know how to get out of."

"Which was?"

"She was being abused by a relative. On a regular basis."

Par for the course, Jenny Lancaster thought. As good a ploy as any to say it was someone else. But hardly sustainable.

"What was your reaction to being told this?"

"I told her to tell her parents. There was also the local helpline, but I advised her to tell her parents. She said she couldn't. She was terrified of what her father would do. You'll be aware he had a prison sentence a year or two ago for violence. She was terrified he'd do something violent and get sent down again."

"Did she give the name of this person who was supposed to be abusing her?"

Supposed! He noted the tendentious choice of words! He'd sometimes come across cases of the police making an assumption of guilt and by selective wording and choice of evidence pursuing the assumption, sometimes in the teeth of common sense. This was the first time it had happened to him.

"She did," he agreed.

"So what name did she give you?"

"Officer. This girl's private life has been destroyed by an abuser. She's had her diary read – which is going to make her feel intruders have walked all over it. She came to see me in confidence. Of course you must have the name so that the abuse is stopped, but I must ask you in the girl's interest – so she doesn't completely lose faith in human nature – to keep the source of information secret."

The constable's response was uncompromising. The network was not in the business of keeping secrets, she said. Secrecy was what got abuse started; it was the beginning of the web.

"The victim is caught, trapped like an insect waiting for the spider, waiting for the hands – "

She checked herself.

"Your duty is to assist the investigating team in any way you can. What happens after that is the team's affair, not yours."

It was the battle she had fought all her life against all that was cobwebby, entrapping. She was a crusader for openness, come what may.

Kendal paused. The overwhelming common sense of the Act meant that everything would have to be revealed.

"The name is that of her uncle, her father's brother, Peter Southwell. She goes to his house once a week to baby-sit while Southwell and his wife work a long shift at the factory. He gets home first because the wife stops off at the supermarket. It's then that the abuse takes place."

The constable checked her notes.

"He's her uncle on the father's side."

And said it as if to say, "And you're her uncle on the mother's side!"

"Pauline was terrified her father would turn violent and attack the brother and get sent to prison again. So though she was desperate about the abuse she was just as desperate about it coming to light. I told her it would have to come out, and the sooner the better. She left in a pretty sad state, I'm afraid."

To Jenny Lancaster it was indeed a sad state of affairs. One paedophile blaming another.

"I understand articles of the girl's clothing were found in your house, Mr Connaby. How do you account for that?"

It was the final confirmation. *His wife had told the police!*

"I account for it by telling you you've been misled, constable. You and I know by whom. Pauline did leave her jumper in the office. I think it fell off the schoolbag it was draped round. Any other item you may have heard about is fantasy."

He leaned across to the inter-com.

"Let me put an end to your hopes, constable."

He had been attacked, and couldn't avoid a certain satisfaction at what was to come.

"The interview with my niece was audio-taped. If necessary I shall make a copy available to you. And all the time my niece was here that door to my secretary's office was ajar and my secretary was present. I'm sure you'll wish to verify that."

He pressed a button. Mrs Soames came in.

The officer asked her a few questions, recognized the solidity of the defence.

She glared at her papers and across at Kendal. Against all her hopes her target had scuttled to safety. False allegations by victims were not unknown, were usually a matter of displaced identity, often caused by fear.

One consolation, however, was that life was going to get highly uncomfortable for Mr Peter Southwell in the near future.

But she didn't care for the fact that as she left the office the solicitor opened the door for her, elaborately, as though she might bungle that too.

CHAPTER 28

The first blow came at work

It was a fax to Mr Alphonse Fenley at Audley House. He was to see Mr Evans at Head Office as a matter of urgency.

He went later that morning.

Company premises at Audley House, he was told, would be required by Head Office with effect on Friday 8th August. The marine insurance section would continue for the time being and operate from 39 High Street, Kirkhaven.

"How confidential is this supposed to be?"

"Not confidential. Just unofficial. Officially unofficial."

Evans was in an unusually good humour.

"You're aware what 39 High Street is?" Alphonse said. "Dilapidated premises next to a Chinese."

"We've done a survey. The floor area is virtually the same as where you are now."

"Not the working area isn't. There aren't any offices there."

Evans took it calmly. "It's all in hand. The contractors will be in tomorrow. No problem."

It was a hell of a problem, Alphonse protested. It was only three weeks till Friday the 8th – and work on the offices hadn't even started.

Evans shrugged, uninterested.

"That's the decision. I'm just passing it on."

"And you're trying to tell me the staff aren't supposed to know? They're to be moved out and they mustn't be told they're to move out?"

"Got it in one."

The proposal was bizarre enough to be true. There had been similar tales from the Blackpool branch.

But why not, Alphonse argued, why not locate the Head Office extension at 39 High Street? Instead of taking over Audley House? Then there wouldn't be any interruption to the work flow.

Evans raised a finger.

"A point of principle," he said. "The firm doesn't expect any interruption to the work flow, Mr Fenley. You've got almost three weeks, for God's sake! Unless you think the task is beyond you?"

Owen Evans settled back, glad of the chance to put Fenley on the rack. He hadn't been left unaware of the fact that he himself had yet to justify his recent promotion.

"I can't do this to the staff without telling them."

"*I can't do* isn't a remark the firm wants to hear, Mr Fenley."

Alphonse's reply was to the effect that the firm would know who to blame when profits slumped, as slump they definitely would if marine insurance folded. Everybody knew it was the most efficient section in the company.

But Evans' face betrayed only that he knew Fenley was trapped: he would have either to implement the proposals or declare that he couldn't. Either way the man was on the slide.

Alphonse was having a bath after work, didn't hear the person downstairs re-deliver the letter.

As he dried himself he noticed his penis in the mirror. He didn't blame it for being dispirited by the day's events. But Amanda deserved better. And for some reason Robbie Burns came to mind.

Ye wilfu', hangin', droopin' member!
Ye joyless, juiceless, charcoal ember!
Na fiery fucks I'll e'er remember
Till ye ha' thrilled her...

It cheered him up, thinking of Amanda. One day, he promised himself, he'd complete the poem. Was sure it would have a happy ending.

He saw the letter on the doormat. From Amanda.

She'd suddenly been given the chance by Peter Dickson to go on a course. At Blackpool. The person Dickson had arranged to go with had had to drop out at the last moment and no-one else could go at such short notice. She'd rung and rung but Alphonse must have been late home from choir – and she daren't ring him at work as things were – so she'd had to write. She'd be home Saturday, was looking forward to seeing him.

Dickson!

He got dressed, had his meal, washed up, put away.

Dickson!

He read the letter again.

Made himself a drink. Had to check whether he'd had his meal.

Fate had done it again; first the fax, now the letter. First his job, now Amanda.

Life had laid a curse on him. He was paying the price of someone else's folly. Or for being Alphonse Fenley.

Then he remembered there was an extra choir practice because of the concert on Saturday.

He talked to choir members. He sang. Even chatted to Albert and Beryl, knowing they knew the family.

They made no secret that they were dismayed she'd gone to Blackpool. It was to do with this university, they said. Gallivanting off like that just because it might come in useful!

"She'll find out how useful universities are one day! When she has to come back to the hotel to make a living!"

Much as he hated the idea of her going he couldn't agree. Amanda was being true to her creed – of being Amanda. He couldn't blame her

But driving home in the darkness afterwards he imagined another car interior. Amanda, grateful for the chance of the course, was laughing at Dickson's jokes, her eyes meeting his, not minding how close they sat or whether Dickson was glancing down at her knees...

He saw the car drawing up at the hotel. And Big Dick and Amanda exchanging room numbers...

Before going to bed he had calmed down. Could look at it rationally. You couldn't waste a place on a course like that. Someone had to fill the vacancy. And Amanda was as bright as any of them. Live your life, my dear, he'd have told her, live it fully and freely. One day, like eagles, we'll couple where our flight paths meet; we'll whirl around each other in delight for a while, then part, you on your life's journey, me on mine.

In the night such rhetoric sounded naive. She'd gone on a course that someone in his position could have done with going on. And people like him in the firm hadn't even been told the course was being held.

Later on, in the desperate hour, he faced another reality. A vision of Amanda's bedroom, every detail, every stick of furniture as clear as if he was there. Amanda was in bed, awake. A tap at the unlocked door. He heard the door open, knew who'd come in. He heard the whispers, the creak of extra weight on the mattress, the gentle rhythmic pushes, the sighs, the ecstatic up, up, up -

He writhed out of the nightmare.

He hated his nature, his jealous personality. On the one hand there was Amanda, open, brave, curious about life, your top-board girl, daring to leap and take her chance; on the other was himself, cringing at the side of the pool of life. Yet it was no fault of his, he thought, that things were bad at work. Somewhere at the highest level of management an idea had taken hold that posturing was more important than production, that rooting out good practice in favour of what was untried would bring home the bacon.

Yet regarding Amanda, she would now inevitably compare him to Dickson, a man on the down as compared to a man on the up. However much she assured him to the contrary she'd think of him as a man who couldn't penetrate her -

He got up early and went to work.

When he enquired about progress at 39 High Street the secretary at Head Office had little information. Alphonse asked if the workmen had arrived. She'd try to contact Mr Evans about it, she said, and ring him back.

No, she told him later, the workmen hadn't arrived yet. There'd been a mix-up over dates. Maybe they'd be able to get started by the end of the week. But one thing Mr Evans had asked her to make clear: Friday 8th of August still stood as the date by which Head Office would take over Audley House.

CHAPTER 29

"He'll see you now, Mrs Southwell."

Audrey Soames showed her in, switched the tape recorder on in her office.

"I expect I'm the last person you want to see, Kendal," Freda said. "I'm grateful to you for sparing the time."

The sisters never having got on very well, Kendal had seen relatively little of his sister-in-law. He'd always rather liked Freda; the sort of woman his wife had never had the sense to become.

"I was favoured with a visit from the Special Offences team," he said. "The woman did her best to get me to confess to abusing Pauline."

Freda closed her eyes, apologised for her role in the ordeal.

He went through the story again, how Pauline had come to his office desperate for help because of her uncle Peter, how difficult it had been for him, Kendal, to take action with the girl virtually paralysed by fear of her father's reaction.

It was tragedy all round, he said.

"And the tragedy for me is that Valerie believes it's all evidence of my guilt! She even threw in a pair of knickers for good measure."

In the end he'd had no option but disclose the culprit's name. Pauline's welfare had to come first, whatever the short term explosions.

"The policewoman got quite upset when she realized she was on the wrong trail."

"Why Pauline named you!" Freda exclaimed. "I can understand why she didn't name the other – but why you? Who'd only been trying to help?"

She turned away.

"But what can you do? There's Paul, there's his brother, there's Pauline! You can't bank on any of them doing the sensible thing!"

Kendal let her recover. He knew all he wanted to know about unreliable partners. At least Freda was trying to be straight about it.

"Something I'd better tell you, Freda," he said.

The woman braced herself for more bad news.

"I shall probably sue Paul."

He let the shock sink in. The woman had had pain enough without this.

"I don't blame you," she sighed. "It must have been horrible for you."

"I'm also applying for a divorce."

She looked relieved at that.

"I wonder you didn't divorce her years ago," she said. "I know Valerie's my sister, but – I think she's quite wicked!"

It was Kendal's turn to feel shocked. A simple enough remark. A sentiment he had been hearing on all sides, and one he'd come to believe himself. But to hear it from her only sister!

"And after telling you that," she said, "I've come to ask a favour."

It was about Paul, she said. He was still being held after the attack on his brother. She wanted him bailed. Mainly for Pauline's sake.

"He'll be calm enough now. If you could use your influence? I'd be more than grateful."

Kendal was willing to help. He made a note or two of the details. The man must have been extremely provoked, he said, having his daughter abused like that. He'd see what he could do.

"You might even have him back home tomorrow."

Freda made a face.

"Not that he's any great catch. Him or any of them. But I've got to make the best of what I've got."

CHAPTER 30

"Excuse me, madam."

The store detective was waiting for her.

"I believe you may have goods you haven't paid for."

Valerie was in the trolley foyer just beyond the inner set of automatic doors.

For a moment she was without a word in her head. She'd been apprehended. By a man young enough to be her grandson.

Was asked to accompany him to the manager's office.

Like watching herself in a film rehearsal.

Her red paisley bag. They wanted her to show them what was in it.

She lifted out the three bottles of red wine. Saw them placed side by side on the desk.

"Three bottles of St Emilion, madam?"

He asked to see her till receipt. Traced down through the items.

Why were the bottles not receipted? Why were they in the bag and not in the trolley with the other items?

She refused to answer.

Hadn't she read the store notices, they asked. We always prosecute.

She would reserve her defence till the police came, she said.

The police officer was soon there.

The facts, she agreed, were probably as the store detective had stated. But she hadn't tried to conceal the bag. In fact, she couldn't have been more open about it if she'd wanted to get caught. As to her motive, all she could say was that she and her husband rarely drank wine. She supposed she must have been distraught. Her husband had recently been investigated because of child abuse and it had nearly sent her out of her mind.

Certainly she would make a statement, she said. She would write it herself, and wouldn't sign it until she was satisfied with it. Her husband was a solicitor so she knew all about making statements.

Anyone who knew her would testify, she wrote, that she had never been a drinker. If she had taken the bottles, and she couldn't remember doing so, it must have been because of the stress she was under. She would never have opened them. She would have stood them in a row at home to look at because red was such a comfort. Any woman whose husband was under suspicion of child abuse needed comfort.

"Is a bit weird," the manager agreed.

He had been shown a copy of Mrs Connaby's statement as a matter of courtesy.

"We tried to get her to modify it a bit," the officer said. "But no way..."

Company policy was quite clear, the manager said. An example must be made of anyone caught shoplifting.

Not to worry about that, the officer said.

"She's already admitted doing it. Couldn't have been more helpful, really. Almost as if she wants to go to court."

CHAPTER 31

With Cecily away Robert had had to prepare for the concert single-handed. For days he'd risen early and gone to bed late. The food, tables, notices for car-parking in the paddock, the seating, the microphone and speakers, finding volunteers for the wine, flowers, the tickets, the washing-up – everything that organisational man needed to organise had been organised. For Robert the best part of the concert was over. He'd had his enjoyment. It wasn't a case of working now for future pleasure. For Robert the work was the pleasure. When the organising ended the occasion lost its point

Alphonse arrived early. The sky was a blue of many shades, there were deep green conifers, hedges of birdsong, the smell of hayfields and walked-on grass. Here was a place where things went well, where he could escape the foreboding of life.

He loved the old red-brick house in its cap of brown-red pintiles, loved the Edwardian ironwork, the intertwining plants on the terrace, the white-framed windows, the glass that reflected the colours of evening. And he'd swap it all for a glance at Amanda's face. Amanda was his colours, his scenery. And she was in Blackpool.

"Heard from Cecily?" Alphonse asked.

Instinctive, almost a revenge for not being contented like Robert.

"Had a letter this morning," Robert said.

Made it sound like a gift.

"Emilia's doing some painting. Got a contract to complete, apparently."

For Alphonse the remark conjured up the walk through the park, Emilia noting the fallen blossom, he and she talking but not small-talking, the two of them jousting ideas.

"Cecily sends her love," Robert added.

"Mainly to her old man, I expect," Alphonse said.

He wanted to make up for his unkindness. Wished there was no such thing as betrayal. He wished couples could stay in harmony, that relationships were inviolate.

"I suppose they'll soon be home," he said.

Robert gave a final look over the rows of chairs on the lawn ready for the guests.

"The children will be glad to be back, I expect," he said.

Cars crunched in at the front of the house, rocked over the grass into the paddock, disgorged their passengers. The few people Alphonse recognised seemed greyer, less vivid than when he had known them a decade earlier, as though the years had been a journey through dust.

From his place in the tenor section on the terrace he scanned the rows of chairs now fast filling up. He didn't expect to see Amanda because he was a person who had to wait for things. Everything happened late to him, and never when looked for. But he hoped she'd come.

The choir was ready, the audience was waiting. Dr McDonald came forward to welcome the guests and appeal briefly for funds for the restoration of the church roof.

"Ladies and gentleman."

"Ladies and gentlemen," an echo said.

He'd brought another loud-hailer.

"I've got a short announcement to make."

As though he was cajoling people at a street market.

Dr McDonald stared, disbelieving. Southwell was launched into what he had come to say.

Some people here, he said, would have heard him slander Mr Connaby a few weeks earlier, accusing him of child abuse. It was a false allegation.

"It was me own brother who was the culprit."

He'd done his brother over for it and now he was going to get done for doing him over. He wasn't bothered about that. He'd been done before. It was one of those things. He apologised sincerely to Mr Connaby for what he'd said, and for any harm or embarrassment he'd caused. It was no excuse for what he'd accused Mr Connaby of, but he had been almost out of his mind hearing his daughter had been abused. He felt clearer about things now. Was glad he'd had the chance to put the record straight in public.

But he'd keep well away from Gerald Paine tonight, he added. He'd lost one loud-hailer. Didn't want to risk another.

When he finished excitement broke like applause. Alphonse marvelled at the man's self-assurance, a man who hadn't even bothered to change out of his working clothes, in front of the crowd, indifferent as an aristocrat. Then the man was striding off, heels confident across the lawn, the gravel drive.

Valerie Connaby seemed to remember something. A moment or so after Southwell's car rumbled away hers was heard leaving.

The weeks of rehearsal flowered.

Gerald plucked crescendos and diminuendos from the hearts of his human instruments, setting all to time and pitch and balance, each last chord was pulled out to its instant and snapped into silence.

The evening deepened. Madrigal followed ballad, lullaby was balanced by shanty. Sometimes melodies were scratched across by the scream of swifts overhead, sometimes edged by warblings and drawlings from the hedges. Alphonse was glad to be part of the fellowship, loved its temporariness, this moment of making music.

But when the interval came and there was still no Amanda, and the second half began and the early stars appeared and Amanda still hadn't arrived he felt what a fragile refuge music and birdsong and evening stars were. With Amanda the day was full; without her, an evening of good things was ruined. He hated her for being so necessary. Hated himself for being a fool, turning her into a goddess to take away a man's independence.

The concert drew towards its close. The programme had been well composed, all credit due to Beryl and Albert.

Peace be with all souls that slumber.

An invocation he hadn't heard before rehearsals began. Now, because Jean might be above in the darkness, it was one of his favourites:

There they rest, the weary-hearted,
Those whose life was joyous boon,
Those who fainted e'er their noon,
Myriad shadowy hosts they number.
Peace be with all souls that slumber...

He sang it to Jean.

He saw them arrive.

Like conspirators.

Saw the glance between them. Arriving late, we two, what fun!

She in a smart skirt he hadn't seen before.

They were at the back of the audience, invisible because of the choir lights.

He refused to try to discern them. The music was what he had practised for, was as important to him, he told himself, as her diving had been to her.

It was the final item. "Jerusalem" swelled out into the night. The audience stood and joined in:

I will not cease from mental strife

Nor shall my sword sleep in my hand...

It had been a good evening, a good programme. He was not going to let his enjoyment be compromised by someone coming late.

Till we have built Jerusalem

In England's green and pleasant land.

The choir took a another bow.

By the time Alphonse was down off the terrace she was there to meet him, she and Dickson.

Her eyes were as they always were, alive with love.

It had been traffic and roadworks all the way from Blackpool, Dickson explained.

"I think he thought he was at Silverstone," Amanda said. "He knew I wanted to get back to see you. I just had to shut my eyes at times."

"So I drove her straight here," Dickson said. "I told her, `We'll never do it, duckie,' I said. `You'll just have to hear me sing in the bath instead.'"

"Oh!" she said.

Alphonse was vaguely amused, relieved at such a simple explanation.

"At least she's all in one piece," Dickson said. "And managed to hear the end of it."

He said cheerio. It was time he got home and saw his family.

"See you Monday, Peter," she said. And waved in her whole-hearted way as though he was someone special.

People were stacking chairs. Some stood about, chatting, reluctant to let the evening go.

"Missed me?" she asked.

"Oh, more than words can tell."

He made it sound like an exaggeration. It was too raw, too turmoiled, what he felt. She was back, and not yet real.

"Been ever so busy," he said, "getting ready for the concert and everything."

But he wanted her to sense it was only half meant, a bridge over what was too tender to say, that he had been dead without her.

"That's all right, then," she said. "I shouldn't want you to be jealous or anything. Peter might take me to see the Weston branch for a day."

He was instant reassurance. Fine, he said. If it would widen her experience it was all to the good.

"I wouldn't want you to think I was making it a priority or anything, Alphy," she said.

"It won't alter us," he declared. "It wouldn't be fair, keeping you all to myself."

But she was killing what was between them.

"That's what I like about you," she said.

Her eyes were melting. And couldn't see what she was doing to him.

"You don't make any demands."

She put her arms round his neck and kissed him. Publicly. Mouth to mouth, holding him close.

Everyone would say: Alphonse and Amanda are in love. They're boy and girl and in love!

Someone would tell Emilia.

He didn't feel sorry for Emilia. Emilia had been deliberately awkward, silent when she could have spoken. Now she'd have to put up with it. Anyone seeing Amanda would understand.

"Shall we call round at the flat?"

"If you like."

She sounded easy, knowing what he meant.

Traffic light lit her face. She was more beautiful than the rest of the evening put together.

"Amanda!" he murmured.

She didn't lean and kiss him as he'd hoped.

"I shan't be able to stay long," she said.

She didn't elaborate.

"One day you must show me where you used to live," she said. "When you were little."

He took it as a deflection. She was in one of her contemplative moods, needed space to sort something out.

"Give me a few minutes," she said. "You make some coffee."

It was poured out by the time she came out of the bathroom.

There was music in the background; he'd taken one of the wall bulbs out to soften the light.

She sat with him on the side of the bed.

"So you didn't miss me too much, then?" she said.

"I thought about you every day. And wished I could be with you. But life goes on."

"Certainly does."

Her voice was quiet.

"Your life has gone on too?" he asked.

She was silent. He assumed she had pushed her days to the limit as was her custom.

She took her skirt off and spent a moment or two smoothing and folding it.

She had already taken off her knickers. Then she lay smooth and shapely for him.

"Come on," she said, lying down. "See what you can do."

He knew he'd be hard enough.

"Norwich," she laughed. "Nickers Off Ready When I Come Home."

He loved her cheerfulness.

She pulled him on top of her. She still had her shirt and bra on.

After a while she said, "Aren't making much progress, are we."

He wouldn't hurt her, wouldn't force it in.

"Last time I was wet enough," she said, "and you weren't hard enough. Now it's the other way round."

She edged away and sat up.

"Third time lucky," she laughed. "We'll be looking forward to it by then, won't we?"

He pushed her down, not trying to force her, but to signify his potency. He felt exultant, sensed how it would be to penetrate her, how simple the act between a man and a woman, how ultimate.

He kissed her, sat up with her, still kissing her.

"I'll know what to expect – one day," she said.

Yet how strange, he thought. There was nothing about him to attract the loveliest girl in the world, yet here he was, getting dressed beside her.

He was glad she hadn't been ready. Now they were even stevens, a bond of failure between them.

He watched her slip her knickers on, push her feet into her shoes, shake her hair into place. But when she put her skirt on she took more care, looked around for a mirror to see herself, stood in a more ladylike way than usual. It rather amused him, but his heart sank.

He didn't know her. He knew who her mother and father were, her grandparents, knew she lived at the In Concert hotel – but Amanda wasn't of any of it. For the moment she was a local girl, known by the neighbourhood. Come the autumn she'd have gone away into her future. Call it Thrunes, call it university, it would be her world. Not his world.

He seemed to see himself and Amanda getting their clothes on in a room like this, a bedsit with long magnolia walls, a window overlooking a supermarket. A couple drawn together by fate, unaware that fate had already decided their parting. He felt sorry for them, hoped they could make the most of what they had left. A woman he loved had already been taken out of his life – and fate always rode tandem. It had taken Jean. It would come back for Amanda.

"Poor Alphy," Amanda said, noticing his face. Her features lit like sunset. "I'll be all right next time. You'll see."

CHAPTER 32

It was to be a private chat, Kendal told her. He didn't want it recorded.

Audrey Soames was uneasy. Mr Connaby was a good boss, easy-going, thoughtful; but this gossip about child abuse was getting too much to put up with. Loud-hailers and public accusations, and now this latest about his wife being caught shop-lifting, saying she was distracted by the rumours about her husband. A state of affairs you didn't want to be associated with.

It came to something, she thought, when you felt embarrassed at even being the man's secretary.

She ran her eye down the sit. vac. columns, prayed there'd be something suitable this week. She'd like somewhere to go to before the police moved in.

And now here was that Mrs Southgate with another appointment with him.

Paul was back to normal, Freda said. Back at work in London, grateful to Kendal for getting him out on bail so quick.

"Doesn't he find it embarrassing," Kendal asked, "having me act for him?"

"Nothing embarrasses him. I'm the one who gets embarrassed, what he gets up to."

He liked her candour. He wished Valerie had been more open, less calculating. You could never tell what sieve Valerie's thoughts had been through.

"He's just got to explode every now and then," Freda said. "I tell him he ought to have been a bomb and blown himself to bits. Then I'd have had a quieter life."

"And Pauline?"

The girl felt terrible, she said, telling them it was Kendal. But she was terrified what her dad would have done.

"You were the soft option, Kendal, you'll be pleased to know."

"So how is she?"

Freda's show of composure faltered. Her eyes filled.

"Doesn't seem like my little girl any more."

That remark of Valerie's, she said, saying the abuse was as much the child's fault as the man's.

"I know it's a lie – but once the idea's been put into your head – you wonder if there isn't a grain of truth in it. Then you hate yourself. That's what my sister has done to me. I shall never forgive her. Never!"

And it was what Valerie was trying to do to him, Freda told him. So she could say in court she had done it because her husband had been accused of child abuse.

"You can imagine the headlines. WOMAN SHOPLIFTS BECAUSE OF PERVERT HUSBAND."

Didn't matter how untrue it was, she said. Something would stick.

Kendal leaned closer. "The irony is," he murmured, "the shop isn't going to prosecute."

By what channel he had come by the information he didn't say.

"What's been intriguing me, Freda," he said, "is why she did the shoplifting."

"Mean you don't know?"

"I suppose she hates me," he said. "Hates me." He looked away, couldn't believe what he was saying – what he was remembering. "Yet it was liberating when I realised – I suppose I'd thought this was how married life was, one doing the loving, the other taking it for granted."

Freda looked relieved, said she'd had a marriageful of incompleteness, wanted an end to it.

" I'd wanted a man who'd – explore a thing -"

It was a comfortable silence.

"So what do *you* put it down to," she asked, "her hating you?"

He'd wondered about that, he said. And then it had come to him. It was because he'd made her pregnant and they'd had to get married.

Freda laughed in his face.

"You didn't rape her, did you? I mean, she let you in, didn't she?"

Was the contraceptive let them down, he explained. Valerie didn't want a child so soon.

Freda sat back. "And up till now "I'd been thinking what an intelligent bloke you were! What's she got to hate you for? You married her. You've provided for her, better than ever she was used to. She wanted sex as much as you did. Where's the grounds for hate in that?"

Because, he said, marriage and motherhood had ruined her career.

"She was a hundred words a minute girl, Freda. Had a brilliant secretarial career lined up at Arthur Cable's. But when she had to get married and have the baby – "

Freda felt almost fond of him.

"Married to her all these years," she said, "and still believe that! I was at Arthur Cable's too. You know what old man Cable told me when he heard she was leaving?"

Kendal had a feeling he was about to be read a brief he'd had for years and hadn't read.

"He said he was glad. Otherwise he'd have had to find an excuse to get rid of her."

"On what grounds?"

"Wasn't up to it, Kendal. Couldn't keep her mind on what she'd got to do. Valerie was all right passing exams, useless in a work situation."

Kendal could believe it. Hadn't occurred to him before, but it made sense. "But why me? Why take it out on me?"

"You really want me to tell you? It's because you're successful. Whatever you turn your hand to, you do well. Whatever Valerie touches falls apart – her job, her marriage, friendships. She's vicious because she's inept."

She could see him turning the idea over in his mind.

"She was no good at work," she said. "If something went wrong – a customer complained or anything – the boss knew where to look. Nine times out of ten it was down to Valerie."

It began to make sense.

Valerie had never praised him, never praised anything he did. Not that he minded. He was used to it. But neither had she had a good word for Cecily, or Jean, or Freda, or Pauline. Or anyone. The only person Valerie could put up with was Valerie.

A comfort to know he had done the right thing. Divorcing her.

"Nearer the truth, I suppose, to say Valerie never got married!"

"Yes, Kendal," she said. "Very near the truth."

He felt easier about the divorce. He couldn't help it he'd been born intelligent. No reason why he should have been subjected to spite, any more than a dullard should be goaded for being dull.

"Perhaps it was you and I ought to have got married, Freda."

"I've thought so too, Kendal," she said. "But I didn't fancy you in those days. We generally marry what we fancy, don't we? And end up divorcing someone we can't bear to live with."

They studied each other, a well-made man in his fifties, a woman who didn't disguise herself under make-up. But chiefly they saw a person they could have talked to, listened to, someone they could have been themselves with.

Kendal checked his note-pad.

"Remind me, Freda. What was it you came to see me about?"

"Don't think it was about anything, Kendal. Aren't going to send me a bill, are you? I'd been thinking I'd come and see you again."

He smiled too. Stretched his hand out to her. They were apparently holding hands across the table when Audrey Soames came in to check something in the appointments diary.

CHAPTER 33

Cecily and Emilia watched England loom out of the heat haze shimmering either side of the Channel. Ahead, the cliffs of Dover, like folds of white paper yet to be written on. Astern, green-white lanes of the wake lay across the sea, stretching back to an unreal world. An hour out of France, Emilia's memories of it were already fragmented, scattered like sunlit beads.

"England, ahoy," Cecily exclaimed. "Alas!"

"Cis?"

"I'd begun to hope it had disappeared!" She laughed, embarrassed. "I expect we'll survive.'

An uncharacteristic remark. No-one could have been a better companion or kinder than Cecily.

"I had this wish, that time has gone quicker back home, so everyone's aged and we're just in time to say good-bye before they pop off."

Cecily's hair this last year or two had greyed in a band at the front, as if her face was fringed round with silver; the rest of it as black and curly as ever.

"Don't worry about it," she said. "They'll all be there, large as life." She watched the approaching coastline. "Unfortunately."

"Meaning husbands?"

She wondered if she'd taken Cecily's kindness for granted. Had been too self-centred in grief.

"Husbands," Cecily agreed. "People."

"Robert's all right, isn't he?"

Cecily studied the distant smudge that was becoming the port of Dover.

"You can have him, dear. And welcome."

"Generous enough, I mean? Treats you all right?"

Cecily didn't reply. Emilia wondered if she was being patronising, like finding encouragements for a child.

"You move in," Cecily said. "See how you like it. Only don't give up the day job. He might even change his ways for you."

Her hands were gripping the top of the rail.

"It's the children I feel sorry for," she said, "having a mother like me."

"I bet they love you and Robert like anything."

"You're being a bit of a bitch, dear. You're supposed to be making it easier for me."

"Making what easy?"

"Everything. I like everything easy. I don't want moral choices. I just want a choice."

"To do what?"

"To stay or to go, according to what's best for me."

Emilia held her sister's hand, instinctively tried to soothe the tension. And seemed to see the faces of the children, the worry at Mummy and Daddy splitting apart.

"Why should a woman have to live an empty life," Cecily asked, "merely because she's borne children?"

It seemed incredible to Emilia that her sister should describe her life as empty.

"Empty of what?"

Cecily turned away to Dover.

"The sweet things."

Emilia put her arm round her. "You're the one I feel sorry for. Having a mother like yours."

"What's wrong with my mother?" Cecily asked. "Reel off the first dozen defects that come to mind about the bitch."

"I think of her as a cold-hearted little woodpecker."

"You've hit the nail on the head there, Emilia. Pecked me into marrying Robert. Just because I was preggers."

"Well, if Robert got you pregnant – "

"I think I was the one who got me pregnant, Emilia. But a girl doesn't have to marry the guilty party – if she can off-load it on to someone else. Any rate, I married Robert. For which I daily give thanks to Mummy."

Yet if one considered the children, Emilia thought, Robert was no bad deal. He was gentle and kindly, and funded all sorts of good things.

"The first thing Mummy asked was whose it was. I told her it was mine. Which didn't go down too well. I mean, just because a man ejaculates at a certain moment in your life it doesn't turn him into a father and husband. You might not be able to stand the sight of him next morning. But Mummy tells me it does. She has this idea that sex should only be indulged in at Christmas and birthdays if you're married, and not at all if you're not. Whereas if I see a man I like I feel like enjoying him for an hour. Not in order to have a child by him, or presents. I don't want souvenirs. I want a man, not a gift shop. Mummy's the opposite. According to her a man is what you can get out of him. Though I have to say – the date of her wedding and my date of birth make you think! Any rate, as soon as she thought of Robert – that was me finished."

The ship's wake slid across to port. A breeze cut past the superstructure. The last traces of France had blurred to haze.

"You don't seem finished off to me," Emilia said. "You've got a pretty face, a sense of humour, a pair of knickers for every hour of the day. What more do you want?"

"I want you to persuade me to run off with someone else."

Emilia shivered in the colder air. "What kind of person do you want to run off with?"

"Someone who spends his time living now, not preparing to live later on."

"Someone like Gerald Paine?"

"Goodness, Emilia!"

But it seemed an agreeable suggestion.

"A little like Gerald."

"Only a little?"

"I do believe there's something rather righteous about you at times, Emilia. A lot like Gerald, then."

Below them cheerful bits of foam from the bow wave slipped past. Cecily was reminded of the beach, she and Gerald paddling, Gerald writing the tune of *Oh, I Do Like To Be Beside The Seaside* in the sand, the wave washing in and soaking the back of his trousers.

"Why didn't you marry him?" Emilia asked.

The metal deck throbbed more heavily. Cecily watched the piers and walls of the approaching harbour. The end of freedom.

"I was no innocent like you, Emilia. The first time I missed I knew. I thought, what a stupid – ! And Robert was keen enough."

"You didn't want to pretend it was Gerald's? Offload it, I think you said."

"Robert was flattered to be asked. Pleased to think he'd fathered a child at last. It would have been a shame to undeceive him."

The face Emilia knew so well began to seem like undiscovered territory.

"You mean Zoe isn't Robert's little girl?"

"She is – and she isn't." Cecily's face was honest as always.

"Meaning she isn't?" Her head sang with dismay.

"Not biologically speaking. Otherwise she is. Just in the matter of genes she isn't. Not that it matters. Robert's her daddy and always will be."

"You've never told him?"

"Goodness, child!"

Cecily smiled at her, the kindly elder sister instructing the younger.

"She could have been his, so far as opportunity goes. It just so happens that she isn't."

"Which you're sure of?"

"I'm a woman, dear."

She could see Emilia hovering on a question she didn't like to ask.

"It's Robert's obsession with preparation," she explained. "It cuts out the unexpected. Cuts out the excitement too. Robert took his usual precautions – and Gerald didn't. So one's the father and the other isn't."

"You going to leave it like that?"

Cecily sighed.

"I can't make Robert the father. It's no good you're being shocked, Emilia. Or high-minded. I've got a mother to turn to for all that."

Emilia puzzled it over. So much she'd been unaware of – Cecily having this man and that man. In a car? A flat somewhere? A memory of Alphonse's flat came to her. But Cecily had been with Tom, Dick and Harry – whereas she herself had only thought about it. Her own living had been done in the mind – was probably no more moral than Cecily's.

"A girl can't worry about things like that," Cecily was saying. "As long as the children are well looked after, it's not their affair how they got here."

"Gerald doesn't know either?"

Cecily laughed, as if talking about men was cheering her up.

"Mind you," she murmured, "Robert couldn't have fathered the child if he'd tried. Isn't up to it. Not that I tell him."

"He must have been up to it sometimes," Emilia pointed out. "There's Kelvin and there's Sarah. They didn't pop out of a Marks and Spencer Christmas cracker."

"Nor out of Robert's Christmas cracker."

Emilia stared at her. "You mean they're all Gerald's?"

"It would seem so."

"So Gerald does know!"

"If you insist, dear."

"Though when you say they're Gerald's," she added, "he's only the biological father. Robert's their real dad."

"How can he be!"

"Because they love him. And he loves them."

Cecily saw life so simply.

"It's like marriage, dear. It only needs love. Doesn't matter about the rest. There's no recipe."

If only there were, she thought, if only you could come across a list of ingredients to make the man you wanted.

The chief steward's voice over the tannoy told passengers to go to their assembly points prior to disembarkation.

Ahead were the piers and quays, the cranes and sidings of Dover. To Cecily they were more than the termination of a journey. For a few days she had begun to believe she could make Gerald love her enough to live with her. But as the ferry manoeuvred itself into its berth and came to rest, the gigantic structures around her, the docks, the country itself felt like a trap. Life would go on as before, it said. Switch your engines off and don't make waves. What do your own hopes and desires matter? Don't want to hurt anyone, do you?

They held the children's hands, made their way to the passenger exit. Would Daddy be waiting, Kelvin asked. Emilia left it to Cecily to answer. She was about to set foot on the land of the haunter of bushes, the man who masturbated rather than live his life. But what was she? What did she do instead of living her life? What bushes did she hide away in?

Out of the gangway, on to the quay. Perhaps it would be the birth of a different Emilia.

She smelt the fresher air. Ignoring the stream of people passing by she stood still, hoped she was looking at the sky and clouds of of a different life.

"England," she said. "Here I am."

CHAPTER 34

Emilia closed the door behind her. Her own door. Her own house. The most unwelcome gift of her life.

Yet the pattern of stained glass in the window, the accidental defects to the paintwork, the light from the side window brushing the evening up the stairway, all were friends. Or traitors.

She let the past come back as it wished. It was in every room, every chair, every rug – except that they were only the skin of the past.

And all there would ever be of it.

The hand of the quartz clock slid silently round over its numerals, a pair of her mother's moccasins lay at the hearth, a science periodical was open on the table.

She touched the green and lilac silk scarf that hung over the back of the settee. Unwarm.

The window was dusty with the dust of a dry summer, the room a landscape of shadows and colours her mother had loved.

She went to other rooms. No-one spoke. No-one asked about her day or told her what had been happening here. Yet this was home.

She turned the tap on till the water ran cold. She filled the kettle, took out a single cup and saucer, made a small pot of tea. She took the tray through to the living-room, was glad of the sound of tea-things, anything familiar. It was the other side of grief, that things could look and sound as if nothing had happened.

She went into the hall. The grey-flecked green coat was on its hanger, the coat her mother used to slip on with that characteristic turn, the toss of the head shaking her hair into place, then there'd be that smile as if to say she'd been ready ages and how much longer was someone going to take?

She went upstairs to her mother's bedroom. Put her hand on the brass door handle, could hardly stop herself saying, "Mum?"

It was the heart of the house, this bedroom. The wardrobe; the Mary Rich bowl on the dressing-table glowing like ancient Egypt; the bed, the green and lilac duvet rumpled from the last time her mother slept here.

They were props in a play, needing only the spark, the charge that would restart the action, and her mother would come in and say, "Thought I'd find you here. I've been ready ages..."

How lightly her mother had gone! Slipped away, every treasure, every fancied thing left behind to say *Don't try to please me. There's no me to please.*

What an example, to slip away so lightly from the owning of things, take nothing away but herself.

She'd have to learn there'd be no spark, no charge restarting the past. This was an interlude that would last for ever.

She thought she'd done with grieving. She had remembered her mum day and night, spoken aloud to her and in her mind, had let her imagination take her into the crematorium blaze, seen flames fester the shell of her frame. Had looked into the night sky, had voyaged past stars into the depths and wished her well. But to be back at home and see the known things, the shoes, handbags, her coat in the hall – this was what cut the heart.

Yet a feeling grew this was not the fracture of her life.

Days passed.

She told people she wanted to accustom herself to being alone in the house.

She worked in the garden, deliberately went indoors again to get used to there being no greeting, no presence except herself. She refused to talk to her mother's spirit or to imagine her spirit nearby; and when the phone rang she assured herself it wouldn't be her mother. She wanted to get used to absence, to feel sorry neither for her mother nor herself. Her mother had endured the loss of a mother. She would endure it too, would try to be as serene as the example of these last twenty-four years had taught her.

Kendal's face was leaner but less fraught than she had expected.

"A weight off your mind," she said. "To know they've got to the bottom of it."

The two of them were having tea on the lawn at Emilia's. Behind them the seed pods of the laburnum hung down as its flowers had hung the afternoon her mother was taken ill; to one side was the variegated hedge behind which Valerie had been busy with her camera.

"The bottom of it," he agreed. "I only wish it was the end of it."

She waited for him to explain. He seemed dispirited, remained silent.

"It's pretty straightforward, isn't it?" she said.

She recounted Valerie's part in the abuse affair, her willingness to see him implicated, her influence on Paul Southwell, her hints to the police, her pretence at loyalty until he was found guilty after which she would have been able to apply for a divorce and everyone would have said serve him right and she'd have got a handsome settlement – up till the time the investigation switched to Peter Southwell and that she'd done the shop-lifting in an attempt to smear his name in court...

"That's the bottom of it," Emilia said. "And I should hope it's the end of it."

"Except," he said gently, "she's not wholly in control."

Emilia looked at him in disbelief.

"You're not still making excuses for her! She wanted to destroy you."

"And my reputation."

But he was so mild. He spoke as if it no longer mattered, as if it had receded into fiction.

"The divorce is still going through, I hope?" she asked.

"I shall give her the house."

"Your house?"

The house she had known all her life, Uncle Kendal's house, where she used to go and play sometimes with Cecily.

"Meaning you'll go and live somewhere else?"

He'd pay the insurance and Council Tax, he said, and give her an allowance and a lump sum.

As if he'd done his wife a wrong and was trying to make it up to her!

How little she knew him, this man who had become her father! Of his professional life or the way he had made his money she knew even less, let alone how he could contemplate losing his home to the woman who had set out to destroy him.

She took his hand.

"I've always uncle-ised you," she said. "Which was very nice, having a nice uncle. But as a daughter I don't know you at all."

He scarcely seemed to hear.

"Can I ask you," she said, "how you feel inside, now it's all over?"

He took a moment or two to come back to her.

"I like matters to be fair," he said.

"And are they? Valerie intent on destroying you and you treating her so generously?"

He moved his chair closer.

"It's not me that's hurt," he said. "I shan't be so well off as I was – but no harm done."

Not for the first time she had the impression of matters undisclosed, that he was at the centre of some intelligence network.

"Those bottles of wine," he said.

She waited. If anyone had a right to know it was surely herself.

"I'm not a mind-reader," she said.

Whether it was some kind of stroke, he said, or whether something had boiled over in the brain, so to speak, and put the fire out -

"Whatever it was, she went and bought that wine. Paid for it, I mean. All three bottles. And drank the lot. So someone tells me."

It struck her how calm he was regarding himself, how concerned for the woman he was going to divorce.

She supposed she was glad he was kind-hearted. She supposed she was glad he was her father. And glad he was more content with life. But there were rumours of a sister-in-law. Kirkhaven was a sea of whispers, half-heard murmurs of *Connaby!* If the tidal wave came she hoped he would have sense enough to survive.

CHAPTER 35

She liked to get outdoors, away from memories. And high time she got on with Terry Bracondale's contract.

By the time the sun was up she was ready to leave.

She chose a viewpoint in an alleyway opposite the restaurant. Half-timbered and pargeted, *La Golondrina* was the sort of building artists like to portray, with its tucked-under lower floor and projecting upper, its small-paned windows and flattened doorway arch, the narrow street in front, the ancient church behind. She was experienced enough to know what she wanted from a scene, knew what not to include, knew what potential customers looked for. She worked confidently, soon got the heart of it down on paper. She made notes of colours, sketched in the logo, and by the time the morning rush to work was over she'd done enough to deserve her breakfast.

In the studio the first stage of the painting went well, well enough to let him know it was ready for viewing.

His secretary answered.

Mr Bracondale was away, she said. Wouldn't be back for a couple a days. She would get him to ring when he returned.

Beach pictures sold well too, she'd noticed. The colours were attractive, people liked the idea of deckchairs and sandwiches and sunlit water.

She found a viewpoint at the end of the chalets on the sea wall and started composing: the pier striding out to sea on its long-legged timbers, an elderly couple sunning themselves in deckchairs, in the foreground a mother drying a child in a swimsuit.

She felt more confident, knew how to look, how to focus on a few main objects. She sized up the angles of the deckchairs, the strutwork, the impression of weight on the canvas, half aware that someone had paused to look at her work as passers-by did from time to time. She sketched the woodwork, the tautness of the canvas, the old lady dozing, her book on her lap – then realised.

It was his smell.

Unwashed.

She swung round, brush handle ready.

He recognised her. Full of himself as ever.

"You!"

A nothing of a man. Slovenly. Who had cost her days and nights.

He looked apprehensive but faced her back. Offended.

"What harm did it do you?"

She lunged at him, stabbed his hand.

"Shit!"

He clutched it to him, amazed at a trickle of blood.

She noticed the bruise where Alphonse had shoved his face against the garage. She crouched to get him again, her chair toppling backwards.

He stared at the show of blood.

"I'm going to show this to the police!"

She beckoned him, lowered the brush handle.

"Come here."

She beckoned again.

"I'll show you something."

He took a step. She shot the brush handle out, missed his eye by a whisker.

"Christ!"

He cowered back.

"Never done you no harm!"

He moved away, indignant. The injured party.

"Flasher!" she called. "Pervert!"

He hurried off at that, was part of the crowd.

Her hands shook, but she knew she had won, had conquered something in herself. Almost automatically she continued mixing a dab of purple-blue to fix the colour of the deckchair stripe. She felt giddy. The depression that had weighed her down for weeks had lifted.

It was Alphonse who had done the business. He wouldn't have caved in like that if Alphonse hadn't shown him what was what.

Felt she wouldn't mind seeing Alphonse again some time.

Over the next couple of days she worked at transforming the sketch into a painting. It was curious, waiting. If it weren't for his card she could believe she had invented the contract, had dreamed the man up.

She started looking across at the phone, trying to will it to ring. When it didn't she thought of it as obstinate. Then she'd turn back to her work and tell herself not to be silly. If Terry Bracondale didn't want to get in touch Terry Bracondale could go to hell.

It rang when she was doing a scrambled egg for lunch.

"Emilia Connaby?"

His voice reassembled him, the concentrated eyes, the poise. She could almost smell the aftershave.

He'd been hoping she'd get in touch, was glad the picture was ready to see. Was it possible to meet her this evening? And have a meal at *La Golondrina*? If so, might he collect her at seven-thirty?

That would be nice, she said. She looked forward to seeing him.

He was an emanation from the handset, but emanation enough to make her wonder what to wear.

She was quite hungry, she realised. The first time she'd had an appetite for ages. She'd probably have a lasagne; and definitely a side salad.

CHAPTER 36

She had the door open as he walked up the drive.

"I knew you'd be on time."

He inclined his head. Business-like. Courteous.

How quickly he became himself, she thought. Mr Facts and Figures Bracondale. She found it comforting. Not that she particularly liked him; but she was glad he was what he was.

She showed him the sketch. He studied it, asked a question or two about colour.

"I expected it to be good," he said. "And it is."

She told him how she hoped it would look when finished.

He'd thought of putting it up in the foyer, he said, near the desk. Where it would be on view. Where it might be traceable by the taxman.

"So I'd suggest a cheque for this one," he said. "For you to put through the books."

"What books?"

The businessman in him was appalled. Then he smiled.

"You need help," he said. "We'll talk about it over dinner."

It was a new experience, being managed, shown to a seat, the man attentive. It wasn't her style, but the novelty intrigued her.

She glanced round at the beams, the timbered uprights, the separate tables. It hadn't occurred to her before that so much cutlery, crockery, napkins, to say nothing of the kitchens and the building itself, could actually belong to anybody.

"So how did you come to own a place like this?"

He thought a moment, his face as crisp and unlined as his suit, as if he had brain enough not to have to worry at things.

"When you live in the jungle – you learn to hunt in the jungle."

And what did one need to survive in a jungle, she asked.

"Luck," he said. "Hard work. And if I may say so, intelligence."

"You make it sound easy."

But *intelligence* jarred.

"People work hard at the wrong things," he said. "At the wrong point. And fail. Intelligence is knowing where to apply the work."

"So where do you apply your intelligence?"

"Don't misunderstand me. I don't claim to be intelligent. A key area would be staffing. Look around. Tell me what you see."

Their secluded corner gave her a good view of the upper floor. She saw waiters and waitresses of mixed ages, busy, pleasant. Nothing particularly key about that, she would have thought.

"I always pay over the odds," he explained. "Then the good staff don't leave."

To him *staff* meant everyone in the organisation, from lowest to highest. He worked on a basis of creative loyalty, the staff loyal to him and he to them, and all loyal to improving the company.

The meal came. His conversation was a sort of dialect from the world of markets and money. A business could fail as well as prosper, he said. Sometimes one had to chance one's arm – maybe one's neck.

He didn't enlarge. She found herself making allowances, glad he was not over-talkative. He'd sussed out where the ladders were in business and where the snakes. She found him slightly exciting, a curio who had temporarily strayed in from a wilder land.

"As regards paintings," he said, "I like looking at pictures, but I'm not sure what I'm looking for."

The change of subject was pleasantly abrupt.

"I'm not even sure that I know what I like," he admitted. "Let alone why I like it."

For a moment she felt superior, knowing she could wax eloquent on matters of art. Yet what, she asked herself, was superior about being able to wax eloquent on art?

"Does it matter?" she said. "They're only paintings."

"Once you start looking at them it does."

He sounded quite severe.

"Once you start something you have to learn the language. Like when I asked you to look at the staff here. You didn't see what I see because you don't know what you're looking at. Therefore you can't apply intelligence."

Same with everything, he said, business, art, everything. You had to learn the language. It was the law of the jungle.

It sounded sensible. But she wasn't sure sensibleness was what she wanted to hear.

"As long as you don't rule out intuition," she said. "That's the best sort of judgement."

She could see him thinking the remark over.

"You don't say *I like him because he wears a suit and has grey eyes,* she said. You say, *He's taking me out to dinner. What shall I wear?* You don't like him because he takes you out; you like him before you agree to go. Intuitively."

She felt rather fond of him, seeing him working at the idea like a student.

At the far end of the room Alphonse Fenley came in.

Alone.

Was shown to a table by the window. Was having a word or two with the young man at art college.

She was glad Terry had got them this corner spot out of the way. Not that she was bothered about Alphonse Fenley. If he saw her with Terry – too bloody bad, Alphonse Fenley! You're not the only man in the world!

"Forgive me for asking," Terry said. "Are you divorced or anything?

"No. What about you?"

He and his partner had broken up. They hadn't married, had been together a number of years.

"It was like a divorce. Rosina has found someone else, which I'm glad about."

Partly it was his fault, being away from home so much. Business was no good for family life.

"But you," he said. "A girl like you must have had offers. Unless you've been indoors all your life."

The waiter was taking a lemonade across to Alphonse. Who had, she noticed, changed over to the other seat so he could keep an eye on the door.

"I've been indoors all my life," she said. "One way or another."

She felt irritated. It was as if he was classing her as a commodity, something on a shelf that someone might choose to take off and dust one day.

Then she realised what was going on, Alphonse eyeing the door like that.

Waiting for a girl!

After all their conversations, all their discussions about life! As if none of it mattered! Because of some little trollop he was sitting there waiting for!

"Oh, I've been outdoors as well," she said. "I've had a pervert masturbate in front of me on the cliff."

And in she came. A blonde. Who went over and kissed him!

Terry took his time to respond. Terry, who hadn't let her down, whose behaviour was that of a gentleman.

"Unpleasant for you," he said. "Did it affect you? Afterwards, I mean?"

"I'm over it now."

It was the least of her troubles, she thought. What had it amounted to after all? She could almost feel sorry for the bloke.

But across the room they were holding hands, looking into each other's eyes.

"You weren't so much a person to a creature like that," Terry said. "Just an object."

"Rings a bell," she said, "you saying that."

The waitress arrived with coffee and cream.

"Your painting – I guess it's taken up most of your time?"

"If you mean by that," she said, "has it stopped me falling in love or anything, I can tell you I haven't the slightest intention – I couldn't imagine holding hands and looking gooey. It's a delusion if you ask me."

Alphonse glanced round, almost in her direction. Didn't see her.

"No need to be defensive – "

"Defensive!"

Whether her hand moved involuntarily or deliberately, she swept her cup and saucer into the wall beside her.

"There's nothing defensive about me, Terry Bracondale!"

Coffee drained down the rustic-effect plaster on to the carpet.

It was as if her feelings had exploded over the wall.

Heads turned. Nearby conversation slackened.

Terry signalled to a waitress, who came over with a cloth and bucket. Then the table-sounds of diners too far off to be aware spread back into the room.

The waitress tidied up, made a cheerful remark or two and left.

"I think you must have hit a nerve," she said. "I probably do need to come out of myself."

She glared at him.

"It's not your fault. Even though you did tell me I was being defensive. I suppose my hand wasn't ready to hear it even if my head was."

He let her calm down.

"You were only being helpful," she said, "trying to suggest where I'm going wrong."

She felt tears behind her eyes. Of fury, she supposed. Of a woman scorned.

But nothing to do with this chap who had worked and worked till his girl had had enough and left him.

"Like a liqueur?" Terry asked.

"Why not? I'd love one."

The fiery sweetness pulled her together, put a perspective between her and the couple at the window.

"You must be glad you asked me out," she said. "I've made your evening a bundle of fun."

"I hope I can ask you again."

Suddenly, hearing that, she felt she understood him. The man was a gentleman!

"And I hope I may be able to answer in the affirmative, Mr Bracondale."

But she wouldn't look at him. It would break her heart if he thought she was mocking him. He didn't deserve mockery.

"Show me where you're going to hang the painting," she said.

On their way to the car park she took his arm.

"Just one thing about that picture," she said. "I don't want any money for it."

She wouldn't hear his protests, his talk of the business approach.

"It's for you. For friendship. You've done me a favour tonight. More than you realise."

There was something comfortable in his silences. She sensed his mind was not elsewhere, that his concentration was on being with her. His not-speaking said more than a day of chit-chat.

She asked what type of frame he'd like. And the mount in National Gallery red? It would be ready for collection a week tonight.

"I've enjoyed our evening," she said. "I'm glad you were with me."

He wouldn't come in, he said.

He took her hand, bowed slightly.

He hoped he'd be able to see her a week tonight. It depended how the cards fell in the meantime. If he should be unable to, he hoped she would understand. And forgive him if he couldn't let her know.

She supposed he was referring to the kind of gamble he'd mentioned earlier?

That kind of gamble, he said.

"And if you lose?"

He unlocked the car door. Under the roadside lamps she could believe he came from somewhere alien, a land where knives were always out, always sharp.

If he lost, he said, the painting would be a reminder of a restaurant he used to own. And of someone he was getting to know.

"I don't know you very well," she said. "I hope you come through."

The remark seemed to please him. Or so she believed from something momentary on a face not used to registering surprise.

CHAPTER 37

No vessels moor in Eastborough Haven.

The arms of the haven comprise close-timbered jetties and a breakwater of boulders enclosing an acre or two of water which, except when the wind lies a point or two south of east, is almost always calm. But at a certain time of tide the current generated between the sea and the River East is strong enough to give the illusion of motionlessness. It's as though some plastic substance has been moulded to resemble water, the peaks high, the troughs glassy, and a large red float, the size of a small boat, anchored there to indicate the direction of the tide, can sometimes be pulled under by the weight of the tidal race.

Eastborough harbour on the other hand is upstream, a stretch of half a mile of river with moorings on either bank. Of a Sunday morning the place is crowded with yachtsmen, fishermen, and visitors who go to enjoy the sight of boats on water.

The harbourage nearest the Haven is generally occupied by sea-going fishing boats, sturdy craft bedecked with trawl gear, dahns, fish baskets, and gay with flags, funnel badges and the paraphernalia of rigging. These being heavier craft, their motion is sedate, more of a comfortable roll, whereas further upstream around the yacht station Dragons, Fifteens and Broads One designs are all of a nudge and dip, the boats nervous as greyhounds, their metals stays and masts in a twitter of yachtsong.

Between the trawlers and the yachts, in what would seem a curiously uniform gradation of tonnage, come the cruisers, larger ocean-going yachts whose owners undertake voyages to sundry lands and on their return sometimes write books. It was to this area one Sunday morning that Alphonse drove over with Amanda on a matter of business, that of meeting the owners of *Ocean Swell* to discuss insurance for a round-the-world voyage.

The boat was in a cradle on the river bank, its hull looking as if it had been stung by a mile of sea hornets.

"Osmosis."

Alphonse pushed a penknife into one of the pustules, releasing matter as though from an abscess.

"It's being in water," he told her. "The water tries to seep into something more concentrated than itself. So it starts digesting the hull."

"Will you insure it?"

It would depend on the surveyor reporting that the repairs had been satisfactory. And on his assessment of the boat and crew.

"We'll get it repaired."

Sid Watson, in nautical cap and yachtsman's top, was standing nearby. He waved his pipe vaguely in the direction of the hull.

"We'll grind'em all out and fill'em all in and smooth'em all off."

He made it sound like an afternoon's interlude.

"Want to have a look inside?"

Alphonse followed him up the ladder. It was his practice to see for himself. He rated the design of the vessel and the way it was maintained as more important than trusting to reports and insurance tables, which was what some firms did. It was why his company flourished while others faltered.

His company! he thought. After the way he'd been treated!

But he couldn't not do the job well.

He noted the vessel's heavier than usual scantlings, the locker and forepeak storage, the gimballed galley stove and the fact that the galley was on the port side. He knew he was looking at a well-made, well-designed vessel.

"I'd like to see your route, if I may."

He couldn't help it if the request was unusual. He rated the crew's competence as part of the risk, and knew by the level of business he did that his rates were competitive. Most crews appreciated his interest.

The maps were in their stores hut, Watson said. The other crew member would be along any minute.

Amanda said there was a shop up-river that sold amber. And a teashop. She'd be waiting in the teashop.

Her voice was soft. Alphonse heard more than the words. He felt he needn't be over-long in the stores hut.

He was impressed by the crew, felt they knew what they were doing. Subject to a satisfactory surveyor's report on the osmosis problem he guessed he was on to a good bit of business.

It was a pleasant walk up-river to the teashop, past fishermen's huts, derelict boat timbers, the endless traffic of the river.

She was seated by the window, reading while she waited for him. He knew every curve of her face, but catching her like that, absorbed, unguarded, he was taken by storm all over again. She was all there was of romantic, adventurous things.

He held the door for a couple on their way out.

"Morning, Fenley."

Big Dick and wife. Dickson contriving to look aloof and friendly at the same time.

"Someone in there wondering where you've got to," he said.

Alphonse went in, joined her at the table.

"How did it go, Alphy?"

It went O.K., he said. "Had your coffee?"

She'd been waiting to have it with him, she said. Peter would have bought her a cup but she said no.

A waitress came and removed the coffee things. For two people.

"They wouldn't have sat here, would they?" he asked.

That's where they were sitting when she went in, she said. Frenella kindly called out there was a spare chair.

"But when I said I was waiting for you, Peter said they were just going. So I sat and waited."

Peter! She could sit and chat with that charlatan! And on first-name terms! If you love me, he thought, love my dog! And if I have enemies, hate my enemies!

"I'd rather sit somewhere else."

He looked around for another table.

"I thought you'd like this one by the window," she said.

"I would have. If I felt it hadn't been contaminated."

He went over to a larger table, at the other side of which were two elderly ladies. They stopped chatting, looked as mystified as Amanda when he joined them.

"If you'd been treated like I've been treated," he told her, "you'd know what I mean. But you haven't been, so you don't."

The harshness surprised her.

"Peter was saying how hard you work."

"'Was saying'!" he mimicked. "He's always *was saying!'* Saying one thing and doing another."

He wanted her to defend him, wanted to weigh in with an attack on the man. Yet he felt sick, speaking to her like that.

The waitress came and took the order.

When she had gone he asked, "When was he saying I worked hard?"

"In the office," she said. "Just casually."

"Specially to you, you mean? Or out loud for anyone to hear?"

"To me, I think."

She was puzzled at his attitude, troubled for him. "Because," Alphonse said, "what he says to me in effect is, 'Everything settled down now, Fenley? The staff you've got left, working their guts out, are they? Excellent. Consider yourself sacked.'"

He knew he was being unfair to her and a fool to himself.

"I think he's got a good opinion of you," Amanda said.

"Oh, that's nice! 'I've got a good opinion of you, Mr Fenley. So here's your notice.'"

"You might not be given notice," she said quietly. "Between you and me."

If this wasn't the limit! A young girl in the office could be told something – something confidential about himself – and he, who it mainly concerned, who had worked at the place years – couldn't!

"Has he told you something?"

She looked uncomfortable.

"I'm not supposed to know."

"What did he say?"

"You won't say anything, will you?"

"Don't tell me, then. It's only my job and my pension at stake. I'm the last one who needs to know."

She looked away, unhappy.

The waitress came with the coffee. Kindly Experienced.

"Will that be all?"

She smiled at them. Young lovers. Maybe having their first tiff.

The smile broke the ice for him.

"You needn't tell me, Amanda," he said. "Really. I don't want you to be compromised."

He felt easier, suddenly on the moral high ground.

"If there's any good news I'll hear about in due course. I don't want you to break a confidence."

"It was something I read," she said quietly.

He didn't want to make things bad for anyone, he said. Not even for Dickson, let alone for someone like her. He wouldn't want anyone else dragged down.

"It was on his desk," she said. "I thought it might help. Something about an offer. I didn't have time to see the rest."

He'd been unfair, he said. Unfair to Dickson, and very unfair to her. He didn't know if she could forgive him. He'd never forgive himself.

She took his hand.

"I think you're too intelligent for that firm, anyway, Alphy. No-one in Head Office works as hard as you."

He began to regret getting angry.

"Sometimes I get this feeling – ."

"What feeling?"

That tide-race at the haven, he said.

"That float. Big as it was – pulled under by the tide. I feel – sort of tide – something – pulling me down – "

Hated himself. Less than manly.

Was glad she didn't scoff, that she did him the courtesy of listening.

He affected a smile, made light of it.

"I thought, that's me! Then I saw those chaps – about to go round the world in a boat no longer than this room is wide."

The two women picked up their handbags, gave each other a look and shuffled off.

"Round the world!" Alphonse repeated. "Over water ten times as dangerous as that haven. Compared to blokes like them – all I am is a marine insurer and making a failure of that."

Amanda was looking at him in astonishment.

"But you're you!" she said. "You don't have to be them. Or anyone! You're Alphy. Who I want you to be!"

But she, Alphonse told her, could face those things.

"You do face them. You swim out, where I'm half terrified. You stand up there on the top board and dive head-first off. And I think to myself, what do I do? What dare I do?"

"If I wanted to go out with a swimmer," Amanda said, "I could go out with Richard. It wasn't much fun going out with Richard."

"I still think it's a miracle," he said, "being with you. Me on the way down – you and everyone else on the way up."

"Alphy!"

He took her hands.

"You're the one and only top board girl," he said. "Do you know the length of that board you're on, in my opinion?"

He bent down and measured her foot between his hands and showed her.

"That big," he said, and wondered how sincere he was being. "The shortest board in the world. Where there's only room for one. And that one's you."

The way she was looking at him.

"You aren't on the way down. Not with me you aren't."

Her bare toe was on his shin.

"The things you say!"

Her foot was warm, insistent.

"Why don't you finish your coffee?" she said. "So we can go home."

His hand on the small of her back in the valley of curves.

"Mum kept saying, 'You will take care, Amanda, in Paris'!' 'I'm not a child,' I told her. And you don't want one,' she said."

Amanda laughed, remembering.

"The tickets should come in the morning," he said.

She turned on her stomach, watching him.

"I couldn't tell her we've been doing it for weeks. Could I? So she'll just have to worry. Poor old Mum."

"I paid over the phone," he said.

She nudged him with her body. She was what she was, an innocent. Compared to her his own complicated motives were little more than selfishness.

He was aware of the smoothness of her back under him, the nape of her neck, the softness of her hair against his cheek.

"Careful," she giggled.

CHAPTER 38

Documents!

The thought hit him, woke him up. He looked at the clock. Half past two.

How could he have been so stupid! Evans and Co had kept him busy, no doubt to give him as little time as possible to get down to it. Was his own fault. He'd kept his nose to the grindstone so long he hadn't noticed what they were up to. Had been faffing about over a bit of business at Easthaven when he ought to have been preparing an audit!

Was out of bed, was making notes.

No good telling them how efficient his section used to be. He could see their reaction: Efficient? Who're you trying to kid, Fenley?

Would be the easiest thing in the world for them to rewrite history, lose a few files, alter documents. Soon be made to look inefficient. Pension, references, prospects – all would look decidedly dim. He'd be the sacrificial lamb. Customers would be dismayed to see the chaos of the premises they were going to dump him in. He'd never keep staff, loyal as they were at the moment. Would lose the kudos of being in charge of the most profitable section of the company. Be in charge of a failure. Then they'd bury him.

The more efficient side of his mind took over. He noted what information he had at his fingertips, what he'd need to find, what to research. Was able to assemble, at least in embryonic form, relevant documentation since the last audit. Knew where to find lists of clients, policy details, policies laid off against other companies, evidence that cover levels were appropriate – every transaction, outcome, approximate turnover, projected profit . . .

By the time daylight streamed in over the supermarket he'd got it clear in his mind. A clearing-up report. Which some people were going to wish hadn't been written – especially when the annual inquest was held in the boardroom.

"Be a copy for you, Evans," he thought, "and one for you, Dickson. And you, Presdel. And each of the directors. And the MD. And one or two other names will be interested."

He was surprised no-one had requested one. No, maybe not surprising. Someone, some little clique, had got his reputation in their sights, got the torpedo ready to fire. Come the hour, come the attack. Then they'd justify the way they'd treated him.

"Shame I've only got a couple of weeks left," Amanda said. "I might have been able to find something out for you."

She was pleased at the lift in his spirits, hadn't realised how important work was to him. It was more than the place where the wages came from. Seemed like a contest between him and something beyond his control, a sort of demon that happened to look like an office job.

They were on the beach having an evening swim. Out on the raft her friends were diving, swimming, messing about in deep water. Amanda was happy swimming with him nearer the shore. She seemed to take each day's happiness as it came, unconcerned whether tomorrow would be happy or not; but for Alphonse tomorrow governed today. Even a forecast of rain next week brought its clouds. He hated his turn of mind, admired Amanda for being free of such cowardice.

He'd swum enough, sat on the beach watching her.

She looked well, bursting with health. Her life unfolding like summertime. Wished he could be light-hearted like her, enjoying the little things. A gift he hadn't got. But he loved it in her.

"What were you looking at?" she laughed.

Water glistened from her swimsuit down her legs, illustrating curve and shadow. She dried her throat, her armpits, shook the excess from her hair till her face glowed.

"Hm?" she insisted.

But rather than confess that he envied her, her openness, her body, he said, "I forgot to tell you. Everything's laid on. We're all ready to go."

He wouldn't hear of her offering to pay her way. She'd only got a couple of weeks at Head Office. Then it was visiting friends and relations. Then Thrunes.

"Haven't got you for long," he said. "It's the least I can do."

"You've got me for ever, I hope," she said.

"I know I have," he smiled.

In the gleam of moisture down over her calf he saw the image of a river. Its speed pitiless.

"Going to be the best few days of my life," she said. "So far."

She leaned over him, shook her damp hair against his face till he seized her up and ran with her into the sea.

CHAPTER 39

A fax emerged.

"From Peter Dickson," Tina said, her voice having to compete with the sawing and hammering and sanding the other side of a plasterboard wall.

"Congratulating you on the smooth change-over."

Alphonse put a hand to his ear. She repeated the message, amused at the look on his face when she said "smooth."

"He wants to see you after work. Says he'll come round."

"What time?"

She skimmed down to, "About five-thirty."

"Reply *After work is seven*," Alphonse said. "I'll be happy to see him then."

"Well, the first part is true," Tina thought.

Doreen took the phone call. It was from the marine surveyor.

The interim finding was that *Ocean Swell* was O K overall except for the hull.

"Owners say hull will be ready for inspection in three to four weeks," she told him.

"Repairs will be completed to the surveyor's satisfaction," Alphonse said. Formally.

Doreen smiled. She liked her boss, his workmanlike mind. The staff knew he could never do less than a workmanlike job.

"If I was going to be dismissed this lunchtime," Alphonse had said once, "I'd still work as normal all the morning."

He assumed, probably correctly, that his staff would support him.

"Everyone gone home?"

Dickson looked round at the empty desks.

"Even the workmen, unfortunately," Alphonse said. "Nothing like the whine of a well-tuned sander to overcome this lonely feeling."

Dickson laughed, eased himself into a chair across from Alphonse. He was a big young man, sandy hair, pale blue eyes.

"Going to take a little while yet to get the place ship-shape," he said.

"Mustn't grumble," Alphonse said.

Dickson took it as an amiable reply.

"That's the way to look at it."

"What's a bit of lost business to Head Office?" Alphonse said.

Dickson had no more superiority than this, he believed: that he was in a lucky run whereas he, Alphonse, wasn't. But if Lady Luck were to turn away a moment, things could be very different.

Dickson took him literally.

"Losing business?"

"I'm not losing business. I work all the hours there are to get business. More hours than I'm paid for. But when you're bottom of the firm's priorities it seems to show."

"You haven't had it easy," Dickson acknowledged.

"Other departments get perks. We get kicked out of our premises. But we still generate more profit per unit than any other department. As that audit I sent you makes clear."

He smiled his hostility. He knew Dickson hadn't come out of friendship.

"You certainly dotted the i's and crossed the t's. Came as rather a surprise."

"Bit of a surprise to Evans, I hear. Looked as sick as a toad, someone said."

"Must have taken you quite a time, preparing something as comprehensive as that?"

"Not office time, if that's what you're worrying about."

Alphonse had long been adept at interpreting Dicksonspeak.

"I notice you don't deny what I said about Evans," he added.

Dickson shrugged. "Mr Evans will no doubt respond at the appropriate time."

Which meant, Alphonse suspected, that Mr Evans would shortly be having his balls chewed off.

"More to the point," Dickson said, "I've been wondering if you'd like a change of venue."

His voice softened momentarily. Wanted it to sound like an offer.

"Another one?"

Alphonse knew what this was Dicksonspeak for: he was going to be moved here, there and everywhere till he got fed up and resigned. It was their revenge for him doing the audit. But he was surprised at the speed of it.

"What have you got in mind this time?"

Dickson involuntarily checked that they were alone.

"It's embryonic at the moment. But it would need someone like you – someone of your calibre – to see it through if it did come to anything."

Leisure Nation, the parent company, was looking to open another small boat insurance branch elsewhere in the country.

"We've noted what your branch here has done. The feeling is there's no reason why another such branch shouldn't be a success as well."

Alphonse waited, suspicious.

"With you as manager," Dickson said.

"Where's elsewhere?"

Dickson drew an imaginary triangle representing Britain on the desk top.

"The Blackpool-Fleetwood area. Probably based at St Alfreds. The north west. We understand there's money in the area. And boats. So naturally they need all the insurance they can get."

He wanted it to sound like an irresistible offer.

"Would need someone energetic. Someone who knew what he was doing. I'd hope to persuade the firm to put promotion money into it, advertising and so on, to make it a goer."

The more he talked the more convinced he seemed of the feasibility of the project.

"It's a nice part of the country. You'd do what you've been doing here. And have a free hand to do it. What do you say?"

St Alfreds. Three hundred miles nearer Thrunes than he was here at Kirkhaven. Yet all it amounted to was talk. No witnesses, no facts and figures, nothing in writing.

"Forgive me for being cautious," Alphonse said. "What about something in writing? Like salary. Expenses. Resettlement award."

Dickson was already shaking his head.

"Let me put it like this. If you take it on, it'll succeed. If you don't, I won't be able to persuade the board to back it. In fact I wouldn't even put it to the board. I'm not putting my neck on the line for a failure. Either it's you for the job – or it's a no-no."

"Have you asked Evans if he'd like to do it?"

Dickson beamed, briefly.

"There's a certain amount of project money in the firm at the moment. If this project isn't proposed the money will go elsewhere. But if you accept – who knows? You might become area manager of the St Alfreds, Kirkhaven and Norwich branches combined. I don't promise anything. I can't foresee the future. I merely float the idea. It's up to you if you accept, and up to you if you sink it."

And what, wondered Alphonse, do you get out of it?

"When do you want to know by?"

"First day back after Bank Holiday. At the latest. I shall need to have got a package together by then – and you're the chief bit of the package. If I don't hear positively by then I'll assume a negative."

"You'd guarantee at least present salary if I take it?"

Dickson paused over a question he wished he hadn't been asked.

"I'd guarantee present salary," he agreed.

Alphonse saw him to the door.

"All this is strictly in confidence. Nothing goes forward till I've got a package. Then there'll need to be a site found – and a bit of market research. But until I've got a package nothing moves. And you haven't heard a word about it!"

He smiled the top-dog-to-lesser-dog smile.

"Nothing is forever."

He glanced around at the improvised office.

"As well you know, Mr Fenley."

It was a pleasant evening, the sun still bright, the air warm. He felt like a walk. He could cover the two miles, cook his meal and still have time to get his things ready for the trip to Paris.

Generally he avoided the Audley House route home. He might be recognised as the man who used to be manager, who'd been chucked out of a handsome Georgian house into a nondescript slum next to a take-away. It was what powerlessness meant: putting up with conditions other people shuddered at.

But this evening, with Dickson's proposal turning over in his mind, he let his legs find the way, and found himself within sight of the sash windows and columned portico, the fanlighted door and red brick facade of his old office. It was a curious feeling, being dispossessed. Like seeing your girl out with another man.

"Alphonse Fenley!"

She was sitting back from the pavement, sketching the house from beside a shop driveway.

"Emilia B!"

An old pang went through him. Those green eyes. Those cynical kissable lips. Wouldn't be long till someone snapped her up. Except that Emilia wasn't a snap-uppable girl.

"What are you doing," she asked, "crawling about here this time of day?"

"That's where I used to work," he said.

"Used to?"

"I was kicked out. I'm in the High Street now, next to the take-away."

"Still in work, then."

He didn't pursue it. She still had the knack of looking down on him.

"So what made you pick Audley House?" he asked. "Hoping to see me?"

He loved it, the look of total scorn. And tried not to grin at winding her up. He surveyed her canvas. The shape and colour of the building were depicted almost by default, as was her method, her concern being with irrelevant little details. He presumed she knew what she was doing, he murmured.

"It's what people seem to buy – pictures of notable places. Like *La Golondrina.*"

He fancied she said it with rather a ring.

"Know what the name means?" she asked.

"Need it mean anything?"

"It's Spanish for the swallow. So someone told me. Quite apt for a restaurant, don't you think?"

"You're not usually such a fund of information," he said. "I didn't think you usually knew what day of the week it was."

She laughed, not wanting to.

"I know what day of the week it was, Alphonse Fenley. It was Tuesday. Enjoyed your meal there, did you?"

He stared at her. Knew she knew.

"I didn't see you there!"

"You didn't see much of anybody there. Gone in for baby-snatching, have you?"

"She's nineteen."

"What's her name?"

"Amanda. Who were you in there with?"

"Never you mind."

"Have you had sex yet?"

"Don't be so damned blunt."

"Have you?"

"No, I haven't. Have you?"

"So I'm told."

"How many times?"

"My calculator's broken."

"Thought you had, the way you were all over her. Revolting little sod."

He felt equal to her now, enjoyed her insults.

"I'd have had it with you," he said. "Except you kept pulling the shutters down"

She didn't reply, her attention apparently back on the front elevation of Audley House. Alphonse waited to see how the painting developed.

"You don't have to stay," she said. "You can bugger off as soon as you like."

"What's his name? This bloke you were in there with?"

"Clear off."

"Give us a kiss."

He laughed and walked away.

Hardly raising her voice she called him back.

"Remember that bloke on the cliff?"

"What – Wally?"

"I didn't know you knew his name?"

"Wally the Wanker."

Knew it wouldn't please her. Was glad it didn't.

"Any rate," she said, "I saw him the other day. He stopped to watch me paint."

"Did you say anything?"

"Told him to clear off."

"And did he?"

"He had the gall to tell me he hadn't done me any harm."

"So what did you say?"

"I stabbed at him with a brush handle. Got him in the hand. He was gone like a shot."

He was pleased for her.

"Think he'll tell the police?"

"Can't tell. He still looked a bit bruised round the face from that time you did him over."

The recollection of it was in her mind, how nervous she'd felt. And Alphonse going for him like that.

"Better be off," he said. "We're going to Paris Saturday. I've got my washing to do tonight."

"Enjoy your honeymoon."

"She's off to university soon."

She could hear the way his voice drooped.

"Not the end of the world," she said. "She'll be home at Christmas."

"Maybe," he said. "May be so."

He wandered away.

"I'm glad I've seen you," he said over his shoulder.

Emilia mixed touches of paint to get the effect of sunset on brickwork. When she'd got it right she allowed dabs of colour here and there to make their contribution. As for Alphonse Fenley being worried or pleased about anything, these weren't on her palette at all.

CHAPTER 40

Trolleys, notice signs, the platform itself, everything began to slide past. Eurostar was on its way.

For a while it picked its way through the city, then they were into the suburbs. Then the Kent countryside.

They gathered speed. Sometimes on a curve they could see the front of the train ahead, a great white technological worm devouring distance, winding its length through copses, round hills, across mile after mile of countryside. Then to chalkier soil, the land laid bare by cuttings, embankments, naked of turf, sprouting posts and pylons, fences and walls; then, a gigantic mouth in a hill, a rectangular maw into which the train rushed without pause, its vast length pouring into the underworld.

"They've left the lights on!"

She was only half serious.

"I thought it was going to be like the Tunnel of Love."

"You've been to too many funfairs."

She laughed. "You sound like my mum."

He laughed too, not wanting to sound like her mum. Nor to think of her escapades with boys, her young body adventuring in the dark, her mouth responding to other young mouths.

Outside, an occasional low-intensity light slipped by, illuminating a hint of cable, a recessed arch. For long minutes there were no lights, only darkness fleeing past into darkness. This was the underworld, man-made, concreted, but the underworld for all that. Alphonse wanted it to be a death and a birth. Wanted to leave his judgemental self behind, wanted to begin finding joy in trifles, to see more in life than achievement. Let the old self die, he hoped; let my new self be born.

He looked at his watch. Had fifteen minutes to bring it about.

Amanda reached up and switched on a couple of pre-focused lights under the overhead rack.

"Like being under the shower," she joked, her hair bathed gold with light.

He laughed too, determined to be delighted.

So what was French for shower, she asked.

"Douche?" she laughed. "Sounds a bit personal!"

He loved her unreservedness, her flitting from wave top to wave top.

A sudden dawn; night to sunshine in two seconds.

"Whee! We're on the continon!"

He wondered if the miracle had happened, if his old self had been left behind, crumbling somewhere back in the underworld.

The train hurtled on, increasing its speed through the countryside of Northern France. A voice over the loudspeakers told them they were going a hundred and eighty-six miles an hour. Landscapes came, whirled past, joined the hundred other landscapes now behind them, unaltered as if they'd never moved, had never offered for view their farmhouses and rivers, their barns and gardens.

Not wishing to sound like her mum he felt less easy with her. He had always complimented her looks, her vivacity;

now he was afraid of boring her, felt that continual praise might be as boring as continual anything else.

He unfolded a map, rested it on the pull-down flaps and pointed out Boulevard St Michel and St Germain, and La Rue where their hotel was.

"A lot of places close in August. It's when the French go on holiday."

"As long as you're there," she said, "it'll be magic."

"I'll be there," he joked. "Till death us do part."

A vista of high-rise blocks, balconies, shapes of steel and concrete. The train slowed, wound through the outskirts of Paris, drew to a halt at a make-shift dropping-off point in the Gare du Nord. Passengers disembarking found little help, few directions. France had seen the influx from England, shrugged its shoulders and turned away.

Alphonse and Amanda collected their haversacks, made their way down and waited under the broad-arched Art Nouveau ceiling of the metro.

A stainless steel train droned in, the locomotive clean and polished as a watch.

Amanda watched the people, older men in suits, the younger ones more ritzy, generally more well-to-do and Mediterranean; the women somehow neater, more conscious of flair than their English counterparts.

He could only guess at the impact Paris was having on her, the conversation she couldn't understand, newspapers she couldn't read, the unfamiliar posters – yet he had a feeling that beneath the foreignness she was already at home.

They were in a road where shopkeepers stood at the doorway of their shops, cajoling passers-by to enter.

"If you give them the eye," he warned, "you could find yourself in trouble."

"I don't give them the eye."

"You don't see French girls taking such notice of them."

"They've seen it all before."

The large stripe-aproned manager of a furniture shop swept his hat down into a bow in front of her.

"You like to look round, madame?"

She stopped, smiled at him, glanced into the shop.

"No, I only want to see."

Alphonse wondered if he wasn't beginning to feel rather like her mum, as if he had a child by the hand who had a world of things to see for the very first time. But it was what they had come for, he reminded himself, to stop and stare at things over the Channel. He stopped and stared with her – at the three- and four-storeyed stone-faced houses fronting the pavements; their balconies and wrought iron balustrades; the great carved street gates; the cars parked and packed in every conceivable place and other cars elbowing in, nudging this car forward and that one backward to make a space...

"Isn't that La Rue?" he heard her saying. "Where the hotel is?"

She smiled at him fondly as if to say, "I'll look after you, my little lost one."

A dark blue awning bore the name of the hotel. The outer glass door was closed against the traffic, the inner one open.

The door to days and nights together.

They checked in, were given their keys. Made their way up a spiral staircase and found their room.

He unlocked the door.

"Chez nous," he said. "Our own little house. Where we can really get to know each other."

"Where's the loo then? I'm bursting."

They found themselves in the Latin Quarter with its street music, restaurants, groups of wandering tourists. Alphonse and Amanda wandered with them, enjoyed the easy-going nature of the crowds, the warmth of the evening, the brilliance of the shop signs, the wonderland of coloured lights, coloured signs, colourful clothes. But what he liked most was watching Amanda, enchanted out of her skin with it all.

He was proud to be with her. Whatever the Latin Quarter had to offer it had little to equal Amanda. It seemed others thought so too, by the glances in her direction, the occasional whistle.

He was glad she was besotted with him.

The Seine at night. Lit and shadowed like a film set, its ripples flickered like mirrors on the white stone banks, under the arches of bridges. Approaching them, bright as a dream, a sight-seeing cruiser showered the river with light, its superstructure a confection of lamplight, its wake a phosphorescence. For a moment they felt part of its glory; then it receded, was replaced by another, the river broken into brilliances, the water dark, polished.

"Like it?"

She shook her head, too delighted to answer.

The centre table ran the length of the restaurant and was made up of numerous separate tables pushed together and covered with white cloths.

"Two only, Monsieur?"

They grinned at each other, glad to be seated.

Jollifications from a group of students at one end. A couple of musicians with violin and guitar trying a note or two at the other. Green-leaved plants in earthenware pots around the walls, along the tables baskets of bread, salads, bottles of wine amongst the candles.

She nodded, her eyes brilliant.

He knew what she meant, that what he'd read to her about a certain restaurant having atmosphere had turned out to be true.

They ordered; they drank; they ate. And drank again.

The musicians were also singers, mainly of love songs. As the meal progressed they serenaded this lady...that lady...Amanda.

She sat up to them, gravely pleased at the attention, courteous when the song ended, allowed her hand to be kissed.

"No wonder they applauded," he said. "The toast of Paris."

"Toast!" she joked. "Couldn't eat another thing."

They ambled back through the Boulevard St Michel. A fountain rushed and gushed its waters over a gathering of stone figures. He asked her to pose beside it for a photograph, and snapped her when she twisted round to see where the spray was coming from.

"Squiffy? he asked."

She took his arm to steady herself.

"Course not."

She stopped in the street and kissed him, swayed as they were kissing.

He realised how alive he felt.

For years the negative part of himself had tried to pull him under. Now it had gone. He'd made himself conscious of his failings, his preoccupation with Dickson at work, his jealousy of Amanda and Dickson going off on that course together. Like a snake discarding a skin he had flung an unwanted self aside.

"Enjoying yourself?" he asked.

She laughed a little, sighed, rested her head on his shoulder.

"I feel as if we're married," he said.

"Oh, don't spoil it. I'm enjoying every minute."

The sluices that wash the gutters of a night-time opened. Her attention elsewhere she stepped in, water up to her ankles. He photographed her laughing, emptying her shoe as if it was the funniest thing ever.

"I'll remember this room," she said.

Modest in size, blue and white striped wallpaper, a pair of brown rexine armchairs, a veneered chipboard wardrobe. But with the curtains closed and the lights on either side of the headboard it felt cosy.

They undressed.

She wanted him. Accepted his help getting her blouse undone, her bra off.

Her wet hair reminded her. It was on her mind that she had been too abrupt saying to him *Don't spoil it.* It wasn't what she meant. What she had meant she couldn't recall.

She knew she'd make it up to him.

He felt her arch up under him, heard her moan, felt her subside, quiver again, and subside.

He kissed her in the slant of street light across the pillow, her hair streaked about her face with sweat, breath heavy with wine.

When she came round she turned to him, almost in sleep.

"You do it the best," she whispered. "No-one's done it as well as that."

She smiled, her body a tingle of satisfaction.

Heard him whisper back, "Better than Richard, you mean?"

Her eyes were too heavy to keep open.

"Too rough. I told you."

"What about the others?" he whispered. "Was I as good as them?"

His voice seemed a long way above. He deserved the truth, but the memories she wanted were too far out to get to, even for her Alphy.

"There was only Bertie."

"Bertie?"

"That boy at school."

Then she was near the surface enough to be amused.

"Don't think he knew what he was doing."

Alphie's arms were round her, his fingers stroking her neck.

"Do it often?"

She felt like a kitten, purring, half asleep again, her master finger-tipping her neck.

"Only when I went out with them. Not often."

The sweetness of sleep was in her mouth.

"Like you and Emilia..."

She sank too deep for thought, her mind encountering emptiness, underwater miles of emptiness.

The hours dragged by.

Sleep was a wave that ran up the beach and receded as he went towards it, foam that vanished in the sand.

There was a train, pushing itself through earth and re-appearing.

A great white needle – unstitching!

He was awake. The oneness that had been himself and Amanda had come unstitched.

He imagined her first time with Bertie.

Tried to imagine the bed. Or mat. Or standing up at the back of some shed. And next day – how had they met next day? With a look that sang across the classroom?

She turned in her sleep beside him.

He thought of her smoothness, the curve of her unbetterable body. Maybe when she was old she would deny it, this hunger, this urge to have a man into her.

Desire was the heart of it! The most delicate bloom desires the bee.

He turned to her. Her body was cool in sleep.

He kissed her damp forehead, her cool lips; and said good-bye.

He had lost, but knew why he had lost. What he had considered special had been so only in his mind. Others had found her special too; or hadn't considered her special. He didn't feel her past diminished her. But his expectation could never be what it was.

He felt he could come to terms with it. There would be no quarrel, no inquest or raking over the coals. Neither would he be unkind. He had said good-bye in his mind; no need to do so in his mouth. By and by the distance between himself and her would increase. They would be as ships that had passed in the night.

It was torture for all that.

He fell asleep, slept the sleep of the bereaved.

A hand was on him.

Insistent. Coaxing.

He turned. She had slept well, her eyes glowed, she was under him in a moment. There was little to do. He kissed her with every show of love, but the Amanda of his dreams, the young goddess from the edge of the world, had gone. Had probably never existed.

Their mouths joined, their bodies arched, convulsed. Nature was spent.

He felt liberated, no longer in thrall to her. He felt more himself, more manly. And this new detachment attracted her more than ever.

"I wish I wasn't going to university," she said. "Tell me not to go and I'll give it up."

"What does your dad say?"

She laughed. "He says a little baggage goes a long way."

Another time she said, "I'd be a fool to go and miss the chance of seeing you every day."

"You've got to go," he told her. "It's your future and you must obey it."

He knew it was good advice, the only proper advice, but he wanted it to sound like a punishment because what she had done deserved punishment.

It was the only time he saw her near to tears.

"For your sake, then," she said.

They were in the undercroft of La Sainte Chapelle.

They admired the blue and gold-starred ceiling, its gilded ribs, its golden arches, its scarlet-bordered stone. Red and gold pillars sprayed out bouquets of vaulting to form a roof whose function was to support the more famous chapel above.

Whether it was the blaze of blue, red and gold, or the human scale of what was otherwise mysterious, he couldn't tell. He felt an identity with it, this rich man's interpretation of the stable of the Nativity.

He wanted to tell Amanda. Wanted to say, "I'm affected by the holiness of this place."

But knew the pain of two minds not in tune.

He looked around. Listened. For the moment Amanda and he had the place to themselves.

"Take your shirt and bra off," he said. "I'll take a snap."

Like an order.

"Alphie!"

He was waiting.

"I can't!"

"For me you can."

He was preparing the camera.

"Be quick. Against that pillar."

He went close, the camera ready.

"Before anyone comes," he said.

Not that he cared who saw her bare breasts. Richard had seen them. And that boy at school. Let everyone see them. And all the better in a chapel.

She undid some buttons.

"As it's for you," she said.

She dropped the clothes to the floor.

"Pose as if you're combing your hair."

They could hear people coming in.

"Alphie!" she whispered.

He snapped her.

"Turn away a bit."

He was on his knee this time. Took another snap.

A man and a woman and their child were in the nearby aisle. Staring.

Amanda went the other side of the pillar.

"You do boss me," she whispered. "Don't you?"

He helped her with the bra, brushed her shirt down at the back.

"You don't really mind, do you?" he asked when they were outside.

She took his arm.

"As long as it's for you," she said.

He felt mean, having such a calculating mind. He'd captured her in the high tide of love, was preserving the image so he could remember.

"A kind of abuse," he admitted later.

"I'd – do – anything for you – dear," she sang. "You won't need a photo tonight."

But it was tomorrow he had in mind. The tomorrow without her.

In the darkness of the underworld fragments of his discarded self had reassembled, the defect-ridden structure he hoped he had said good bye to. Or maybe he hadn't altered even for a moment, perhaps could never alter, could never discard what he hated and make a better man of himself.

They made their way towards the Luxembourg Gardens.

The incident in the chapel was on her mind.

"Would you ever dare do something for me?" she asked.

"Anything specific?"

"If it became necessary, I mean."

"As long as it wasn't diving off the top board."

She accepted his assurances easily, was happiness itself with him. And he was preparing to jettison her.

"I wish I could dare to be as nice as you," he said.

She was serious in a moment.

"Don't you change, Alphie," she said. "Ever! I've got you just how I want you."

It was their last evening. They were back in the Restaurant of the Long Table.

Like meeting an old friend. They commented on the yellow wall lamps, the terracotta wall troughs, the smell of watercress and coffee. The worn-out face and long-suffering eyes of the manageress gave no hint of recognition; whereas at the desk by the door the patron, sleek and pink-cheeked, greeted them as he greeted everyone, as if they were friends come back from the dead.

The waiter brought soup, fresh baguettes.

Alphonse poured the wine.

"To us!" Amanda said.

"To us!"

The musicians strolled up. The guitarist, bearded and with grey-flecked hair, strummed a few bars from the next number. The other was taller, his eyes engaging with those of the customers, flitting away to the fiddle strings and back again, black into the depths of the women's eyes.

"You sing to lady?" he asked Alphonse.

A courtesy really, for having sung to his girl the night before.

"Go on, Alphy."

She sounded full of the devil.

He recognised the air, had sung it at the promenade.

He got to his feet.

He was on his own high board now. Unpractised, unprepared, about to sing to a roomful of strangers. But he had a charge of pain, a cry waiting to burst. He had said good-bye in his mind. And couldn't say good-bye.

Plaisir d'amour
Ne dure qu'un moment.
Chagrin d'amour
Dure toute la vie.

His voice relaxed; he was able to sustain the notes. The guitarist nodded, approving.

J'ai tout quitte
Pour l'ingratte Sylvie;

Elle me quittes

Et prends un autre amant.

He sang to Amanda. She wouldn't understand the words. Those who did would think he was joking.

The violinist improvised a passage, brought him in for the last time.

He held her hand, a troubadour with a love-song.

Plaisir d'amour

Ne dure qu'un moment.

Chagrin d'amour

Dure toute la vie.

He kissed her. Diners applauded, the musicians were kind. He felt he had done his dare. And had said good-bye.

"What did the words mean, Alphie?"

The two were in bed, had explored their pleasure to its limit, were settling towards sleep.

"The pleasure of love doesn't last a moment; the bitterness of love lasts a lifetime."

She stroked his neck. "Lots of songs have silly words. I loved the way you sang it to me. All those people. I wouldn't have dared."

He slept better that night. Was aware of pain; and the numbness that kept it at bay.

When he got home on Bank Holiday Monday a note from Emilia:

> *"If you can spare the time when you get back from your honeymoon come and see me. Not that I want to see you particularly.*
>
> *Emilia."*

CHAPTER 41

"Didn't take you long to get here!"

She stood the other side of the threshold in her painter's overall. Unwelcoming. He felt as if he had turned up late at a clinic.

"Your note said you didn't want to see me. So I came."

Emilia was taller than Amanda, less feminine. He was still fond of her, though she was someone you'd have to subdue intellectually, someone you'd have to argue into being affectionate.

"You'd better come in."

"Not if you don't want me to."

She seemed about to retort, "I don't want you to," but stepped back and showed him into the living-room.

Those same armchairs. The settee Jean had sat on, the hearth she used to sit in front of. A familiar geography he'd never be part of.

"It's about this."

She handed him a package loosely wrapped in brown paper tied round with string.

"Am I supposed to open it?"

"As you wish."

He pulled the paper off. The painting of the ship of death.

He took it over to the window to see it better. He remembered his thoughts once about lady painters, and regretted them.

The picture was different now it was finished. When he'd seen it before he had thought of it more as an hallucination, a nightmare unlikely to come true. He'd been shown something startling on a bit of paper, a sort of rumour no-one could put faith in. But Jean had died. The nightmare had come true.

This bit of paint was all there was of her.

He studied it a long time. Emilia didn't mind him taking a long time.

He handed it back.

"Caught me at a bad moment, actually."

She kept her arms in her apron pocket.

"Dear me! Honeymoon not go too well?"

His gesture might have agreed with her, but otherwise he didn't reply.

He studied it again, knew what a tribute it was. And now here it was framed and wrapped. A person's life. Tied round with string.

"She's been in my mind lately," he said.

"That's why I wrote," she said. "She'd have wanted you to have it."

Gone to all that trouble to frame it and get it ready to give it to him?

"If you'd like it."

"Christ!"

He put the picture down. The illusion of recognising the girl he'd known at school had faded.

"You'll have to judge where to hang it," she said.

He loved her for being so immovable, so aloof.

"What will you – ?"

It was an unfinishable question. Was no longer his business.

There'd been a brief coming together. Now it was as if he'd never come back, as if the two of them had always gone their separate ways.

He looked into the room again, the landscape Jean had lived in. Knew he was no longer welcome.

"I suppose I just take it and go," he said.

"I think that's the idea."

He picked the painting up, got as far as the door.

"Seems wrong, somehow."

He couldn't help looking at it again, the blood-red scarf of a sea, the ship itself, its destination, sunrise, dawn, colour.

Her hand was on the doorknob.

"Maybe not as wrong as you think."

The evening sun poured into the hall, lit familiar blemishes in the paintwork.

"So when's the wedding?" she asked.

But to him it was a wound, not doorstep talk.

"You're sure about this?"

For a moment the hostility in her face lifted.

"I can't bear to look at it. So you can have it."

She wanted to go indoors, shut him out of her life.

"Can't I – "

He meant make some kind of recompense for it.

"Bugger off, Alphonse. I've got a life to live."

CHAPTER 42

He'd been in touch with Dickson, had made the appointment. Come the afternoon he worked less late than usual, locked the premises, drove over to Head Office.

He went over his strategy in his mind. He'd think of the meeting with Dickson not as an interview for a job but as about taking a decision for the right reasons. Based on judgement, not out of fear or favour. Whatever transpired he would emerge as a person he could live with.

He glanced at the facade of Head Office. Immediately ahead, on a plinth the height of the wall rustication, a statue of the founder of the original bank, the face devoid of sympathy, the eyes sightless. Alphonse had seen it often, had ignored it as he might a hoarding or street sign. Now it was a symbol, a metaphor of the unknown.

He gave it two fingers.

He checked in at the desk.

Rita rang through.

"Mr Dickson'll be ready in two minutes," she said.

Doll-like as ever with her ceramic cheeks and expressionless eyes.

The hall was as palatial as in its Regency days, its ceiling duck-egg blue, the walls turquoise, mouldings and cornices picked out in white. That old man on the plinth outside, he thought, knew what he wanted – and how to get it.

"She's in that one."

Rita indicated the door Amanda had gone in last time he was here.

"She didn't half enjoy Paris."

He couldn't bear to talk about her.

Last time he had seen a goddess in a short black skirt and a white blouse, a creature from the mists of the world. This time – she was almost his wife. And soon? She would be at university. And that would be that.

He tried to shut her out of his mind. She was too great with him.

"Found any amber yet?" he asked.

Rita looked around at the carpet.

"You made that up. You'd been seeing that film."

"If you feel about with your bare feet you sometimes find some."

"I asked my friend. She said it came out of the sea. She said you were having me on."

A message from the office.

"Mr Dickson will see you now," she said.

He passed the aquarium as he went. A dignified circular fish with its mouth on one side of the perimeter and its tail on the other rose from behind plants as bright and green as plastic. Last time he had been in need of a comfortable, threat-free world. Not any more. This time he was going to be master of himself. His decision would be his own, arrived at freely.

Dickson was seated with his back to the window, a device designed to give him an advantage, except that in the evening the light illuminated his face more than Alphonse's.

"I've decided against," Alphonse said.

"On what grounds?"

"It's too vague. No job description, no indication of salary or conditions, no area of operations -"

Dickson raised a hand.

"We know all that. This is a new venture. We don't know how big it'll grow – or if it'll grow at all. The area of operations is up to you. How you go about the job, how you build the business – all up to you. That's why I want you in the package. We'll continue paying your salary and so on while you find out and report back what the prospects are."

"What about my job here in Kirkhaven?"

"We shall have to advertise. Naturally."

"For a replacement?"

"Insofar as anyone as good as you can be replaced."

And what of Doreen and Tina and the other staff?

The insurance office was a going concern, Dickson said. As long as it remained a going concern staff would be needed.

Alphonse maintained what he hoped was a faintly hostile attitude. But the first hedge had been jumped: his staff, verbally at least, had been promised some security.

"And if the St Alfred's venture turns out to be a flop?" he asked. "What happens to me?"

"Why should it be a flop? This job hasn't flopped. As your report pointed out, it's become even more profitable. Why shouldn't a new business do the same?"

"Because it is new. And I don't know, and you don't tell me, how much commitment the firm has got to making it succeed."

"I want it to succeed!" Dickson said. "I don't want to be associated with failure any more than you do."

Which, Alphonse pointed out, wasn't the same thing. Dickson might leave the firm, might even as they were speaking be on the look-out for another job. And if he left, the firm might not be in the least committed to the new business.

That, said Dickson, was where trust came in.

"Trust!"

Alphonse laughed. The bare-facedness of the business world took some believing.

"After the way I've been treated? That's where something in writing comes in, I think."

Dickson's large-moon face seemed to brighten.

"What if you had something in writing?" he asked. "What sort of thing would you want?"

"A proper contract. Terms and conditions and salary laid down in black and white. And a commitment to funding from the firm."

Dickson seemed to demur.

"I take it," Alphonse said, "I shall be asked to resign my present post. Formally. Therefore I should want a new post to be offered. Formally."

Dickson took an envelope from a drawer, withdrew some typewritten sheets.

"Something like this?"

He handed them to Alphonse.

"If that's what you want," he said, "we can go ahead now."

Alphonse glanced at the folded papers. He'd need time to study the conditions, he said, and take advice.

"That kind of time is a luxury we haven't got."

"Then you can forget it. I'm in no hurry."

Dickson sighed. Here he was, a man patiently giving up his time trying to assist a less fortunate colleague into a more prosperous world, and what was the response?

There was money available, he explained, new project money, but only till the end of the month. There were only five days left to benefit from it. If this department didn't get it another department would.

"How much money?"

"Confidential. As you well know."

He well knew it indeed. And also well knew that a package would already have been drawn up needing only his signature for them to go ahead, a signature tantamount to resigning from his present job.

Dickson shrugged, didn't disagree.

In that case, Alphonse asked, seeing that no research or field work had been done for the firm to have any idea whether the venture would be viable, why commit money to something that would as likely fail as succeed?

Dickson slapped the table.

"Exactly! That is the point. Of course no research has been done. Because who's to do the research? An expert. And who's the expert? You are! Show me anyone better. Show me someone with more experience in the field or in the office! You're the person I want to go and do the field work. I don't want to trust someone else's judgement – who might not have half your skill and know-how."

So what would the contract be for, Alphonse asked. Market research?

"And for setting up the new business. And running it."

"And what if I find there isn't any business?"

"There will be."

"But what if there isn't? What happens to me?"

The firm would probably fit him in somewhere, Dickson said. "But the uncertainty'll make you dead keen to make sure there is business."

Alphonse slid the papers back across the table.

"Do you want me to say no now, or think about it and say no later?"

Dickson got to his feet.

"I want you to think about it and say yes."

He checked his watch.

"I've got a consultation for half an hour. I'll have coffee sent in for you. When I come back I'll want a decision. If it's no, the project is off."

He left the papers where they were.

"But just remember one thing. Your present contract is a month's notice either way. As you say, the new job may not be permanent. Neither may your present one be."

Which, Alphonse said, he took was a threat.

"Take it how you like," Dickson said. "And take this too: the job may not be exactly where you want to work, but it's a job, equivalent to your present one. If you refuse it, you'd have a poor case, legally speaking."

He'd lost. Was in no position to safeguard his staff further whatever he did.

He'd done his best. Now it was of no benefit to his staff for him to remain. They would merely suffer by association. Already, because he'd been hounded out of Audley House, his staff had been hounded out too. It would be kinder for him to go away.

Someone brought in a tray of coffee things.

Alphonse had no doubt but that the enterprise Dickson was suggesting was a ploy to get rid of him. Once at St Alfred's he wouldn't get the funding he needed; the firm would let him struggle a few months till it was obvious the project had failed, then he would be dismissed – as a failure. How high then his chances in the market?

Give Dickson his due, he thought. The ploy might be cruel, but it was well thought out. Whether he opted to go or opted to stay, they'd got the finger on him.

"Didn't like it?" Dickson asked, noticing the untouched coffee.

"I can't sign your form," Alphonse said.

He paused for the disappointment to sink in.

"Because I haven't been able to read it and wouldn't know what I was signing to. But I'd be willing to sign something like this: I am willing to relinquish my present post subject to the period of notice stipulated in my contract with Leisure Nation in order to assume an equivalent post in the St Alfred's area... and then insert dates and terms and so on."

It was the concession Dickson wanted. He nodded a sort of approval.

"I'll write it in handwriting," Alphonse said. "If you've got a piece of carbon paper for copies."

He knew what he was writing was fair and business-like. And he also knew that in the event of a dispute it was odds on the firm's interpretation would win.

He completed it, signed it, dated it, gave the top version to Dickson.

"I've done this in good faith," he said. "I should like to think the firm is going to act in good faith too."

"Oh, naturally," Dickson said.

He glanced at the paper.

"Tell me. Strictly between ourselves."

He had accompanied Alphonse to the door. He paused, spoke confidentially.

“What persuaded you to change your mind on this? I mean, you were totally opposed at one time.”

Alphonse faced him back.

“I’ve given you my signature, Dickson. I’m not giving you my blood.”

He sat in the car, seat belt not yet buckled.

He had signed his job away. Whether he had done the right thing, he couldn’t tell. Nor be clear what his motives had been. Dickson had held the cards, had played them hard.

He took a last look at Head Office. In front of him, stone-faced, sightless, the statue of the founder.

The sun had shifted, the shadows gave the brows an illusion of focus, an effigy of Fate itself.

Whom fortune deserts, it said, *I will not spare.*

CHAPTER 43

Finally, she knotted the cord and cut off the excess. She peeled a sticky label, affixed it to the back of the picture.

For Terry Bracondale. "La Golondrina." With all good wishes. Emilia Connaby.

She put the painting in one of the personalised carrier bags Terry had advised her to go in for now that her work was becoming popular, ready for him when he called round later. She looked forward to him calling round later.

She went over to the desk, studied the sketch of Audley House . She wondered why some people preferred a morning light and others an evening or midday light in a picture. Every shade had its challenge for an artist; but sunset lent a charm that might not be present an hour or so earlier or later. Maybe the suggestion of warmth in a sunset appealed to those who liked to believe life was more rosy than it really was. Not that it mattered what they liked so long as this Peter Dickson chap liked it.

She set to work, recreating the tones of the scene from notes scribbled on the sketch. She recalled the evening, Alphonse wandering past, his mind elsewhere. As usual. She remembered there'd been a hesitation about him, guessed he was uneasy about something.

Serve him damn well right, she thought.

Come the evening she cleaned and dried her brushes, cleaned as much of the palette as necessary, and had a bath. And decided against going out.

She found herself looking at the view across Kirkhaven. Ages ago Alphonse had been intrigued by it, wondering if the threads of streetlight and criss-crossing beads of traffic had an influence on her. He'd thought of it as an urban swamp, she recalled, out of which the creatures of the night hauled themselves, and into which at dawn they slithered back.

The notion amused her, that one's character might be influenced by a view from a window. Alphonse was a fund of fanciful notions. Little wonder his world collapsed around him from time to time. He constructed it of such improbable things.

The town didn't look much like a swamp at this time of day, the sun on its way down, west-facing surfaces brushed with rose and apricot, the streets canyons of blue-grey shadow. She presumed Alphonse would be amongst it now, in his flat, or out with that schoolgirl. She wasn't going to bother her head wondering where Alphonse Fenley was. He'd shown her how much he thought of her.

The doorbell rang.

"You're on the dot," she said. "As always."

Smartly dressed, as always.

She liked a man who didn't let you down.

"I expect you're surprised I haven't changed," she said.

She didn't want to go out. Unless he'd booked somewhere he couldn't unbook?

"I'd like to cook us something instead."

He'd ring *La Golondrina* and let them know, he said. He seemed pleased with the suggestion.

"As long as you don't expect anything as good as you get in your restaurants," she said.

He seemed at home in a kitchen, knowing when to keep in the background, helping where she told him to help, enjoying it, enjoying getting to know her.

Then she remembered.

"I ought to have asked you straight away!"

"I'm back," he said.

"Safe and sound? And out of the jungle?"

"And glad to be in your kitchen."

She guessed he wasn't going to elaborate.

"You really are safe?"

She scanned his face. Realised how relieved she was.

Eventually, accompanied by wine and oven-warmed rolls, the meal began.

The conversation flowed over unworn pebbles.

Rosina had left him, he explained.

"I think she was tired of me. Or tired of me not being there. But I was building the business. And neglecting the business at home. The next thing I knew – !"

Emilia observing him: a sharpish nose, an oblong face, grey eyes. His face was pleasant enough, she supposed, but if asked to identify one of the more elusive denizens of Alphonse's swamp she guessed she wouldn't have to look further than the gentleman in front of her.

"If you get a minute to spare, one day," she said, "I'd like to do your portrait."

"That's if you'd like me to," she added, seeing a certain hesitation on his part.

"To go in an exhibition?"

"Needn't do," she said. "Just from me to you."

"I'd like that," he said. "Very much."

"That's what we'll do then, Terry," she said. "One day."

It was the first time she had called him by his name. It felt like catching him. She looked forward to seating him so, turning his head so, to get the right emphasis on this and that feature. Would be a way of getting to know him, capturing him from the jungle

He'd brought chocolates. She opened them after the meal while he undid the painting.

He looked at detail after detail, asked how they'd been achieved.

"Only a square of board," he said, "with a bit of colour on. Yet you make it look like this. As if you could walk in it."

Naive though his comments were she knew she wasn't in the company of a fool. He was absorbed by the picture, held it this way and that as if by concentration he could get to its essence.

After a while he laid it aside.

"Must be satisfying," he said, "being able to capture scenes on a piece of card like that."

Emilia smiled to herself. Thought how Alphonse would have gone ahead at the coincidence. "Fate is a sandwich," he'd have said. Or some such tosh. "First you give a picture to this man; then one to that man! It's life echoing itself!"

And was irritated to think Alphonse and his stupid ideas should have surfaced at all.

"Well," Terry said, "we'd better get on with the washing-up."

"We'll do the washing-up afterwards," Emilia said. "If you like."

He stared. Took her meaning.

"As long as you realise I've never done it," she said.

He didn't say it was a surprise. But it was obvious it was.

"If you've got any contraceptives," she said. "I haven't."

He wasn't sure. Didn't think he had. Wondered whether there were any in the car. Doubted it.

"Not nowadays," he said, patting his pockets.

"Unless you can be careful?" she suggested.

He wouldn't hear of it. Risk was one thing, he said; folly was something else.

He tried to think where there would be a dispenser. Emilia couldn't suggest anywhere.

They caught each other's eye, the two of them thinking about contraceptives and looking puzzled. She was glad he had a sense of humour.

She'd washed up and cleared away by the time he came back.

"A pleasure I've deprived you of, I'm afraid," she said, meaning the wiping up.

She hoped he'd be luckier in bed.

In due course it appeared they'd both been lucky in bed, a pleasure heightened for Emilia by feeling she was now even stevens with Alphonse Fenley.

CHAPTER 44

Alphonse's belief that Amanda would one day find someone else eventually came true. Female students found her quick and good fun; male students noticed other qualities; and when she sometimes met Alphonse at vacations she shared with him the joys of the youthful community of Thrunes. Alphonse had little of sparkle to regale her with in exchange. The setting up of a business in a far-away town, the tussles with management, the crises of the day-to-day fight for survival – dull stuff compared to the dazzle of her brave new world. A few years later, shortly after taking her degree, she married her tutor, and from that happy day Dr Goodchild's life was guided by management skills of quite a different order from those he was accustomed to teach.

But she never loved anyone as much as she had loved Alphonse; and although Alphonse became attached to this girl or that girl there was never another by whom he was so swept away. Nor ever a day but some recollection of Amanda beguiled him. Those who believe the mind to be a rational thing may conclude he had only himself to blame. Sometimes he wondered what his real motivation had been, as opposed to the reasons he'd paraded at the time. He hoped it was some deeper instinct warning him that in the long run they wouldn't have been happy together.

Eventually he almost believed it, except when the grief of their drifting apart hit him.

He returned to Kirkhaven only for visits. In later life he and Emilia became better friends. They occasionally met, occasionally corresponded.

Emilia didn't marry Terry Bracondale. It was a happy relationship. They followed their own paths, pursued their separate careers, lived as partners when he returned, and for Emilia it felt as near love as a person of her independent nature was ever likely to feel.

Her swings of feeling regarding the uncle who turned out to be her father did not return; she loved him in both relationships. She saw her mother's point of view in wanting a baby; she admired her dad for wanting his wife's happiness; and was glad that the wishes of both had been granted. It was only when she mused on the secrecy of the engendering that she had a twinge of unease, and then was harsh with herself for being so puritanical as to have such twinges

Gossips who enjoyed the rumours of Kendal Connaby's involvement in child abuse were silenced by Peter Southwell's trial and imprisonment. But after Kendal's divorce they were pleasantly outraged at a possible liaison between him and Freda, mother of the girl the trouble had been about in the first place. Better informed than most on the matter was his secretary Mrs Audrey Soames who, unable to obtain another post, failed to resign the one she had, despite the unseemliness of working for a man under such a cloud.

"Can't say a word," she might whisper to a friend. "If you knew half that went on! Another appointment with her this week! A whole hour together! And that door kept shut!"

A week or so before he left Kirkhaven for ever Alphonse called in at a newsagent's for a paper, being in the habit of scanning employment ads to see if anything attractive was on offer. The man in front of him paying for a packet of cigarettes was Gerald Paine.

Alphonse asked him if he'd like a lift.

"I wonder if you'd be ever so kind and drop me round at Park View," Gerald said. "Just want to see if there's any mail."

To see if there was any mail? At his own house?

"Don't tell me you haven't heard."

"Heard?"

"I've moved in at The Warren."

"With Cecily?"

"And Robert. You must be the only one who didn't know."

A menage a trois?

The most ordinary set-up in the world, according to Gerald. But he hadn't sold Park View, which was why he sometimes dropped in to collect any mail.

"So you're actually living at The Warren?"

"Cecily's idea," he said. "Said things were reaching crisis point between her and Robert. Told me I'd better do something about it."

"And Robert – ?"

Didn't seem to mind, Gerald said.

"Cecily told him if I didn't move in she'd move out."

Robert had proved a decent old stick. Had organized the move in there like clockwork.

Alphonse asked where Cecily would have gone if she had moved out.

Gerald shrugged. "Anywhere. And taken the kids."

That was what decided it, he said. He couldn't let her take the children away from Robert.

"The old boy dotes on them. I think they mean more to him than they do to me."

"Robert's happy about you being there?"

Seemed to be, so far as Gerald could tell. They all got on well together. Cecily had a night with him occasionally.

"She likes him better now. Makes quite a fuss of him. I tell her, don't you make me jealous!"

They went into the music room. With no choir in there Gerald's antique chairs and decrepit old furniture were all the more noticeable.

"Some of these could tell a tale."

That old armchair for example. He indicated a worm-eaten relic of a Windsor most people wouldn't give house-room to. Old Jameson the brewer had left it to him.

"He'd sit and yarn, telling me some tale or other about the beer, every now and then he'd lift his great leg and fart and carry on telling me about the beer, then fart again. Like a duet. He'd say, what the hell are you laughing at?"

Gerald moved the chair back into its corner.

"I think of him, poor old boy."

And that little pink button-back chair, Gerald said. Belonged to little Miss Edwards. In the church choir.

"She always told me she'd leave it to me. Never got round to marrying anyone. Told me a yarn or two'd make your hair curl!"

He laughed, kept Miss Edwards' confidences to himself.

His eye lit on a shabby rust-upholstered chair near the window – then realised the time.

"Mustn't keep you."

As they left he gave his chairs a last look round.

Alphonse could only guess what murmurs from the past they evoked. He felt the world was bigger for having Gerald in it, a man who treasured worm-eaten old lives.

They dropped in at a pub. Had a flagstone floor, old-fashioned furniture and an ancient piano. At one end of the bar an elderly, well-wrinkled, well-rouged woman was occupied with her thoughts; at the other, Gerald was ordering drinks, the mirrors and glassware at the back of the bar twinkling in what light there was. As a pub, Alphonse thought, it wasn't much to be saying good-bye to, but it was part of the land he knew.

"So what's it to be tonight, my love?" Gerald called out. "Wine, blackberry juice, drop of my blood?"

The old bird's lipsticked mouth parted in a smile of yellow teeth.

"Gerald, my darling!"

Like a corpse at a resurrection.

"Fancy seeing you here!"

The thin face softened, glad of the attention.

"You wouldn't really part with your blood for me, would you, Gerald? Oh, I believe you would!"

The voice was thick, the words slurred.

"I'll have a rum and blackcurrant, my darling," she crooned.

Gerald winked, took her drink and his own to the piano.

"Fancy you coming in, Gerald. You've made my day!"

She shuffled across on his arm.

"What are you going to sing for us, then?" he asked.

"Oh, I can't sing," she croaked. "You sing. Something for me."

He sat at the piano, played a bit from a song, looked up at her as if she was a young girl.

"You look a treat, tonight."

"Gerald!"

He started singing, caught her eye, loving the foolery of it.

We could make believe,
I love you,
Only make believe
That you love me...

"You devil!" she cooed.

She went to drink his health, almost toppled over.

Gerald grinned, his eye kindly on her made-up old face.

She hung on the piano towards him, her voice following his like an invalid.

Others find peace of mind
In pretending;
Couldn't you, couldn't I, couldn't we
Make believe our lips are blending
In a phantom kiss,
Or two or three?

"Oh, if only I was younger," she sighed, looked round indistinctly. Then laughed, wet lips smudged, a straggle of hair down her face.

Alphonse joined them. It was part of what he was saying good-bye to, a life that would go on without him, would soon have forgotten him. Sooner or later this too would become part of the blur of everything that had passed. And if, later on, certain sequences of what he had lived through came to mind he guessed he might have to ask: was it really like that? Or have I painted it all too vivid? A dream in a fever?

It was dear, for all that. And with the pain of Amanda in his mind, the pain of being with her, the pain of life without her, he joined in as they sang the song again:

Others find peace of mind
Peace of mind
In pretending;
Couldn't you, couldn't I, couldn't we

Make believe our lips are blending
In a phantom kiss,
Or two or three?
Might as well make believe
I love you,
For to tell the truth,
I do.